About the Author

Natalie Tambini has more than thirty years' experience as a national newspaper and magazine journalist. She created and wrote Cosmopolitan's 'Confessions' columns, supplements and books and interviewed countless celebrities during nine years at TV Choice and Total TV Guide – infamously missing a slot with Julia Roberts. Her work has been syndicated worldwide, and she has acted as ghostwriter for several celebrity columnists on women's magazines.

Her fascination with murderers and the need to understand them stems from a childhood passion for Agatha Christie novels while growing up in Norfolk and Hampshire. She has also interviewed many victims of crimes as a real-life journalist, and those who endured miscarriages of justice, including an innocent man who spent 20 years on death row.

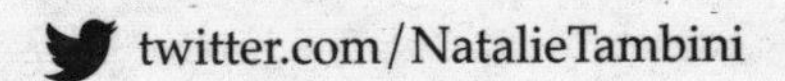
twitter.com/NatalieTambini

THE NAIL SALON

NATALIE TAMBINI

One More Chapter
a division of HarperCollins*Publishers* Ltd
1 London Bridge Street
London SE1 9GF
www.harpercollins.co.uk
HarperCollins*Publishers*
Macken House, 39/40 Mayor Street Upper,
Dublin 1, D01 C9W8, Ireland

This paperback edition 2023
2
First published in Great Britain in ebook format
by HarperCollins*Publishers* 2023

A catalogue record of this book is available from the British Library

ISBN: 978-0-00-858855-7

Printed and bound in the UK using 100% Renewable Electricity
by CPI Group (UK) Ltd

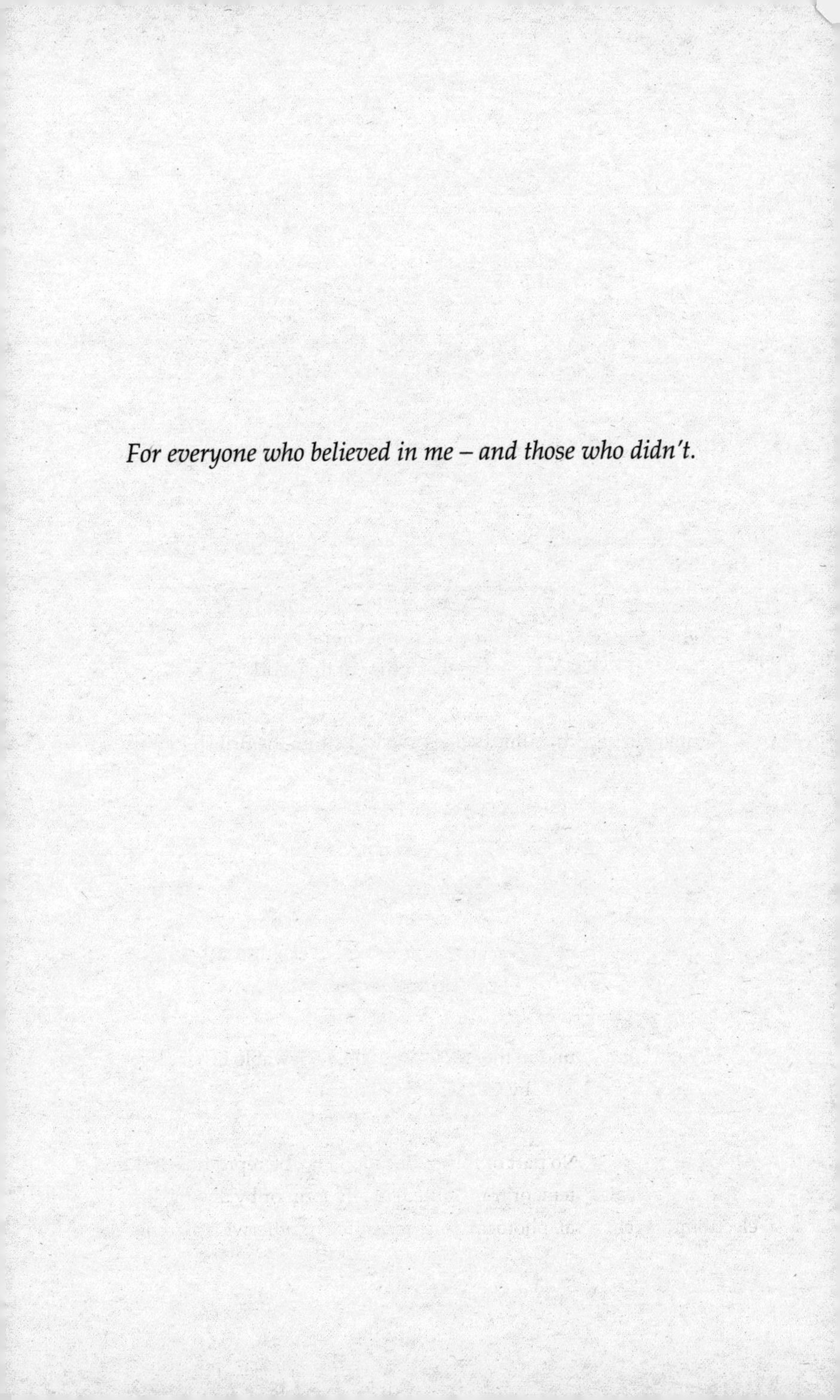

For everyone who believed in me – and those who didn't.

'She's dead. Wrapped in plastic.'

Pete Martell, Twin Peaks.

Chapter One

MELINDA

She's been having the funeral fantasies again.

The ones where she swaps the Canderel for ricin or Novichok or some other deathly poison that she dreams of buying on the dark web.

She tells me, in hushed whispers, that a friend says there are *hit men* available. It's never going to happen, of course. She's far too anxious to go poking around the murkier side of the internet. This will end up like all the others – in a messy divorce with an obscenely huge payout. Enough to cover the housekeeper, the nanny, the Botox, the fillers, the Prada. She'll get the house anyway.

And that's when the rot really sets in. Soon it's daily trips to the hairdresser, to me – here in the nail salon – and slipping a vodka into the Evian to fill the gaping vacuum. I've seen it all a thousand times before.

But Soozie hasn't hit the divorce courts yet. She's still officially in the 'making a go of it' stage, even though she loathes her husband, Simon – forties, blondish hair, works out, pretty handsome as far as City bankers go – who has been having pretty wild sex with a brunette twenty-something for the last year and a half.

Soozie doesn't know that. But I do. I know all about their lives. Not just what they tell me.

Day after day, I listen to their stories as I file, paint, polish. I'm their confessor. I know *everything*. Just the occasional, sympathetic 'oh' is enough to unleash another torrent. And today, Soozie is on a real roll.

'It's just so *unfair*,' she wails. 'This dinner party has been arranged for *weeks*. Now he's saying the firm needs him in Manchester overnight. Overnight! On a Saturday. So I'll have to host it on my *own*.'

I make a sad face. If only she'd seen what I have. Simon in the back of his car, the brunette astride him, pumping up and down, pink flesh pressing against the damp glass. Not to mention their twice-weekly trysts they used to have at his secret second home – a secluded mock-Georgian mansion, Riverdell, on the nearby, private Crown Estate. The estate where Soozie longed to live, but Simon insisted they couldn't quite afford.

Soozie gazes down at her blue nails. 'He doesn't give a flying fuck about me.' We both know the Manchester trip is a lie.

But listening to her isn't enough. My clients keep coming back because they genuinely believe I'm their friend. Their closest friend, I've been called.

I can't do without them. It's not just the money. I feed off their lives, their emotions. Their pain is my drug. Their joy, too. I soak it up, letting it run through my veins, feeling every betrayal, every divorce, every new baby, every school exam, every failed university application, every elderly parent whose mind is being eaten away by dementia. They rarely ask much about me. I like that. And I do have a soft spot for a few of them. Especially Soozie.

'Well, we'll have to make sure this is the most fabulous dinner party ever, honey,' I say brightly. 'What's on the menu?'

'Black cod.' She's not cooking it, of course. Some Nobu-trained chef is doing the catering. 'And there's a *vegan*.' She spits the word out. Soozie briefly embraced the whole clean-eating fad, before the lure of a steak and garlic butter became too much. 'I mean, *honestly*. I'm putting up with all this from the girls too. They won't touch dairy. As if life isn't complicated *enough*.'

It's the first time today that she's mentioned the twins. Both are complete teenage brats. Simon adores them and they know it. I've seen them climb into his Range Rover, all waist-length blonde hair, pink lipstick, tiny waists, fake tan and heels, and he drives off like he's won the lottery. And poor, irrelevant Soozie, with her creases and pot belly that no amount of sit-ups seem to shift, and the ever-present glass of wine, is yesterday's news.

She wasn't always like this. When she first came to the nail salon, five years ago, she was full of joy. Talking about how giving up her career in celebrity PR to be a full-time mum was the best move she'd ever made. How looking after the girls was the best job in the world (even if, as far as I could see, all she did was tell other people what to do). I didn't follow her then. Her story was too familiar, too commonplace. I didn't feel that connection. But when the twins started coming in, that's when I knew she'd be on my list. And Simon too.

It's always been my tactic – become their confidant, and then casually suggest other family members might like a session. Soozie came with the girls at first. But soon they were coming on their own, and that's when I began to breathe in their stories like a rush of terrible oxygen.

Her nails are dry, and Soozie's in no rush to go. But I've had my fill for the day. Even though I'm not on the guest list, I've got a dinner party to look forward to.

Chapter Two

The reflection in the bathroom mirror needed attention. Her face was fine. He was always careful about that. But as Detective Chief Inspector Sue Fisher let her silk robe fall gently below her shoulders, the livid bruising on the tops of her arms glared back, daring her to expose it to the world. She ran her fingertips over the marks where his fat, thick fingers had been, holding her, shaking her, and for a moment she was back in the living room, his voice distant and hollow as he ranted and seethed. Sue couldn't even remember what the latest tirade had been about. Spending too much time on jobs with her colleague Mike was usually behind it.

There was a little arnica cream left in the tube and she smoothed it over her shoulders, trying not to wince. Sunlight streamed in through the bathroom window, and her phone said it would be thirty degrees today. Even the water in the cold tap was warm. This summer had been the hottest on record so far, and to Sue's horror it showed no signs of abating. It was easy to cover up at work; people expected a shirt and jacket, but on her days off it was harder to explain a long-sleeved T-shirt when everyone else was sun-worshipping in strappy tops.

He was still asleep in bed. He'd be sorry, of course, there would be texts, tears, flowers and the broken-record promise to stop drinking. Keen not to wake him, she tiptoed around the bedroom, dressing as silently as possible, hoping that their son Tom hadn't heard the row. Being fourteen, he spent most of his time zoned out with headphones, oblivious to everything going on in the world.

On the way to work, Sue cranked up the car stereo, shouting out the words to 'Mr Brightside' as she screamed into a void.

The office was unusually quiet for a Tuesday morning. Mike, her deputy, was late as usual, but Sue didn't care. Tipping some of the murky brown liquid from the communal coffee machine into a cracked green mug, she was still logging on to her computer when the boss, Chief Constable Steve Biller, strode in.

'Missing person,' he said, throwing the file onto her desk. 'Reported early hours of this morning. Another underage runaway. Check it out, Sue. Rich kid. Probably putting on her parts when daddy wouldn't pay for a limo. Went AWOL once before and turned up like the proverbial bad penny having stayed the night in a Travelodge. Last seen 7am Monday. It's been twenty-four hours, so…'

'I'll get straight on it, sir.'

Sue picked up the thin file. A girl's face stared back at her, the full Instagram experience. Big hair, pout, green eyes, flawless – and obviously photoshopped – skin, looking far older than fifteen.

'I miss the days when kids looked like kids.' She sighed as Mike quietly slid into the seat opposite, his hungover eyes shaded by dark glasses. 'Good night? Twelve pints and a curry?'

Mike shook his head. 'Wine,' he said weakly. 'It's the Devil's work.'

'Oh, the *date*! I forgot. How was she? Anything like the photo?'

'No. And nothing like her description, either. I tell you, Sue, you're so lucky to have Rob. This online dating lark is a nightmare. I had to drink two bottles just to get through the evening.'

'How did you end it?'

'At Wimbledon tube. Thanked her for a lovely evening and said I'd be in touch. She wants me to go horse riding. In Richmond Park.'

Sue looked up from the file and grinned. 'Why not? Beats staying in watching *EastEnders*. You should give it a go.'

'And she's got kids. Three of them. All under ten. Two different fathers. Didn't mention that in her bio. Too much baggage. Anyway, who's this then?'

'Anna Littlejohn-Eaves. Fifteen. Lives in Kingston. The very posh bit. Tillingham Estate. Last seen yesterday morning. They've tried the local hospitals.'

'History?'

'Done it before, a year ago. Went out partying, stayed in a Travelodge with a mate, then rang Mummy at 7am to go and pick them up, completely unaware of the fracas she had caused.'

Sue took a slurp of coffee. 'Come on. We'd better go and see the parents.'

Chapter Three

MELINDA

He's never been to the salon. Doesn't even know it exists. But the twins have put me on to Daniel. Soozie's twins. Sky and Star. The fifteen-year-old brats – with the ridiculous names and more spending money in their Prada bags than I'll ever have in a lifetime – waft in just as Soozie's leaving. She's popped in for me to touch up one of her nails. And a chat. They've been in the coffee shop opposite. Sky still has the remnants of a soya caffè latte on her top lip.

'Do you girls want me to wait?' ventures Soozie hopefully. 'I could give you a lift?'

'I told you, Mum, we're going shopping,' snaps Sky, rolling her eyes. 'We'll get an Uber.'

Soozie looks deflated. 'OK, well don't be out late. I'll see you at home.'

I watch as she closes the door behind her. She hesitates for a moment, her fingers resting on the handle as if she's coming back in, then walks down the street towards the car park. Sky stifles a giggle. Poor Soozie. The girls are just cruel to her. And she knows it.

They don't glimpse the disappointment in my eyes. To them, I'm just 'staff', in the same invisible category as their housekeeper, the chef, their personal trainer – but they can't resist showing off when a captive audience of one is present.

'I met Daniel online,' brags Sky, as I begin removing the immaculate gold nail polish I applied three days ago. 'He's taking me out in London this afternoon. Told me to meet him in Leicester Square. Three o'clock. By the Tube.'

Soozie clearly doesn't know. It's a Monday in August, the school holidays, and she rarely had any idea what they were up to until she checked their pouting Instagram feeds.

'What's he like, this Daniel?' I ask.

'Probably a paedo,' Star says sulkily.

'He's not,' snaps Sky. 'You're just jealous. I've seen pictures of him. He's nineteen. A YouTuber.'

There is time. I have two clients booked for the afternoon whose stories have long gone cold. I can easily cancel. And to hell with any walk-ins. Daniel is worth a follow. Soozie won't be winning Mother of the Year any time soon, but at least I can keep an eye on Sky for her. Strip away the nails, the makeup, and she's just an insecure little girl. Fragile. I remember how that felt at fifteen.

The girls flounce out, Star with purple nails, Sky with bright red. I flip the sign on the door to 'closed' and pull down the blind.

My salon is on a Surrey high street, Cobshott to be precise, where bankers' and footballers' wives, plus a handful of top 'creatives' – whatever the hell they are – dominate the handful of council tenants yet to be squeezed out. Vast, sterile mansion new-builds rise up from the ashes of old cottages. This is a land of triple garages and bifold doors, of interior designers and Range Rovers, of a quest for perfection and inner pain the like of which I never saw back home in Great Yarmouth.

There aren't many of us who make it out of the seaside town. The singer who did the jungle and the M&S ads, whatshername – Myleene Klass, I just googled it – maybe a few others. I never fitted in there. But here, in Cobshott, they love me.

My clapped-out mini is parked around the corner. I can't afford to live here, of course. Renting the tiny salon costs a small fortune, though I did a good cash deal with the owner. But image is everything. Reality is a bedsit twenty minutes' drive away, in Surbiton, the heart of suburbia. They'd never believe it, my clients. One room, with an overflowing wardrobe and a tiny TV. A sink in the corner. A dingy grey bathroom with damp, threadbare towels piled up, shared with five others. Mice in the kitchen and a solidified KFC bargain bucket, left on the table by two of the Kingston University students a couple of days ago. It's the closest place I can afford to Cobshott, near enough for me to have an easy, cheap commute, and right by the fast train to London. To my sanctuary. Where I can be me.

I find a space in the street nearby, lock the Mini carefully and walk up the weed-strewn front path. It's an old Victorian terrace, and I'm in the basement. The only blessing is there's no damp. Down the stairs, key in the lock, and I'm in. Now, what to wear?

My wigs live on a long shelf above the dressing table. I have everything – curly blonde, red bob, hipster, even clip-on man bun. Today I'm going for the shoulder-length brunette. First, some foundation. The cream darkens my skin tone and I set it with powder. Draw on my eyebrows and lighten my lids with MAC shadow in Nylon. Pale lips. Jeans, a baggy blue top, padding to make me more portly, and a thin baggy jacket. Trainers. Nothing too noticeable. I need to disappear into the Leicester Square crowd.

The train is half-empty. I take a window seat and gaze out as summer flashes by. Semi-detached houses quickly give way to terraces, then tower blocks. Run-down, brick council flats jostle with the steel and glass outline of new London. The Shard appears, reflecting sunlight against a crisp blue sky. Down the Tube, where tourists puzzle over the coloured train arteries connecting London, and parents are inflicting the horrors of a commute on half-terming kids. It's hot, too hot, and I spill out into Charing Cross road, with its familiar smell of urine-dried pavements and diesel fumes.

Outside the Hippodrome Casino seems a good place to wait. I lounge against the wall and scroll through my phone, furtively glancing round at potential Daniels. There's a nervous young lad in a baseball cap, clutching a cheap bouquet of wilting roses in plastic wrap. A handsome but slightly shifty-looking guy in his mid-forties, wearing a suit and a coat with the collar up, despite the stifling heat of the day. The lad meets his equally-terrified-looking date, and they disappear into Burger King. Classy. Two-thirty. Three o'clock. Then four. The shifty-looking guy has gone, replaced by irritating, fat American tourists loudly asking where they can find Lie-cester Square.

I'm starting to worry a little now. London is no place for a fifteen-year-old, especially one who thinks she's streetwise. I check Sky's Instagram, wishing I'd thought of it earlier. There's a shot of her and Star in their Cobshott pool, posted half an hour ago, all smiles, drinking cocktails on a giant inflatable unicorn and hashtagged 'summerdaze'. The shadows show it's late afternoon. And there, right there, are the freshly painted, bright-red nails with the two diamantés. She's home, and she's safe.

For a moment, I'm relieved, but then anger begins to boil in the pit of my stomach. She's lied to me. She's made me feel like a *fool*. I'm here, sweating, tense, wasting my time trying to look out for her when she hasn't even left the house. She's invented Daniel to wind up Star, and I've fallen for it.

I'm heading back to the Tube, furious and fed up, when I spot her in an alleyway. A newbie. Couldn't be more than sixteen. Long, carefully curled chestnut hair, ironed clothes, clutching a small rucksack but with a harrowed, fearful look in her eyes that spice, heroin or any other street drug has yet to numb. Sky might not need my help, but this young girl does. And she needs it now. Maybe this afternoon won't be a waste of time after all.

'You OK?' I say gently, crouching down beside her.

She shakes her head, but her green, desperate eyes meet mine. There's an asthma inhaler in her hand and she's wheezing.

'It's all right, honey,' I add. 'I'm Sally. I help out with London's homeless. Haven't seen you around before.'

'Just arrived,' she says, in a soft voice, politely taking my hand and shaking it. Well-mannered. I like that. 'First time. I'm… Karen.'

I gesture to a homeless man on the pavement, frozen, zombie-like, in the foetal position, his filthy, shoeless feet and stinking clothes resting on a urine-soaked newspaper. 'You've got to be careful on the streets, Karen. He's on spice. That's what it does to you. And there're a lot of dealers ready to push you into it. For free. At first.'

She agrees to a coffee in a nearby Soho cafe, one I know has no CCTV, where sweet, kindly Sally listens to her life story. From Margate in Kent. Absent father. An alcoholic mother who starts the day with a vodka. Severely asthmatic. Scars she hates from surgery to her belly when she was a baby. A second coffee, this time with a veggie 'bacon' sandwich. And cake. Soft Victoria sponge, with jam and cream, just the sort a loving parent would bake. She's fifteen, she's started talking and now she can't stop. Tears, pain, sexual abuse, it all tumbles out. I hug her, feeling her pain, more alive than I've been for months. I've been wanting another lost soul to help, to join my family. And Karen is perfect.

My long wig is itching, my makeup sweaty, the padding is making me overheat, and the anticipation makes me feel like I'm about to burst. But outwardly, I'm just sweet, calm Sally, the one person in London that Karen can trust. At last her words begin to dry up, her throat thick, and she gazes out at the warm drizzle now conveniently coating the shiny London streets.

'Weather's taking a turn,' I say softly. 'We really do need to sort you out a bed for tonight. It's too dangerous on the streets. Drugs, rape, even murder. And the hostels aren't any better. That's why people choose to sleep out here. They think it's safer.' My voice drops to a whisper. 'But it isn't.'

She clutches her rucksack to her chest like a teddy bear and puffs at her inhaler.

I sigh deeply. 'Look, I don't normally do this, but why don't you come and stay at my place? There's plenty of space and you can have your own room. We've chatted for so long, I trust you, and it's getting late. Tomorrow morning we can phone round to find you somewhere permanent. And a job, with training. A new start.'

Karen hesitates, but only briefly. On the pavement outside, a frozen spice addict suddenly stirs, and soils himself.

Her gaze flicks back to mine. 'Are you sure?' she says. 'I won't be any trouble.'

'Of course.' I smile. 'It's a bit of a walk, as it's on the

other side of town, but we can chat on the way to Waterloo. Then just a little train ride. Much nicer than the Tube.'

We leave the coffee shop, squeezing through the hordes of people spilling out of pubs onto Soho's warm streets, down to Trafalgar Square, and I point out where she'll be able to see the giant Christmas tree in a few months' time. Over the busy Hungerford footbridge, where the City skyline glitters in the failing light, towards home. The drizzle has stopped, and the summer sunset bathes London in gold, the colour Karen had always dreamed it would be.

Chapter Four

Sue swung the car out of Kingston police station's car park, joining the queue of traffic heading into the town centre. The seat belt pressed uncomfortably on her shoulder, sending spikes of pain shooting across her chest and down her arm.

'You OK?' Mike asked, as she involuntarily winced.

'Yeah. Just an old shoulder injury. From badminton. Plays up sometimes.'

They spent the rest of the journey in comfortable silence, Mike nursing his hangover and Sue silently hating herself for putting up with Rob. He'd never threatened Tom, or been anything but the doting dad in public, though distant in private. Sue knew that if he laid a finger on him, she'd walk out for good. Everyone loved Rob. He was handsome, charming, with a quick wit – the perfect party guest. Successful too, running his own locksmith business and giving up his Wednesday nights and Sunday mornings to coach kids' rugby. She'd met him eighteen years ago, when she locked herself out of her flat, and fell in love instantly. No one else ever saw his dark side.

'Turn left here, boss. This is it.'

Mike's voice snapped her back into work mode. She swung the car into the private Tillingham Estate on the outskirts of Kingston-upon-Thames, where open white gates marked the entrance to a world of huge gravel driveways, upmarket new-builds and ubiquitous bifold doors.

The girl's home was classic new money; a double-fronted mock-Georgian affair with a triple garage and self-contained flat above. A squad car was parked out front, and the front door wide open.

'Thank God you're here,' snapped a painfully thin woman standing in the doorway, framed by two ornamental bay trees in oversized blue pots. Her streaked-blonde hair was pulled back into a ponytail, her face barely moved with Botox and she was dressed in the new-money uniform of Lululemon gym kit. 'I'm Zoe Littlejohn, Anna's mum. She's been gone for a whole day and you're not doing anything about it.'

'DCI Sue Fisher,' Sue said formally, shaking her hand. 'I assure you we're doing all we can to find Anna. Can we go inside and talk?'

Zoe led them through a wide, cream-tiled hallway into the kitchen, a hangar-like, sterile space where she perched on a bar stool at the central island, her fingers wrapped around a pink mug. Apart from a couple of framed photos on a shelf, the place reminded Sue of a show home, with none of the unopened post, unwashed coffee cups and piles of paperwork that littered her own kitchen. But behind her superior demeanour, Zoe's eyes were so filled with pain that Sue found herself softening slightly.

'I know you've explained it to the uniformed officers,' Sue said gently. 'But if you could take us through everything, step by step, that would be really helpful. When did you last see Anna?'

'Yesterday morning. Monday. About 7am. I didn't see her, but I heard her go downstairs. Paul – her stepdad – was leaving for work and said she told him she was going to meet friends in Kingston after breakfast.'

'How did she seem?'

'He said she was fine. Just Anna. You know teenagers, they don't say much.'

'Had there been any arguments?'

'No.' The word came out a little too forcefully for Sue's liking. 'None at all.'

'And who else is in the household?'

'There's just the three of us. Anna's an only child. I've called all of her friends and no one has heard from her.'

'Where were you when she left?

'I was still in bed. Stayed there most of the day. I-I wasn't feeling well. Had drinks with friends the night before. So I didn't hear her leave. Paul had already gone to work.'

'What about staff?'

'We have a live-out housekeeper, Zelda. I can give you her number. She does everything.'

Sue picked up one of the framed photos. It showed Zoe and Paul standing either side of a slightly younger Anna, their arms around her.

'That was taken in the Maldives. Three years ago.'

'Do you have some more recent ones?'

Zoe reached into her pocket and pulled out a gold iPhone. 'Here's her Instagram. There are thousands.'

Sue took the phone and scrolled through the images. Even if they hadn't been photoshopped, the girl really was very pretty, with stunning green eyes. 'It would be useful to have some that aren't so posed,' she said. 'Holiday snaps, that kind of thing?'

'I'll find some.'

'What about her birth father? We'll need his name and address.'

Zoe's gaze hardened. 'James. He was Paul's best friend. So things have been ... difficult.'

'How long have you and Paul been together?'

'Eight years. Since Anna was seven. James took it pretty badly. He hasn't seen Anna for years. Said he just had to walk away for his own sanity. Though within a year he'd got his secretary pregnant and started a new life. That's why Anna changed her surname and took Paul's. I had to go to court to get the house. And maintenance. Anna tried to stay in touch at first, but James wouldn't return her calls. Or mine. Too busy with his new family, from what I hear.'

Zoe's perfectly manicured fingers tensed around her pink mug.

'What about security?' Mike added. 'I noticed a CCTV camera on the front of the house. Are there others? We'll need to see those tapes. And we'll need to chat to Paul.'

'Only that camera, but it's a dummy. Paul's at work.'

Mike paused. 'Must be important if he's had to go in when Anna's missing.'

Zoe took a swig of what Sue suspected was vodka. 'He's not taking it seriously. Says she's being a "silly girl" and we're making far too much fuss. Thinks she'll turn up in a Travelodge again like last time. Or Ibiza. I've told him her passport is still in the safe.'

Sue met her gaze gently. 'And what do you think?'

'I just know something's wrong. She's taken her rucksack. And her spare asthma inhalers. She only takes all that when she goes on holiday. I don't know what else is missing. Her iPhone is registered to me so I tried tracking it, but it's switched off.'

'Can you show us her room?'

The sweeping, open-plan staircase led to a vast upper floor, carpeted in cream, and Anna's room was in the far corner of the house. Sue had never seen anything quite so pink. Or a teenage room quite so immaculate.

'She's a very tidy girl,' Sue remarked.

'That's the thing,' Zoe replied. 'It's usually a tip. She won't allow our housekeeper in. But last night, when we started to worry about her, I opened the door and found it like this. Zelda says she's even changed the bedlinen.'

'What about boyfriends?'

'None that I know of. Unless they shinned up the drainpipe.'

'Would you still have the used bedlinen?'

Zoe shook her head. 'Zelda assumed Anna had wet herself or been sick and didn't want to say. She found the sheets on a boil wash in the machine.'

As Zoe headed downstairs to refill her mug, Sue pulled on a pair of gloves and opened Anna's chest of drawers. 'Something happened in this room, Mike. Get Forensics in. And we need to pay the stepdad a visit.'

Chapter Five

Karen wasn't my first. Or even my second. Karen was the third girl I'd helped. All teens, all homeless, and so far not one had registered a flicker of interest in the press. They disappeared, escaped their old lives, and no one gave a shit. Except me. I kept my charitable work a secret.

Sometimes, when I was bored, I'd flick through the missing persons' websites. Only Number Two showed up, and then only once. Cindy. Age fourteen. Last seen in Manchester, boarding a train to London. A close-up of her sweet face, red hair scraped back, and haunted eyes that had seen far more than they should. I knew how that felt.

I remember being nine or ten, sitting on the back doorstep of our well-kept Victorian terraced cottage in Great Yarmouth when the cat, Smokey, wandered past. As I reached out to pet him, a car backfired. Spooked, he sank his claws deep into my hand, drawing blood. I yelped.

'Stop it, Smokey,' my mother said vaguely, in her thick Norfolk accent, as she pegged out the washing. 'Give him a smack. Don't let him hurt you.'

I'd felt it before, a darkness that meant bad things might happen. Whenever I'd sensed it, I'd pushed it deep inside me. Not this time. The rage rose up through my belly, burning, blinding me to everything except my father's face. I grabbed the cat and ran upstairs.

My mother saw Smokey fall. He lay on the path, splayed, as a spreading pool of deep red blood emerged from his crushed, twitching body. She was too repulsed to touch him.

'D-don't look,' she stammered, seeing my face peering over the window ledge as she threw a tea towel over him. 'There's been an accident.'

My father came out of the house and hunched over the cat, prodding him to see if he was still alive, while I gazed out of the window, numb. The searing anger had gone, and I felt nothing. Not a single emotion. Dead, like Smokey. Anaesthetised. Drugged with something so powerful that it could take all the fear, the rage, the hurt away. Night after night, I'd prayed to feel like this, and killing the cat had done it.

I came down the stairs, disconnected, there but not there, blurred around the edges. They stared at me, silently, and for the first time in my life I saw guilt in my father's eyes. Fear too, and a searing sadness. Even my mother, usually so detached and frozen, had paled and a thick tear dripped silently down her cheek as the blood, the deepest red I'd ever seen, seeped across the flagstones and onto the tips of her pink slippers.

'He fell,' I said simply.

I sat down cross-legged beside Smokey, peeling back the reddening tea towel to look at him. Neither of them said a word. This, like everything else, would never be spoken of. My mother stepped out of her slippers, pulled her heavy cardigan around her and disappeared back into the kitchen, followed by my father. I heard the hum of their voices, low and hushed, but not their words. Most of the time they both zoned out of life, just existing, going through the motions. The alarm clock at seven. Him going to work, coming home, eating his tea. Bed until she fell asleep, when he tiptoed across the landing to my room.

I don't know how long I sat there, stroking the cat's body as he turned as cold as stone and his open eyes clouded. I barely noticed him when he was alive. In death he was a comfort.

It was sunset when my mother and father came out of the house with a shoe box, lined with newspaper. She picked up her slippers, now stiff and red, and put them gently in the dustbin.

'We need to bury him now,' she said simply.

My father sobbed as he scooped up Smokey and we buried him at the end of the garden. That's when I realised what I'd done. As he forced the spade into the hard earth, over and over, the pain, the guilt, the fear, the shame, it all came flooding back. Hot, thick tears swelled in my eyes but I would not let them fall. I picked up a stick and after my father went inside I jabbed it into my thigh until it bled, hating myself, hating him, until the physical pain numbed my mind.

The next day, my father didn't go to work at the town hall. He took me to the beach and bought me a twirly ice cream on the seafront. Strawberry, my favourite. With a flake. And we sat by the yacht pond watching the little remote control boats whizzing by. He promised me I could have the piano lessons I'd been asking for. It was a good day. The only day I remember spending with him. After Smokey, he didn't touch me again. They carried on living their predictable, empty life. Dinner at six and a tablespoon of Milk of Magnesia before bed at ten.

That was the only time I ever saw my father cry. Not even at his mother's funeral, when he sat, stony-faced and ashen, unable to look at the coffin. Not even at *my* mother's funeral, as he joined the pallbearers to shuffle towards the grave, her vacant silence pressing down on his guilty shoulder in death as it had done in life. As they lowered her into the cold earth, I promised myself I'd escape this lifeless hell and make a sanctuary, a place for girls like me who didn't have anywhere to go, or anyone to turn to. The misunderstood. The misfits. The ones who wouldn't be missed.

~

It's a hot Wednesday morning, just over thirty-six hours since I met Karen, but I open the salon as usual, turning on the TV screen that keeps clients amused while they wait. That's when I see it. Karen's face, right there on Sky News. I freeze. Turns out she's not from the run-down Margate council flat that she told me about. She's Anna, from the posh Tillingham Estate in Kingston Upon Thames, just a few miles from Cobshott, and her family won't rest until they find her.

My hands start to tremble. They show CCTV of Karen – sorry, Anna – leaving the train at Waterloo, and a shot of her walking alone through Charing Cross station – on her way to Leicester Square, not that they know it – but then the trail 'goes cold'.

No one cared when the first two girls went missing. Now they're saying Anna's mum is going to make an 'emotional plea for her daughter's safe return' alongside her estranged father. My panicked mind races. What if they trace her to me?

The salon door opens and Soozie breezes in, a twenty-pound note in her hand, laced with the remnants of her morning cocaine. 'Darling!' she says. 'I hadn't forgotten I owe you this.' She glances up at the TV. 'Have you *seen* this missing girl? I know her parents. Well, the mother, anyway. The girl was at nursery school with the twins. She's on their *Facebook*.'

Given that Sky and Star have several thousand Facebook friends, most of whom they don't know, this doesn't surprise me.

'It's terrible, isn't it?' I reply, trying to stay calm as the TV shows a poker-faced, thin blonde woman sitting at a press conference, and a tense, forty-something man, flanked by police.

'That's her!' Soozie squeals. 'The mother! My god, she's had some work done. And the real dad. James. He's now estranged from her, from what I hear. Always seemed nice. Used to collect Anna from nursery sometimes. Worked in advertising.'

I reach for the remote and turn up the volume. 'Somebody must know where my baby is,' the thin woman sobs, staring directly into the camera. Beside her, the grey-haired dad sits silently, his green eyes filled with terror, exactly like Anna's, and I'm suddenly hit by a ghastly wave of nausea.

'B-back in a sec,' I stammer, pushing through the rear salon door into the tiny courtyard, where I vomit copiously on the ground. Every pore in my body is sweating, and as I stare at the remnants of last night's pizza, I hear Soozie's voice calling softly through the door.

'Melinda? Are you OK?'

I grab some tissues from my pocket and wipe my mouth. 'Food poisoning,' I reply. 'Sorry, honey. I'll have to close the salon today.'

'Can I get you anything?' she ventures. 'Some water? An Uber? Tell me your address and I'll book one now. Or I can drive you?'

No, no, no. I need to be alone, to *think*.

'It's OK, Soozie. Just put the "closed" sign on the door for me, please. I'll see you for your appointment tomorrow.'

'If you're sure. Take care, darling.'

She totters out of the door, stiletto heels clicking on the polished stone, while on the TV the green-eyed man sobs for his daughter's safe return.

Chapter Six

It was 10pm before Sue finally made it home. He'd texted, of course, apologising for his 'outburst', as he put it, and promising never to do it again. 'If only you didn't spend so much time at work…' The usual line. The feeling that somehow, underneath this twisted, toxic mess of a relationship, it was her fault. Maybe he was right. Maybe she did spend too much time at work. She hadn't replied. But she arrived home on time and opened the front door to the sound of soft jazz, a table set for two and the smell of her favourite dinner, coq au vin.

'I saw you on the telly,' Rob said softly, taking her coat ever so gently from her shoulders. 'Thought you'd need a good meal and a big glass of this.'

He handed her a gin goblet full of red wine. 'Tom's staying with a mate,' he added. 'And before you say it, I've checked. He's definitely there. Come and eat and you can tell me about your day.'

He wouldn't mention last night, of course. Neither of them would. What had happened would be swept up like yesterday's newspapers, discarded and forgotten. Until the next time.

'So, the missing girl,' he went on. 'Alive or dead?'

'I can't call it,' Sue replied. 'She switched off her mobile when she left home, so we can't cell site that, unless someone turns it back on.'

Sue took a huge mouthful of chicken, which Rob had clearly ordered in. 'It's the sheets,' she went on. 'The girl had boiled her bedsheets. Forensics are sweeping the room. I know something happened in there.'

'How are the parents holding up?'

'Badly. The mum is downing vodka like water. Her ex – the real dad – turned up wracked with guilt that he's had nothing to do with Anna for years. And as for the stepdad ... he went to work and acted like nothing was wrong. Shock can do that to people.'

The wine was going straight to her head, and in the soft light Rob topped up her glass with a gentle smile. He was so handsome, no doubt about it, but the prickling pain in her shoulders screamed at her to stand up, walk out and never return. 'Look, Rob...' she began, but his mouth was on hers before more words could come out and they had sex right there in the flickering candlelight, a whirl of confused emotions making Sue feel more alive, more needed, than she had ever felt before.

~

'Now who's hungover!' Mike grinned as she sidled into work five minutes late on Wednesday morning, last night's red wine still staining her lips. Sue mustered her best withering look.

'I've just been talking to Kim, the FLO,' he added. 'She's got her concerns about the stepdad, Paul. Nothing concrete, just a feeling. He doesn't have any previous.'

Sue nodded. The police Family Liaison Officers, or FLOs, were positioned to support the family, but spending so much time with them often unearthed suspicions and secrets.

'So we've got no more leads on CCTV?'

'Nowt. Uniform are still talking to people in the Charing Cross area.'

'What about the appeal?'

'Usual nutters claiming they did it. Couple of potential sightings but they're weak. One woman says there was a group of girls on the Tube heading to Canary Wharf and one looked like Anna. We're checking the Jubilee Line CCTV. But one anonymous caller reported a girl in a Soho coffee shop, deep in conversation with a middle-aged woman. Sobbing, apparently. That's why she caught their eye. Reckoned it was Monday evening, about 5.30pm. Had a similar rucksack.'

'Which cafe? Don't tell me, Starbucks or Costa.' Sue was immensely proud of the fact she'd never frequented either of them. Anywhere. Even for a takeaway.

Mike flicked open his notebook. 'Nope. Independent one. The Coffee Bean Factory. You'll love this. Website says the coffee is special because the beans spend six weeks floating their way over here on traditional boats. Probably in sacks hand-woven from yak hair.'

Sue smiled. 'Utter bollocks. But let's find out for ourselves and pay them a visit.'

The supposedly fast train into town seemed to take forever, eventually crawling within sight of modern London, glitzy and domineering over the drab brown council blocks. Sue and Mike sat in frustrated silence, though as they drew to yet another unexpected halt outside Vauxhall, the broken aircon mixed with the August heatwave and Sue's hangover to leave her sweating and tense. Hot beads of sweat prickled on her forehead and a familiar panic rose up from her stomach to her chest.

'You OK, boss? It's boiling in here. Take your jacket off.'

Mike reached his arm around Sue's shoulder to help, but she pushed it away roughly. 'I'm fine. Just hungover. Back in a minute.'

Fortunately, the mid-morning train was half-empty, and Sue made it into the stinking toilet before she vomited. She clutched the sink and stared at her pale reflection in the mirror, unable to control the hideous flood of thoughts in her head. Had Tom heard what happened? Would he turn out to be like his father? And most intolerable of all, would he have so little respect for her that he'd leave at eighteen and never speak to her again?

Sue had no answers, only questions, and the more she tried to push them away, the more they spiralled. Rob loved her, she was sure about that. He couldn't help the outbursts.

Growing up with a violent father had scarred him too deep. He didn't mean to hurt her. He just lost control sometimes. Always when he'd had a drink. She pushed the tap to rinse her mouth, but the smell of the disgusting grey water that spurted out made her vomit again.

She'd thought about leaving, when it first happened, shortly after they moved in together. It came out of the blue, fifteen years ago. She'd been out with the girls and got home around midnight. Suddenly she was on her back on the sofa, Rob pinning her down, his face thrust against hers, the smell of wine on his breath, spitting bile at her so fast that drool fell from his lips. Her arms felt like they were going to break. But the pain was nothing compared to the shock and fear. All she could think about was staying still, staying silent, making herself as small and invisible as it was possible to be, protecting the three-month-old baby growing inside her.

It was over in seconds. She should have left then. But as he released her, the tears began to fall. Proper, agonising tears that came from the heart. How he'd seen his father do far worse to his mother. How he'd promised he'd never be like that. How sorry he was. How he hated himself and how he knew she'd never forgive him. She hugged him close, trying to protect him from the overwhelming rush of emotions that engulfed them both. And she stayed.

Gingerly she took off her sweat-soaked jacket, wiping down her damp arms with loo roll. She wasn't proud of the pale, bruised reflection that stared back at her. Most of the time she hated herself far more than the twisted love-hate feelings she had for him. But she was proud that she'd put plenty of bastards behind bars. Bastards who hurt people. And he'd never hurt Tom. That was what really mattered.

The train jolted, and Sue's panic began to subside. She was on the move, no longer trapped in the maze of her own thoughts. She had a missing girl to find.

Chapter Seven

I'm still shaken up by what happened yesterday. I could so easily have cracked, told Soozie everything and given the entire game away. The police hunt for Karen – sorry, Anna – is still all over the TV – not to mention social media, where her friends have started a desperate campaign, #findanna. But I can't have the police poking around in my life, stopping me from helping lost souls. They'd never understand. And there are so many more still out there who need me, the mother they never had, to care for them while they get back on their feet and set them free, starting a new life with me and their siblings as their family. Safe and loved. I can give them that.

I'm their fairy godmother, undoing their pain, undoing my past. All I ask for is their loyalty, their unconditional love. That's all any mother wants. I know how it feels to have parents who crush your soul with their actions or their silence, forcing you inwards to a place where nothing and no one can reach you, cowering until the darkness comes, spewing its rage and hate, exploding like a shit-filled supernova. Caring for them, being their mother, sets me free from the prison where I've spent much of my life, where I'm all smiles on the surface but inside I'm often so desperately alone. It feels good to be needed. That's why I help them. And because nobody, not a single, bastard soul, helped me.

Soozie's back, and I'm finishing her nails. I have to ride this out, make sure it's business as usual. Behind me, I've changed the channel from Sky News to *Bargain Hunt*. Trouble is, Soozie won't stop talking about Anna. She's convinced a serial killer is on the loose.

The salon door opens and Cleo strides in, the ideal distraction. She's wearing a polka-dot mini skirt, with legs that most of my clients would kill for. Long, lean, utterly toned from hours in the gym. But it's her shoulders that are the real giveaway. They're just too angled, too square to be as feminine as she longs to look. The Adam's apple, too. I'd never tell her any of that, of course. To me, she's perfect.

'Cleo!' They air kiss, Cleo tossing her long red hair over one shoulder and Soozie holding her freshly-painted pink nails safely in the air as she sweeps out of the door. 'How are you, darling? Coffee soon?'

They've never had coffee. They never will. But bumping into Cleo regularly at the salon for the last two years means they keep up this pretence of a friendship. And Soozie likes to tell everyone that she has a trans friend. It's so much more on-trend than having a gay one.

Cleo places her thick fingers in the bowl of warm water

and smiles. Her wife Helen will be back at home now, in their small suburban semi, exhausted after a day of caring for two under-fives. She's small, mousey – just like her husband, thirty-something Charlie in his work clothes, coming out of the council offices in a nearby town.

The address Cleo had given on my registration card didn't exist, so as the weeks passed I'd coaxed her into talking about work. Cleo hadn't seen me board the bus, her dark hair short and brushed back, her men's suit crisply tailored, or notice as I followed her down the dark street to a front door, where she scooped two toddlers into her arms and mousey Helen shrilled: 'Daddy's home!'

'I've had a *hell* of a morning,' says Cleo.

'Your brother?' I venture, raising an eyebrow. I don't want her to sense I'm stressed.

'Exactly. You won't *believe* what he's done now, the bastard.'

I look up from her nails and open my eyes slightly wider, quizzical.

'He's put the house on the market. *On the market*. Says he needs the money. I told him, that's Mum's old house and I don't want to sell it. I won't *let* him sell it.'

'Oh, honey. Can you stop him?'

Cleo sighs. Her gaze drifts to the window.

'He says if I don't agree, he'll tell Helen. About me.'

'But that's blackmail!'

We sit in silence for a few moments, Cleo's eyes filling with tears. Over my shoulder, the lunchtime news has started and I try desperately to block it out. 'Have you thought any more about, you know, telling Helen yourself?' I say gently.

Cleo shakes her head. 'I can't. She won't understand. And then there's work…'

It's been six months since Cleo's brother found out the boy he'd grown up with was trans. I thought he should know. She only dressed as a woman one day a week, when she came to me. Everything else about her life was too staid, too rooted in fear and in the past for her to come out and be the person she really was. Fifteen months of listening to her airing the same old fears was making me unhappy and frustrated. I wanted Cleo to be herself, to escape the prison she'd made for herself and not leave her real soul in the shadows. A few secret snaps on my iPhone and an email sent from an internet cafe ten miles away were enough to do it. I thought her brother would feel the same as me, and talk Cleo into telling her wife. He didn't. I've regretted sending that email ever since.

'Anyway, I'll have that Powerful Pink again,' Cleo sighs, casting her watery eyes over the rainbow of bottles.

She always comes to me on a Thursday morning. Helen doesn't know she works four days instead of five. Or about the hotel room that Cleo rents by the hour, round the back of Waterloo station, with its peeling paint and dirty, stained bed. That's where she transforms herself, stripping away the browns and beiges and flat shoes and replacing them with colour and drama and heels. By 6pm, it will all be gone. But for those few hours, Cleo is herself again.

'Do you really think he'd tell your wife? About you?'

Cleo shrugs. 'I've told you he said I'm repellent. That Mum would be turning in her grave with disgust. So, yes, I think he might. Unless I let him sell.'

I stroke her huge hand gently, massaging in some oil.

'He's a pig. And I hate to say it, honey, but even if you let him sell, he could tell her anyway.'

She looks down at her nails and swallows hard. Her pain floods right through me, making me feel alive. I wish it didn't.

'Sometimes I want him dead,' she whispers.

I nod. 'Well, if it ever comes to it, Cleo, I do know where to find someone who could help with that.'

The shock on her face tells me I've stepped way out of line. 'I'm joking, honey,' I smile quickly, letting my face fill with warmth, allowing her to relax. 'Now, let's get this Powerful Pink on.'

Chapter Eight

The Coffee Bean Factory on Soho's Greek Street was everything Sue hated. Uncomfortable designer chairs, lairy zig-zag decor, ridiculously overpriced coffee and 'home-made cakes' that clearly weren't. No CCTV. And the last thing the balding, fifty-something owner wanted, having rebuilt his trade after the pandemic, was any negative publicity.

'What makes you think she was here?' he snapped.

'There was a sighting,' Mike said firmly. 'And may I remind you that it is an offence to obstruct police inquiries. So unless you have something to hide – other than the potentially illegal workers staffing this place which I am currently overlooking – I'd start talking if I were you.'

The owner reddened. 'Juanita,' he said. 'Over there. The barista. She was working the afternoon and evening shift. Juanita, come here. These people need to ask you some questions.'

A thin, olive-skinned girl in her twenties nervously approached the table, her sleek black hair pulled back into a ponytail, brown eyes quizzical.

'We're looking for this girl,' Sue told her, placing a photo on the table. 'And we think she was in the cafe on Monday afternoon.'

Juanita glanced at the photo and looked away. 'I no know,' she replied in a thick South American accent.

'I know it's difficult,' Sue said patiently. 'But try and think back to Monday.'

'It so busy,' replied Juanita, her eyes darting nervously about the cafe.

Sue leaned forwards across the table and picked up the photo of Anna. 'Look, Juanita, I'm not going to ask about things like national insurance numbers or visas. I just want to find a missing girl. She could be in terrible danger. She could be being held somewhere. This is our chance to save her. So, please, just tell me what you know.'

The barista glanced across at Mike, who nodded reassuringly. 'They sit there,' she replied, pointing at a table towards the back of the cafe. 'I see the rucksack. She hold it like baby.'

'Was it definitely this girl?' Sue pressed, pushing the photo across the table.

'Yes, I sure. It her.'

'Can you describe the rucksack?'

'It look like the one on TV. In the news. Blue, with teddy bear on the zip.'

Mike opened a photo on his phone. 'Like this?'

'Yes. It the same. I see the rucksack on TV.' She gazed down at the floor, her eyes wet. 'I too scared to ring.'

'It's OK, Juanita,' Sue said softly. 'You are helping now. Who was she with?'

'A woman. Brown hair. The girl do all the talking. They here for a long time. I no seen them before.'

'Did you see the woman close up?'

'Yes. She buy cake. For the girl. Brown hair. Maybe age thirty. Or forty. I no know. I see her eyes. So blue. Bright blue.'

'What was her voice like?'

'British, I think. You all sound same.'

'What did she say?'

'She ask for the cake and say "thank you, honey". No else.'

'Did you hear what they were talking about?'

'No. The cafe very full. But the girl cry sometimes. The woman nice to her. She give her hug.'

'How long were they here?'

'Must be a couple of hours. I no sure.'

'Did they leave together?'

'I no see. I go for my break and when I come back, they gone.'

'What time was that?'

'I go 6.30pm. Come back 7pm. On the dot. The boss no like us be late.'

'What about the people sitting near them? Were they regulars?'

'Regulars?' Juanita looked confused.

'People who come here often.'

'No. Everyone all different. Lots of holiday people. *Turistas*.'

Anna had been here, Sue was sure of it. 'We'll need you to help us draw a picture of the woman,' Sue said. 'If we can find her, we might find Anna. You must come to the police station with us now. And don't worry. You're not in any kind of trouble.'

'You promise?'

'I promise.'

Still unsure, Juanita went to collect her bag and coat. 'Watch she doesn't make a run for it,' Sue whispered to Mike, who followed her out the back of the cafe. From what she'd heard, there was every chance Anna was still alive.

Chapter Nine

I'm in bed at a Premier Inn a couple of miles from the salon. It's surprisingly cosy, with soft purple and white bedding, recessed lights and views over fields with horses. Much nicer than my flat. That's how I spend my Thursday afternoons. I'm a little in love with Cleo, you see. She intrigues me. Someone else who just doesn't fit in. A wonderful distraction.

'Shall we see what's on TV?' She smiles, curling her bare legs around mine. 'It's almost five. I've got to go soon.'

I don't let her touch me, or even look at me naked. She wants to, but I enjoy giving her pleasure. I get my release after she's gone, or when I'm at home. A psych would tell me I'm obsessed with control. Screwed up by my father. Maybe both. Maybe they'd be right.

Cleo loves classical music. She has a first in music from Cambridge, plays the flute – though I've never heard her – and we've been listening to Bach's Goldberg Variations all afternoon, her iPhone plugged into a speaker. Every week she introduces me to a piece I haven't heard before. My father never did get me the piano lessons, but he arranged for me to use one in the local pub every Saturday morning before it opened and I'd hammer away on the sticky, beer-stained keys, teaching myself from a second-hand grade one book until the podgy landlord unlocked the doors for the day and told me to go. Cleo says music is just subconscious counting, and she's right. Whenever I need to zone out, I listen to Bach, mostly, or Chopin, my mind transported to a rolling seascape of rising and falling musical notes, where nothing else can reach me.

The Variations have ended, and she picks up the remote control, flicking through the channels, stopping on Sky News. That's when I see it. My face. Well, sweet Sally's face, but it's right there on the TV. 'Police are hoping to trace this woman,' says the reporter, as an artist's sketch fills the screen. 'They believe she was with Anna shortly before she disappeared, in this coffee shop in Soho.'

It's the eyes that terrify me. The hair, the lips, none of them really resemble mine. Maybe the shape of the face does, at a push. But the eyes are identical. Even down to the shade of blue. My throat tenses with fear. I should have put my brown contacts in. It had to be that barista. I should never have gone back up to the counter for the cake.

'Oooh, they've found a *suspect*,' trills Cleo, and suddenly I want to be anywhere but here. 'In that missing girl case,' she adds.

My throat is so dry that no words come out. 'What case?' I croak.

'You know, silly. That teenager who disappeared. Anna something. It's been all over social.'

Cleo is starting to deeply irritate me now. Speaking like she's a hip teenager, not a shy, flute-playing civil servant living a half-life. But I can't let her see that I'm riled.

'Yeah, I read something about it. Maybe the woman was trying to help her.'

Cleo paused. 'Maybe.' She looked back at the screen, where the artist's impression gazed out. 'I don't think so. Look at those eyes. They're psychotic. I know nuts when I see it.'

The sketch is all over social media. And the news. Anna's friends are split into those pleading with her to get in touch, and those who want 'her captor' to let them know where she is. I wish I'd never met her. Sometimes the fear of the police tracing me, wrecking the secret life I've built, is overwhelming, and I have to lie on my bed, eyes screwed shut, waiting for the terror to pass. If I was Soozie, I'd have a drink. But I don't touch alcohol. I've never liked that feeling of being out of control.

Sally had to go, of course. I'd already burned the clothes in my fireplace, and now the wig had gone too, just a few charred remains scattered in the grate. It was like saying goodbye to a close friend. She'd helped me with Number

One. Tanya. Sixteen. A kid from Middlesbrough who'd grown up on the wrong side of the tracks. Drug addicts for parents. In and out of care. It was finding her mum dead in a bedsit – overdosed on shitty heroin three days earlier, a needle still hanging out of her arm, her dehydrating skin turning black – that sent her to London, looking for a way out. She met Sally, and never had to go back.

It's been twenty-four hours since I first saw the sketch, and my blind panic is subsiding a little. I've worked out an emergency exit plan. The thought of using it is stressing me out, but I'll only do that if I have no choice. I can't let them catch me. I won't. There are too many souls who will need me, souls I haven't met yet. And if I don't keep trying to help them, keep undoing my past, that twisted, blackened void inside me starts to open up, drowning me in memories, dragging me back to a place that I cannot go.

So for now, I've got to make sure it's business as usual. Soozie is back in the salon. She wants diamantés added to her fingertips.

'I had coffee with the mother yesterday,' she tells me.

'Which mother?'

'*The* mother. Zoe. The one whose daughter has gone missing.'

Under the table, my right leg begins to twitch nervously, but I keep my hands steady.

'Really?' I reply carefully placing a diamanté in the centre of her thumbnail. 'What did she say?'

Soozie's voice drops to a whisper, even though the salon is empty. 'She was pissed. Very pissed. Vodka in the coffee cup. Kept blaming herself for Anna running away. Said she should have done something sooner.'

'Done what?'

'I don't know. But she's in a bad way. Maybe she feels bad that Anna hasn't got a relationship with her dad. Zoe ran off with his best friend and it all went tits up.' She glances around again, checking the coast is clear, with an irritating self-importance. 'Paul. I've met him at a few charity balls. *So* handsome.'

I think of Anna, baring her soul to me in the coffee shop. How it started when she was in primary school. At first it was helping Paul to make a 'secret milkshake'. Soon it was more. Much more. How he'd threatened to tell her mother about their 'affair' if she spoke out. I'd done the right thing. She couldn't go back to that.

'Did you hear they're looking for a woman?' Soozie went on. 'That's got to be a good sign. Zoe's hoping maybe this woman found her somewhere to stay and now Anna's too embarrassed about all the fuss to come home.'

I place her hands under the nail dryer. 'I wonder.'

Chapter Ten

'Got another date tonight, Mike?' smiled Sue, as they drove towards the private estate. Ahead, the sun was setting, turning the warm Friday evening into hues of pink and gold.

'I wish. And I wish I'd never let you talk me into trying that horse riding. The physio says it'll be six months before my shoulder is back to normal.'

Divorced, thinning on top, a portly figure and a broken nose – busted years ago during a run-in on a burglary – forty-eight-year-old Mike wasn't, on the face of it, much of a catch. Not to mention the ex-wife who had screwed him over in the courts for such a huge maintenance payment that he now lived in a tiny ex-council flat in Kingston, where the walls were so thin that he constantly had to turn a deaf ear to the dubstepping and drug dealing next door. Sue had never been on Tinder but she was pretty sure he'd be a swipe left for no. And that, she decided, is where online dating got it wrong. Mike was a good guy, a big bear of a man always ready with a witty comment, a hug, a coffee, an anecdote. He was also a damn good detective, and someone who it felt good to be around.

Her son, Tom, liked him too. She'd been so busy in the five days since Anna went missing that she'd only seen Tom once, passing ships, as he headed to school. He hadn't mentioned the 'episode', as Sue silently called it. He never did.

Pinning down Anna's stepdad for a second time hadn't been easy, especially as Sue now wanted to speak to him informally at home. Something about him set alarm bells ringing. Maybe it was the fact he'd appeared too in control at their first meeting at his City office. They'd finally agreed on 8.30pm. Rob would be angry when she got back, Sue was sure of it. There was no way she'd make it home before ten.

She turned into the wide gravel driveway and parked outside the triple garage, quickly sending Rob a short text saying: *On a job. Urgent. Back around 10pm. Love you xxx* followed by a smiley face. She'd texted him earlier, too, warning him she'd be late, but he hadn't replied. That didn't bode well.

Zoe answered the door and showed them into the immaculate kitchen, where Paul was perched on a bar stool with a glass of red wine, still dressed in an obviously very expensive suit and tie.

'Thank you for coming,' he said, springing to his feet and formally shaking Sue and Mike's hands. 'Any news?'

'We've had quite a few calls about the artist's sketch,' Mike replied. 'Plenty to follow up. But we just need to make sure we've crossed all the i's and dotted the t's, so if we can run through your movements again the night before Anna disappeared, that would be really helpful.'

'Sure. Though I've told you everything I know.' He picked up his iPhone. 'I was in the office all day Sunday. Got home about 9pm.'

'Remind me why you were there on a Sunday?' Sue interjected.

'The IT teams are migrating us onto new software and I didn't want any fuck-ups on Monday morning, so I went in and stayed late to test it. There were plenty of people around who can confirm that. But I'm sure you've already checked.'

Sue looked down at her notepad. 'And you said Anna was at home?'

'In her room, yes. She had her TV on. I asked her if she wanted a takeaway curry, but she said no. Zoe was out at a party.'

'Had you planned to join Zoe there?' Mike asked.

'Good lord, no. It was an Ann Summers one. All Tillingham mothers. I'd have been eaten alive.'

Zoe took a deep swig of wine and met Sue's eyes. 'Sorry I didn't mention that to you,' she slurred. 'It just sounded a bit seedy.'

'So what did you do, Paul?' Sue went on.

'Ordered a curry for one – from the Taj Mahal on Cross Street if you need to check – watched some TV and went to bed. Next morning, just before I left for work, Anna was making coffee. Must have been 7am. She said she was going to meet friends later, in Kingston. I haven't seen or heard from her since.'

Sue nodded thoughtfully. 'What is your relationship like with Anna?'

Paul bristled suddenly. 'Fine. I'm not her dad, but we never argued, if that's what you're getting at. She had the odd teenage tantrum, but who doesn't.' He paused. 'Look, what's this all about? Shouldn't you be out there looking for her? If I'm under some kind of suspicion I need to ring my lawyer.'

'There's no need to worry, Mr Eaves,' Sue said soothingly. 'We're just making sure we've got all our ducks in a row. Now, Monday night. You got home around 9pm?'

'Yes. Zoe said she was worried as she hadn't heard from Anna.'

'Were you?'

'No, to be honest. I assumed she was still with friends. If they'd gone to the cinema late afternoon, they were probably having dinner somewhere. There's masses of restaurants in the Rotunda centre, by the cinema. Zoe couldn't trace her iPhone but I thought it was probably just out of battery. And Zoe said she'd taken her spare inhalers, but maybe they were just in her bag when she grabbed it.'

'So when did you start to worry?' Mike asked.

'Early hours of Tuesday morning. But she's done it before so I thought she'd be holed up in a Travelodge.'

'What did you make of her room?' Sue added.

'Zoe and Zelda told me it had been tidied. I never went in there. It just looked like a girl's bedroom to me. Look, I'm happy to help but shouldn't you be out there looking for Anna? Someone must know where she is. What about the woman in the sketch?'

'We're doing all we can,' Sue replied, snapping her notebook shut as Zoe let out a sob before draining her wine and refilling it. 'Thank you again for your time.'

Outside, in the car, Sue gave Mike a knowing look. 'He said Anna "had" tantrums,' Mike said gravely. 'Past tense.'

'Let's put him under surveillance. I want to know where he is, who he's talking to. The works. Voice intercept on all of his calls. And get the team to check CCTV from Soho to Waterloo at around 7pm on Monday to see if she retraced her steps home. Maybe she came back here after all.'

It was gone 10pm by the time Sue pulled up outside her 1930s semi, deep in the heart of Surbiton's Berrylands, her mind firmly on Paul Eaves. Something wasn't right.

They'd lived in the semi since shortly after Tom was born, spending so much to buy it that modernisation was still a distant dream, its faded seventies avocado bathroom rapidly becoming a sought-after vintage item. The outside light was on, the curtains open and Tom was watching *Love Island* with what looked like a bowl of cereal. 'Had a good day, love?' she smiled, flopping onto the sofa beside him.

'Yeah. Had a history test.'

'Did Dad get you some dinner?'

'No. He's been down his shed all night. Said he'd got stuff to do.' He shrugged. 'Suits me.' He passed her the half-eaten bowl. 'Frosties are cool. Want some?'

Exhausted, Sue's eyes were already half-closed. 'No thanks, love.'

'How was the case? You're looking for the missing girl, aren't you? I saw it on the news.'

'Yeah. Anna.'

'She used to go to my junior chess club.'

'Really?

'Yeah. The one in Kingston. Wednesday nights. She was pretty good. Rating of 140, which was awesome for a junior. But she stopped coming. Probably around the time we all started senior school.'

'What was she like?'

'Nothing like that Instagram shot you've been using. She was quiet. Didn't say much. Kept herself to herself. Her stepdad used to pick her up afterwards.'

Sue felt the familiar pang of guilt, remembering how Tom had often had to walk to and from the club because she was held up at work, and Rob was running the kids' rugby club.

'Did you ever chat?'

'Maybe a couple of times at a tournament. But only about chess.' He gazed at Sue's red-rimmed eyes. 'Mum, you're exhausted.'

'I know. But there's a chance she's still alive. I could save her.'

Tom put his arms around Sue and hugged her tight. 'Stay there.' He smiled. 'I'll make us a hot chocolate.'

Five minutes later, a half-finished cup of hot chocolate on the coffee table in front of her, Sue was snoring on the sofa, dead to the world. Tom adored her. To him, she was a single parent, who had brought him up the best she could, not *with* his father but in spite of him. *One day,* Tom promised himself, *I will kill the bastard and set her free. Or earn enough money so that we can escape, move to Spain and start a new life. Somewhere where she can feel the sun on her skin, drink wine in the sun, and smile, without him as the puppet master.*

He reached down to take off her jacket, but the livid red marks on her arm stopped him in his tracks. His stomach lurched, and a familiar rage welled up inside him, a fury with nowhere to go. Tom carefully placed a blanket over his mum, turned out the light and glared out of the French doors up the long garden, where an orange light seeped from under the wooden shed door, its blackout curtains isolating his father from the world.

Chapter Eleven

I turn the grey Range Rover into Cobshott's Crown Estate, its blacked-out windows protecting me from cameras and prying eyes. Blackmailing Soozie's husband, Simon, had been easy. Three texts, a phone call and one meeting on a bench on the South Bank, dressed as a red-haired businesswoman, Beverley, nine months ago, had done it.

'So what do you want?' he'd asked, sweat pricking his botoxed forehead as I showed him the explicit photos of him and his twenty-something secretary on my phone. 'Money?'

'Your place in Cobshott. Riverdell. Where you fuck her. Mia.' Getting into character proved easier than I expected. It was the house of my dreams, the perfect place to create my sanctuary, and I sure as hell wasn't going to blow it. 'I need somewhere to stay for a while. Somewhere private.'

'It's ... it's an investment.'

'Which Soozie doesn't know about. Yet. How much is it worth? Two million? Three? If this gets messy and goes to the divorce courts, your escape plan, your little nest egg, will be thrown into the mix. She'll get a massive cut of that too.'

'I'd rather she had it than give it to you.'

I sighed. 'What I want is a temporary private place, somewhere I can go about my business unnoticed. You give me the keys to the house and the car, let me stay there and never, ever interfere in what I do. You never contact me. You ensure all the bills are paid. You ensure no one comes to the house, including you. No cleaners. No "men coming to do some work". No one. In return, I tell Soozie nothing. And in a couple of years, I move on.'

Simon hesitated. 'Or,' I added, picking up my phone, 'I can text her these photos right now.'

'Wait!' He watched as I carefully placed the phone back on the bench. 'How do I know you'll move out?'

'Because my business here will be finished. When it's done, I'll give you the new keys and the new codes for the alarms.' I smiled. 'And, by the way, should anything happen to me, anything at all, a friend has instructions to hand-deliver a sealed package to Soozie. They have no idea what is in it.'

'This is fucking blackmail.'

'No, Simon, it's a business arrangement. We both get what we want.'

His eyes blazed. 'Who the hell are you? And how do I know you won't tell Soozie anyway when you leave?'

'Who I am is not your concern. As for telling Soozie, you'll have to trust me on that. Like I say, when my business is done, I'll have no interest in Cobshott anymore.'

And that was it. The vast, detached mansion, Riverdell, is perfect. The house of dreams, where my children can escape the pain, with me as their doting mother, starting their new lives. Even a piano for me to practise on. Sometimes I have to be strict, of course – every mother has to – but it's for their own good. I just hope taking Anna doesn't lead the police here and destroy everything I've built.

As a child, I'd pore over my book of fairy tales, marvelling at Cinderella's pretty gown and praying that a fairy godmother would turn up. In my teens, I ached for a long-lost relative to whisk me away to their huge, modern home, a world away from my father and the poky Victorian cottage with its creaky boards and windows rattled by the east wind, until I realised that I'd have to make that life for myself. Now I was doing just that, and being the godmother I never had. I want my new family to live happily at Riverdell for as long as I can blackmail Simon. After that, who knows? Perhaps I can persuade him to buy us a house by the sea in return for my silence. That would be a cheaper option for him than Soozie finding out the truth. And if I make our home perfect, no one will ever want to leave.

I go in and out of Riverdell by Range Rover, dressed as

Beverley. Heels, big hair, skinny jeans and waterfall cardigan. Sometimes Lululemon and trainers. The wardrobe is full of Mia's designer clothes, and shoes to die for, doubtless bought on Simon's credit card. Tens of thousands of pounds' worth. I'd guessed there would be a few outfits there I could use, so I'd told him to leave some of her clothes behind, but this was like winning the lottery. He'd left the lot. Maybe she had nowhere in her poky flat to keep them. Maybe he just bought her some more. Every piece is perfect Cobshott attire, not that it matters. No one sees me. The house is completely secluded, backing onto a forest, with electric gates and a twisting tiled driveway surrounded by trees. Safe. The family home I'd dreamed of.

As the Range Rover approaches, the garage doors open automatically, closing swiftly once I'm inside. I open the boot and take out a Tesco bag of shopping, plus a packet of antibiotics I had in the bathroom cabinet. She'd been coughing a lot, and it sounded like a chest infection. Not good. And the asthma inhalers weren't working. I'd need some more of those, too. But first, dinner.

I love cooking at Riverdell. They have Sabatier knives, every kind of saucepan hanging up over the island, honestly it's like Jamie Oliver's kitchen. Stainless-steel worktops, sleek-grey cabinets, a cavernous American fridge with an ice machine and a single button closes blackout blinds over the – you guessed it – bifold doors. It's a million miles away from our tiny kitchen back in Yarmouth, with thin lino on the floor, beige Formica worktops and a

Hotpoint fridge with minced beef Crispy Pancakes in its freezer.

Tonight I'm making us vegetable stir-fry. We'll both like that. I can't eat meat anymore. When you've seen flesh rotting, putrid and bloated, it puts you right off.

Chapter Twelve

'We've got a breakthrough,' Mike gabbled down the phone at 6am, as Sue stumbled into the bathroom on Saturday morning, trying not to wake Rob. 'Retracing Anna's steps on CCTV around 7pm has worked. We couldn't find her in Soho, but we've got someone who looks exactly like Anna, with the same woman, boarding a train around ten past nine that night at Waterloo. They get off at Surbiton, just a bus ride from her house. That's when we lose them.'

Sue rubbed her eyes. 'So we think the woman was taking her home?'

'Possibly. I've got uniform talking to people on Surbiton High Street right now. Someone must have seen them. It was a warm night, so plenty of punters out on the streets and outside the pubs. We're going through the CCTV on local buses.'

'What about stepdad Paul?'

'You're going to love this. Two days of surveillance and nothing. He goes to work. Goes home. One visit to the GP. Nothing on his phone. But Forensics found a pay-as-you-go burner under the spare wheel in the boot of his car. We've just got access to its text messages. Quite a few sexy ones to someone called Lola. Arranging to meet her at 3pm by Leicester Square tube on Monday, the same day Anna went missing.'

'You're joking?'

'Straight up. Lola texted Paul about 3.30pm to say she's stuck on a train at Raynes Park, and he replied that they'd have to rearrange it. That checks out – someone jumped at Wimbledon so the train lines were blocked. Lots more sexy texts after that right up until they found the phone yesterday, but no meet-up. We have witnesses who put Paul at work that day, but could he have slipped out for an hour? Maybe Anna saw him in Leicester Square with a bunch of flowers and knew her mum was hungover at home in bed?'

'Have we traced Lola? Or is it Anna?'

'The phone is registered to a Mrs Susannah Lightwater in Cobshott. Former big name in celebrity PR. Now a housewife.'

'Sneaky sod. Shagging the local yummy mummy.'

'Chief Biller says the Child Safeguarding Unit is snowed under. But as we're both ex-SGU, we can stay on it.'

'Good. Send a team to bring him in. Now. And you can pick me up in fifteen minutes. We need to talk to this Susannah.'

She heard Rob stirring. 'Go back to sleep, love,' she said gently, kissing his head. 'I've got to go into the office.'

Rob grunted, rolled over and Sue's stomach lurched. She wondered what she'd face when she got home tonight.

Soozie was doing a morning stint at the gym when the call came. Simon hadn't come home last night. Just a one-line text at 2am saying he was staying out with the 'lads from work' and 'hitting a casino'. Lads? How old was he, for fuck's sake? Silently seething, Soozie jabbed at the running machine's control panel, speeding up her pace slightly and sending nauseating waves of last night's Pinot Grigio surging through her body.

Sometimes when her self-confidence was low, which was pretty much all the time these days, only the gym or a trip to the nail salon would help. Or upping her dose of Prozac. Sometimes it didn't. Sometimes it took every ounce of her energy just to get out of bed and go about her day, the hollow emptiness of her life threatening to swallow her from every side. She envied those women who had a purpose, who boarded that 7am train in their suits and their heels, with spreadsheets and PowerPoints on their minds, who relished their new Karen Millen coats and their Chanel bags because they had earned them. Was it someone like that who Simon was seeing? Someone for whom life still held an excitement, a thrill, a goal other than trying to shift a sagging pot belly and trying to hide a loneliness that gnawed away at her very core. She couldn't even think about the girls. They'd been such sweet little things, and she knew she'd spoiled them into self-obsession.

It hadn't always been like this. When she'd met Simon, in his third year at Oxford and her second, they had so much in common. State schools, divorced parents, irritating siblings, a love of jazz-funk, T. S. Eliot and Mykonos. She was reading English, and in with an arty crowd, while he played rugby and occasionally turned up to a history lecture. It was the mid-1990s, when yuppies, suits and brick-sized mobile phones had long since given way to ecstasy, warehouse parties, Britpop and New Labour. They'd had a ball. And when he landed a job in the City and she went into celebrity PR, they bought a huge flat in London's Vauxhall, moving out to suburban Kingston just before the twins were born. Then leafy Cobshott. On paper, they had it all – the cars, the housekeeper, the designer house, the holidays, the huge City bonuses. She didn't need to work anymore, and anyway, dealing with celebrities' egos had become tiresome. Wafting round Cobshott was far preferable to dealing with the fallout of a famous face who dangled his balls in someone's Prosecco 'for a laugh'. Or keeping an actor's penchant for rent boys a secret.

But with each move, Soozie felt an emotional distance between her and Simon opening up, wider and wider. At first she loved having a housekeeper, cleaners, a cook, and life became a heady whirl of parties, Pilates and coffee mornings, joining in with the mothers' competitive boasts about their offspring's achievements – or blaming the lack of them on undiagnosed dyslexia – and complaining about the staff at the £4,000-a-term school. Unlike the others, Soozie didn't look down her nose at the few mothers who chose to work, or had to, when they arrived at the school gates late and stressed. Simon bonded with the dads, helped out at a kids' rugby club – which she figured made up for not having a son – they threw some legendary dinner parties, and Cobshott felt like the home she'd always wanted.

But then prep school came to an end, the girls took the train instead of Soozie doing the school run (even though she offered), and no longer relished her 'interfering', as they put it, in homework or their social lives. Some friends moved away or returned overseas, and without the children to talk about, Soozie realised she had nothing in common with those that were left. Her celebrity contacts were long gone, signed to new personal publicists who guarded them like hawks, her former colleagues feigned interest but cancelled at the last minute every time she arranged a date, and suddenly the closeted Cobshott life she'd created felt like a prison, where each day lay terrifyingly empty before her, a void that no amount of hairdresser's appointments or trips to the nail salon could fill. Simon became increasingly distant, returning home late and leaving early, and soon she was opening wine at four o'clock. Sometimes vodka. The talking stopped, the sex stopped, and they slept in the same huge bed but as far apart as they could, clinging to their own edges for comfort, as if their relationship were now so fragile that accidentally touching each other could break it. The doctor blamed the menopause and gave her Prozac to take the edge off, suggesting she go back to work, or try volunteering, using her PR skills to help a local charity. But as her belly sagged, so did her confidence and her desire to do anything, and she retreated into a caricature of herself, playing bossy, drama-queen Soozie towards her staff, putting her PR face on, never realising that after her fifth evening glass of wine, her housekeeper Miquita heard her crying herself to sleep every night.

Sometimes, on the treadmill, she thought of the girl who once ran naked around the quad, who stayed up all night with Simon just to watch the sunrise over the spires, who insisted on punting down the Cherwell and then fell in. Today was one of those days. The memories crowded out her anger, reminding her of who she really was, but they also tore at her soul, bringing a sadness that she would never feel alive again. It was into this uneasy mix of emotions that the phone call came.

Seeing her landline flash up on the screen, Soozie half-expected it to be him, home with his tail between his legs, a bunch of flowers from the Shell garage and a 'little boy lost' look on his face. She ignored it. But the phone rang a second time, then a third.

'Calm down, Miquita,' she snapped at her housekeeper when she answered the phone, slowing her gentle jog on the treadmill to a walking pace. 'What do you mean, the police are there? Has something happened to the girls? Or Simon?'

'They here to see you, Miss Lightwater. They not say

why. They want to wait. But they say it not about Mr Lightwater. I ask because he not come home. And the girls are in bed.'

'Have you checked their ID? They are police aren't they, not burglars?'

'They police. They show me badge. A man and a lady.'

Fifteen minutes later, an unwashed and mildly panic-stricken Soozie pulled into her driveway, slamming the Range Rover door shut with an unmistakably angry air.

'What's happened?' she snapped defensively, walking into her living room where Sue and Mike were waiting on the sofa, in front of a pot of coffee.

'Mrs Lightwater. I'm Detective Chief Inspector Sue Fisher and this is my colleague DI Mike Barley. We're investigating the disappearance of Anna Lightwater-Eaves and we need to ask you some questions about messages sent from your phone two weeks ago.'

'My phone?' Soozie was puzzled. 'Here it is.' She tossed her iPhone onto the sofa. 'Passcode is 7684. I had coffee with Anna's mum, Zoe, the other day. Anna was at nursery with my girls. What on earth makes you think I've got anything to do with it?'

'Mrs Lightwater,' Mike added gently. 'We have seen the messages. I understand this is difficult, but I need to ask about your relationship with Paul Eaves.'

'Paul Eaves? Her stepfather?'

'Yes.'

'I've met him at charity balls over the years.' An uneasy

mix of anger and fear welled up inside her. 'What do you mean, relationship? What messages?'

'Text messages between a phone registered to you and a pay-as-you-go phone we believe belongs to Mr Eaves were exchanged.'

'I've never…' Soozie paused. Her face paled. 'What sort of texts?'

'Sexual ones. From someone called Lola.' She checked the phone. 'It isn't this iPhone, Mrs Lightwater. Can I see the one ending 0980?'

Soozie froze, her eyes filled with dread. It had to be one of the girls.

'I know this is difficult,' Sue said softly. 'But I understand you have two teenage daughters. I have to ask, would that phone be used by anyone else in the family?'

Soozie sank onto the sofa, her perfectly-manicured hand clasping her face. 'I have three phones. Sky and Star, they're only fifteen… I-I don't know their numbers.'

Sue and Mike exchanged a glance.

'According to your contacts,' Sue said gently, scrolling through the phone, 'it's the number for Sky.'

Images raced through Soozie's head; sickening, vile, disgusting images, and the more she tried to push them out, the more horrific they became. Paul Eaves. The bastard. The sick, twisted, bastard. 'H-have they been—'

'As far as we can tell, they haven't yet met up,' Sue said quickly. 'It appears to have all been online. But we need to talk to Sky urgently. Is she here?'

'Sh-she's in bed.'

Miquita, who had been listening at the door, came in with a tray of fresh coffee and water. Seeing her, Soozie recovered some of her composure and sat up.

'Ask Sky to come down right now, Miquita,' she said quietly. 'No shower, no getting changed, no excuses.'

'Of course, Miss Lightwater.'

Soozie slumped back on the sofa, as sickening images of Sky and Paul Eaves burned in her head. The pervert. The disgusting pervert. How had he got Sky's number? How *dare* he?

They sat in uncomfortable silence, as Sue looked around the immaculate living room, with its white carpet, white silk sofas and cinema-sized TV screen. A tabby cat, Lola, was curled up in an armchair, utterly disinterested in the tension in the room.

Without makeup, and dressed in pyjamas, Sky looked like a lost little girl. Her bravado was gone, and she sat down beside Soozie, her phone in her hand.

'I heard what you were saying,' Sky blurted out in a little-girl voice. 'Mummy, he said he was a YouTuber.'

'Can you tell us about him?' Sue said softly. 'You're not in trouble. How did he first contact you?'

Soozie took her hand. 'I want you to tell the police everything, Sky. No bullshit. No lies. No PR. The truth. You haven't done anything wrong.'

Sky pulled her hand away. 'He sent me a text. Said a friend gave him my number. Maybe a month ago. Said he was called Daniel. And nineteen. He sent me *photos*. There must be some mistake. He's not old. Maybe it's his son.'

'Paul Eaves doesn't have a son,' Soozie whispered. 'Only his stepdaughter.'

'Did he ask you to send him photos of yourself?' Sue asked.

'No. Nothing like that. We chatted. He was nice. After a couple of weeks, things got a bit … sexy.'

'Were you uncomfortable with that?'

'No.' She blushed. 'I liked it. He asked how old I was, and when I said I was nearly sixteen he said it was good because I'd soon be *legal*.'

Soozie gasped.

'And he asked you to meet him?' Sue went on.

'Yes. On Monday. He said we could go for a late lunch near Leicester Square. But some idiot had jumped so the trains were fucked… Sorry, Mum … *delayed*, so I texted him and he said he couldn't wait. I thought that was a bit off.'

'What about since?'

'We've messaged a few times. Sexy stuff. I asked to meet up, but he said he was busy YouTubing at the moment. Some new contract.' She paused. 'So he's like an old man? The one whose daughter has gone missing? Oh my god, I feel sick.'

Soozie put her arm around Sky's shoulder and this time she didn't push her away, burying her face. 'It'll all be all right, Sky,' she said soothingly. 'Everything will be all right.'

'His stepdaughter is missing, yes,' Mike said gently. 'We'll need to take your phone, Sky. Right now.'

She handed it to Sue, her face reddening. 'I've deleted all the messages.'

'That's OK, we can still retrieve them.' Sue sealed it inside an evidence bag.

'Really?' Sky hesitated. 'And I looked at YouPorn. When we were chatting. Because he said it was a good site.'

'Like your mum said, you haven't done anything wrong, Sky. But he has.'

Sky turned to Soozie. 'Please don't tell Dad. And please make Star promise not to tell my friends. She's listening at the bottom of the stairs.'

Inside the evidence bag, the phone lit up and a flood of WhatsApp messages appeared on the screen.

'I think she already has,' Sue replied.

'Star!' Soozie bellowed. 'Come here now. And give me that phone.'

Star appeared in the doorway, her face triumphant. 'I told you he was a paedo. You are going to get *so* many new followers when this comes out.'

'Give me that phone!' Soozie snapped, handing it to Mike. 'I'll have to tell your father, Sky. But like the police said, it's not your fault. Paul Eaves is the pervert. He's an arrogant sod, too. Superior. Always looked down on us because we're not rich enough to own a house on the Crown Estate.' She paused, as another sickening thought swirled into her head. 'Do you think he had anything to do with Anna's disappearance?'

'I can't comment on the investigation,' Sue replied. 'But we are following up all lines of inquiry.'

'You'll need to come to the station this morning to make a formal statement, Sky,' Mike added. 'Your mum can come too. We'll need any tablets, laptops and any desktop computers you've used.'

'Take the lot,' Soozie replied. 'And I don't want to see a word about this on social media, girls. Do you hear me? Not a word. That bastard needs to go down for what he's done.'

Soozie excused herself and went into the downstairs loo, where she stared at the puffy-eyed, haunted face in the mirror and promised herself that she would find out exactly what Paul Eaves had done. All of it. For the first time in years, she had a purpose.

Chapter Thirteen

There's a door from the garage down to the basement at Riverdell, home to a soundproofed 'panic room' hidden behind a false wall. Most of the posh houses have them – I know this from my clients, who see it as a badge of honour that they're rich enough to need one – though it had taken me a while to find it. I'd prepared it carefully, removing the landline, a bizarre amateur radio device, plus the cutlery, crockery and canned food stockpiles which the previous owners hadn't bothered to take with them, disabling the ability to open it from the inside. It's empty, apart from the bed, a pillow, pink sheets and a steel toilet. There's a bath and a sink on the far left. Cold, too, with grey concrete walls, a black tiled floor and a tiny vent linked to a system which pumps in purified air. I'd like to warm it up for her but I need to keep it as cool as possible.

The lights are on a timer which I've set to give exactly twelve hours before darkness. Night and day. The catch is the entrance door. It's like a walk-in safe, thick steel, with a one-way peephole looking out, so I can't see what she's doing.

I make my way down the stairs, carrying the plate of stir-fry, already dreading what I'm about to see. It's her own fault she's in here, I tell myself, over and over, as the guilt begins to claw at my chest. I'd hoped I'd never have to use it. The room was only ever going to be a last resort, somewhere to put a loved one who betrayed me, until they learned their lesson and were ready to rejoin my happy family.

'She has to learn *loyalty,*' I say out loud, as the darkness comes and the guilt is replaced by that rage, that fury that burns so hot, so menacingly that my hands begin to shake. I pause, and breathe deeply. She mustn't see my anger. The face I must present is of kind, thoughtful mother, to show her what she's thrown away. The life she could be living now. All of this, everything I'm doing, is for her own good. She has to learn. It's what she deserves. She's just too damaged to see it.

I tap in the code and it opens slightly. Light slices through the crack into the dim basement, but it's the smell that hits me first. I retch, before pulling a surgical mask from my pocket. Making sure I carry one is a trick I've learned. I can't bear more than a few minutes of this.

She's slumped on the bed, her T-shirt and pale jeans now a whirl of brown and grey, her wrists chained and her feet shackled together with a padlock I bought in B&Q. A short, thick chain attached to it allows her to move from the bed to the toilet, but no further. She's been scratching the wall.

'Hi, honey,' I say softly, through the mask. 'Are you feeling any better today? I've got you some more antibiotics. Don't you worry about the mess. We'll get that cleaned up.'

She sits up immediately, green eyes blinking.

'Thirsty,' she croaks.

'Of course, my darling. Here you are.'

I roll a large bottle of water across the floor. She grasps it and drinks desperately, which triggers a bout of retching and coughing. The shouting, the rage, the crying, the pleading, it has all stopped. She's given up asking why she is here, or when she can go home.

'I've made us some veggie stir-fry,' I add, placing a bowl on the floor within her reach. I've already crumbled some diazepam into it to take the edge off. 'Just how you like it. No peppers. And here are some antibiotics for your chest. Take them on an empty stomach.' I slide a blister strip of six tablets across the floor – I've checked, she can't overdose – followed by toilet paper and a packet of antibacterial wipes. 'Use these for now. I'll bring clean sheets later, and your nice cosy blanket. It's in the tumble dryer. I know it's chilly in here.'

'Th-thank you.'

I hover by the door, as she hugs her skinny, stained legs, rubbing them with the wipes, and rocking from side to side, just like I used to at night back in Yarmouth. Unexpectedly, I see myself on the bed, dabbing myself with tissues, hot tears burning my cheeks, and the memory triggers a sickening wave of fury. But Mother remains calm.

'Veggie sausage rolls,' I add, placing a pack of four on the end of the bed. 'Thought we could share them. But I'd better get this cleaned up first.'

There's a sharp buzz as a fly is disintegrated by the electric fly zapper I've installed on the wall. Most of the flies have gone now. The skin on her wrists and ankles burns scarlet, and she's been picking at a weald on her arm. Discarded plates and empty water bottles litter the floor, which I gather up and stuff into a bin bag. If only the bath was in use. Once the diazepam kicks in, I can change the bedding and wash her properly. Make her look beautiful again.

I would have given her everything, all the things I never had. A caring mother who adored her. A happy home full of life and love. If only she'd joined my family and repaid my trust with loyalty.

She drops the wipes, rips open the packet and stuffs almost an entire roll into her mouth. The sight of her, so dependent, so willing, pleases and repulses me. 'Careful, honey,' I say. 'You'll choke.'

She nods and takes another gulp of water, her attention totally focused on me, which, as always, I'm rather loving. She needs me now.

'So what treat do you want next?' I ask.

'Ch-chocolate.'

'You know it gives you spots, my darling. What about something else?'

Huge tears well up in her eyes. I let them linger there for a moment. 'All right. Chocolate. I'll bring some.'

She smiles, her teeth furred, her breath rank.

'Oh, and I got you a new book,' I say casually, sliding across a Virginia Woolf.

She picks it up. 'Th-thank you.'

'Have you read any of her novels?'

Now she's nodding, fervently, obediently, like the toy dog my father had in the back of his Cortina, and a blinding, red rage surges through me again. I can't let her see that. Control it, Mother. I force a smile behind my mask, my eyes creasing kindly.

'I'll be back tomorrow. Probably. Or the day after. With the chocolate. So don't drink that all at once. We can talk about the book. And I'll bring an iPod with some music. Classical. To continue your education.'

She's swallowed the sausage roll now, and she seems more focused. Her green eyes meet mine.

As I close the door, I hear her whimper.

'P-please don't shut it. Don't go yet. Leave it open. I can't get out. Just so I have some air. I just need air.'

The heavy door clicks closed. I sigh. I had such high hopes for her. We could have been upstairs now, enjoying dinner together on Riverdell's gold-rimmed china plates, fit for a queen. Maybe a movie afterwards, curled up in the cinema room. A dip in the indoor pool with its soft blue lighting. If only she'd let me give her the life I promised, the one I had ready and waiting for her, instead of turning on me. That I can't forgive. Not yet. For that, she must be punished.

I walk back up the stairs, eagerly gulping fresh air as I rip off the mask and open the door into the garage. Back in the kitchen, perched on a high stool by the island, I breathe deeply over and over until the rage slowly recedes, enough for me to eat my stir-fry and think about my exit plan. I'm praying I don't have to use it. Maybe the police will back off. Maybe she'll learn her lesson and become the doting daughter I dream of.

Minutes later, I drive the Range Rover out of the Crown Estate and onto the A3, parking it unnoticed on a gentrified suburban street, ten minutes' walk from my bedsit, where I carefully place Beverley's red wig on its stand, slip out of her red heels, turn on Bach's Brandenburg Concertos, and fall into a restless sleep.

Chapter Fourteen

Paul Eaves was proving a slippery character. Having availed himself of the best lawyer money could buy, he was resolutely sticking to his story that he last saw Anna around 7am the day she disappeared and replying 'no comment' to everything else. Including the evidence from the burner phone.

'They're trawling through his computers now,' Sue told Mike, as they took a much-needed coffee break. 'Still waiting on Forensics, but there's more than enough to charge him with one count of child grooming, and I can't see the judge releasing him on bail in the circumstances.'

'What's your gut feeling, Sue?'

'He abused Anna. That's what my money's on. And that's why she ran away. Reports from the school say she'd been even more quiet and withdrawn for the past few months than usual.'

Mike snorted. 'And they didn't think to act on that?'

Sue looked at him patiently. 'Mike, when you have kids – with a supermodel, hopefully – you'll realise that they all go quiet and withdrawn sometimes. But what confuses me is the mystery woman. My best guess is she was persuading Anna to go home. And if so, why didn't she come forward to help us?'

Her phone beeped. 'It's the forensics.' She opened the file, and smiled. 'We've got him, Mike. His semen is on Anna's mattress. Traces on the carpet too. And spots of her blood.'

They strode back to the interview room, where Eaves was sipping on a coffee.

'So, Paul,' Mike began. 'In our interview last Friday, you told us you'd never been in Anna's room. So can you explain how our forensics team have found your semen in the bed and on the carpet?'

He looked at his lawyer, whose face paled as she whispered 'say no comment'. But Eaves was cornered, and the confused, tortured emotions he'd been keeping under wraps for days came tumbling out.

'I swear to God, I don't know where she is,' he sobbed, waving away his lawyer.

'But you did have sex with her, didn't you?' Mike said.

Eaves sobbed ever louder. 'Just the once. Before that we just … did other things. Messed about.'

'Did your wife know this was going on?

'No. Zoe knew nothing. She was always … pissed. Passed out.'

'Mr Eaves,' Sue said brusquely, trying to contain her

feelings, 'Anna is missing. And right now, you are the chief suspect. So if, as you say, you had nothing to do with her disappearance, you had better start telling us the truth.' She paused. 'You began a sexual relationship with her when she was…?'

'I don't know.' He began to sob again. 'It started a couple of years ago.'

'So she was twelve or thirteen?'

'Yes. Probably. I don't know. I can't remember.' His face burned scarlet and the hot tears left greasy streaks across his cheeks.

'So you had full sexual intercourse for the first time the night before she went missing?'

Eaves put his head in his hands. 'Yes. For the first time. She seemed to enjoy it.'

A wave of anger and disgust surged through Sue, but she remained composed.

'Was that before or after the curry?'

'Before.'

'Did you argue with her after you had sex?'

'No.'

'So, afterwards you went downstairs?'

'Yes. I asked her if she wanted a takeaway but she said no. So I ordered it, ate it and went to bed about 11pm.'

'When did Zoe arrive home?'

'I don't know. Maybe 1am. Pissed. As usual. Fell asleep next to me, fully clothed. And the next morning, when I went to get her some water, Anna told me she was going to visit friends. That's the last I saw of her. I swear on my life.'

'And you expect us to believe that?'

Eaves rubbed his face with a handkerchief. 'Not really. But my life is ruined. Why would I lie?'

'To save you facing a murder charge? Life imprisonment?'

'Murder?' He glanced at his lawyer.

'And you'd better start telling us about Lola. I ask you again, how did you get her number?'

Eaves paled. 'A friend. He'd been chatting to her online. Said she was a game girl.'

'Which means…?'

'Up for some sexy chat. Maybe the odd photo.'

'Who is this friend?'

'I don't know his name. It was on the dark web.'

Sue fixed her gaze on him. Contacts on the dark web were untraceable, and they both knew it. 'We're going through your computers now, Mr Eaves. If there's anything on there, we'll find it.'

'I didn't download anything. There's nothing on them.' He let out another sob. 'I've been such an idiot.'

'Anna was going to tell the police about you, wasn't she?' Mike said gently. 'That's why you made sure that didn't happen.'

'No! That's not true.' He began to wail, a pitiful, whining sound that echoed around the interview room. 'I wouldn't hurt her. I *love* her.'

'We've checked with your office,' Sue added. 'They have no eyewitnesses placing you in the building between 2pm and 4pm on the day Anna went missing. She saw you, didn't she? In Leicester Square? Waiting for Lola?'

He shook his head.

Mike gave him a sympathetic look. Their good-cop-bad-cop routine was working. 'These things happen, Paul. We just need to know where she is. Things will look much better for you if you help us.'

'I don't know,' he wailed, turning to his lawyer. 'I don't know. I'm desperate for you to find her.' Mucus and tears dripped from his nose, and Sue had never seen quite such a pitiful yet repellent sight.

'My client needs a break,' the lawyer said firmly.

'Interview suspended, 10:33.' Sue snapped off the tape recorder and left the room with Mike on her heels. After what she'd heard, the break couldn't come too soon.

This time it was gone midnight when Sue finally made it home. She'd messaged Rob to say she'd be back as soon as she could. Emotionally and physically wrung out, the last thing she needed was grief from Rob for being late back. But to her surprise he was out, and a glow from under Tom's bedroom door told her he was still up, playing chess on his computer.

'Went out about nine,' Tom said, his eyes fixed on the screen. 'He was up the shed, and then I heard the front door slam. Didn't say anything. Sorry, Mum, I'm playing a grandmaster, give me a few minutes.'

Sue nodded and went down the creaky stairs to the kitchen, where the remains of a takeaway pizza lay in an open box, beside half a bottle of red wine and a half-empty wine glass. The soothing relief that Rob was out flooded through her. Glancing through the French doors into garden, she could see the shed was in total darkness. He'd been spending so much of his time up there lately, with the curtains drawn and the door locked.

Too tired to cook, and still hungry after the kebab that she'd shared with Mike on their way home, Sue plonked the pizza box and the wine glass on a tray and slumped on the sofa. Even though she was physically too exhausted to move, her mind kept auto-replaying today's interview with Eaves. She'd been a detective for fifteen years now, and his perverted lust for children sickened her to her core. But what she couldn't shake, and she couldn't understand why, was the feeling that he hadn't killed Anna.

Maybe it was the torment in his eyes. Maybe he was just a damn good liar. Maybe he was deluding himself. Or maybe it was that horrific wail he let out, a noise that she'd only heard once before, when telling a mum her son had died in a car crash. It seemed to come from the very depths of his soul, tormented by not knowing where the girl he loved so much had gone.

~

She woke up with a start, still on the sofa, just after 2am, as a car door slammed. A key in the lock, and Rob tiptoed in.

'It's OK,' he said softly, just as the fear of what might happen next began to engulf her. 'I'll take you up.' With that, his huge arms swept up Sue, carried her upstairs and laid her gently on the bed.

'You're coaching the kids' rugby tomorrow morning,' Sue murmured. 'Don't be late.'

'I won't. Get some sleep.'

She knew better than to ask where he'd been.

Chapter Fifteen

I step off the escalator at London's Camden Town tube station and emerge, blinking, into a brown dusk. Hordes of tourists huddle on the other side of the exit barriers, unsure what to do. They've arrived in the nirvana that is Camden Town and discovered it's little more than a grubby high street, a Vans shop, a twenty-something with an amp playing Hendrix, and the homeless. Lots of them. Filthy clothes, skinny, often shoeless, faces etched with torment that even heroin or spice can't hide. Dressed in skinny jeans, a psychedelic T-shirt, Converse shoes and leather jacket, with short brown hair, no one notices me as I stroll past. I'm at home here, myself, among the outcasts, the misfits, a world away from Cobshott's stripy lawns and artisan shops where music is Kenny G's 'Songbird' and drugs are a neat line of coke on a designer glass coffee table, chopped up with a gold Amex. Music here is raw, visceral, spewing out of the Electric Ballroom, and drugs are a greasy ball of cling film which just emerged from someone's arse, a deal done quickly down one of the alleyways, while the police turn a blind eye.

I'm still hoping I won't have to use my exit plan. But if I do, I'll need a powerful drug, something to knock her out for a few hours. The diazepam isn't enough. Heroin is perfect, so long as I'm careful she doesn't overdose. And this is the place to buy it. I stroll towards Inverness Street and duck behind the handful of market stalls packing up for the night, where two guys are leaning against the wall. I've already placed my order, using a pay-as-you-go burner phone, swapping my twenty-pound note for a wrap. There's always a chance that the police are having a crackdown and my heart thumps rapidly as I walk away, trying not to break into a run. It's in my pocket and I roll the greasy ball around in my fingers, looping back into the busy high street, where the shops are always open late, spilling out onto the pavement with their cheap 'London' T-shirts and tea towels. Tourists pore over the shoddy Big Ben ornaments, hoovering up key rings with mini red phone boxes and black cabs dangling from them, even though the reality of city life is now a mobile and an Uber. Up towards Camden Lock, over the little bridge, where people are packed along the tiny canal side, clutching pints and Pimm's and filling the air with the throng of conversation. This is Camden, and this is home.

I walk on past the lock, skirting the edge of Camden Market proper, with its cobbled streets, the smell of joss sticks and Chinese street food a deliciously heady mix. It's hours since I've eaten, so I stop in the hectic food market, gazing at the huge piles of stir-fry and vivid orange sweet-and-sour, before settling on a bowl of vegetarian Vietnamese pho. All the tables are full, so I stroll up to the statue of Amy Winehouse and perch beside it, the pho warming my belly and calming my restless mind. Beside me, three French students are sharing a silver tray of paella, while opposite a homeless man with one shoe picks at his blackened feet.

I drain the last of the pho and head out of the market, up the hill past the Roundhouse Theatre, pushing my way through the crowds waiting to get in. A vast Morrisons is on my left, and I cut through its car park to a short row of well-kept ex-council flats lined up along the banks of the canal. My key slides in the lock and I sink down onto the shabby sofa. No one notices when I come or go. London's anonymous like that. Not like Cobshott, with its twitching curtains and network of bored mothers texting each other every time a dog craps on the pavement.

This is where I stayed when I first came to London as a sixteen-year-old, not long after my mother's funeral, desperate to start again. Camden was my mecca. I'd heard all about its music scene, its clubs, a place where no one fitted in so everyone did. I'd slept rough for the first two nights, huddled in the doorway of the HSBC bank, until a regular came along, urinated copiously on me and told me in a slurred, drunken voice to fuck off. That's when I met Shauna. I was walking along the street, covered in pee, crying. She was mid-forties, with a weathered face and grey dreadlocks, on the way home from her job in a Camden record store. Took me back to her run-down, ex-council flat and let me sleep on the floor. Even washed my clothes in the sink and found me something to wear. I'd never seen anywhere like it. Tie-dyed throws over everything, joss sticks and candles burning constantly, and the whole room festooned with Buddhist peace flags. In the morning, I slid into bed beside her, begging her to hold me. She was soft, warm and so gentle, like the loving mum I'd never had.

Shauna wanted to go to India and find herself. She'd been single for years, since an ex broke her heart. So we did a deal. I'd take over her job at the music store and pay the rent in cash to her dodgy landlord, looking after the place until she came back. Suited me. I had a few thousand pounds from my mother's will, enough to keep the flat going, and once I felt settled I'd search the suburbs for a place to start my dream nail salon. Six years on, and I'm still here. Camden is home. Cobshott is work. Riverdell is charity.

The flat still looks almost exactly as Shauna left it, with the tie-dye decor, the sagging wood-framed bed, the piles of CDs and the big chest freezer in the corner, covered with her old eiderdown. And paying the landlord a year's rent in cash, upfront, means he leaves me well alone. I'd never bring my children here. They deserve the chocolate-box house, the white picket fence and the garden. They have their sanctuary. This is mine. I open the door and I'm home.

I shove one of Shauna's Fleetwood Mac CDs into the player, open a can of Diet Coke and check Twitter for the latest on #findanna, as 'The Chain' fills the air. My blood runs cold. There's a new update. And a new CCTV photo. It's Anna and me, on the train.

'Police are asking anyone near Surbiton station on Monday night about 21:30 to contact them. They believe Anna arrived there on the 21:12 from Waterloo. Did you see her?'

It's already been retweeted 24,049 times – make that 25,208, it's escalating by the second – and that's just the start. Facebook is awash with it. And Instagram. My throat tenses and I dig my nails into my arm so hard that it bleeds. Tanya and Cindy were a breeze. I thought she'd be the same – an unwanted, unloved, invisible girl who nobody missed. Now the whole world seems to be looking for her. People who've never met her piling in to share her story on their social media like it's their business. People quoting the tweet so their self-esteem gets a boost when it's retweeted. Most of them don't care about actually finding Anna, or the hellish home life she endured. It's the story that gives them a buzz. The retweets, the shares, the follows. This could destroy everything I've worked so hard to build.

I take the wrap of heroin from my pocket and place it on the table, as the music thumps. There's enough to do it. The police are on the hunt and getting closer. I could stay here, swallow the lot, drift away and escape this mess I'm in. *Running in the shadows, damn your love, damn your lies.* But then I think of Riverdell. She needs me now. I can't leave her there to starve to death. What kind of mother does that?

My exit plan would be an act of *mercy*.

Picking up the heroin, I snap off the CD, head out of the front door and back towards the Tube, eager to get back to my bedsit. The clock is ticking. There's so much I need to do.

I'm back in Surbiton watching an old episode of *Strictly,* trying to distract myself from Anna.

My phone beeps. A text pops up.

Can you talk?

It's Soozie. This is unexpected. She has my mobile number for emergencies. A broken nail is usually her excuse. We both know her immaculate nails bolster her fragile self-confidence. One chip, and all the anxiety about her empty, shallow life comes flooding through.

The phone starts ringing then and I answer.

'Soozie? You OK?'

'Mel, you are not going to believe what's happened. I need to talk. Can we meet at your place?'

'No,' I say calmly, ready with the excuse I give anyone who asks. I can't let her see this grubby bedsit. 'I've got friends staying. I'll come to you.'

'You can't. The police have been here. I don't want them to know what I'm up to. Christ, they might be tapping my calls.'

Now I'm scared. Properly scared, a real sense of dread

deep in my soul, but fear is a feeling I understand, and know how to handle. Suddenly I'm right back in my bedroom, waiting for the soft creak of the door, the slippers padding across the carpet. Even so, it creeps up my spine, squeezing my ribs and my breath sticks in my throat. I take a deep breath.

'The police?' My voice sounds hoarse, distant. I clear my throat. 'Why would they do that?'

'They're not. I'm just being paranoid. But after the day I've had…'

'Is it Simon?' My mouth is so dry the words barely come out.

'Oh, no. Nothing like that. It's Sky. But I need to chat in person.'

Sky. Not Simon. Sky. The fear lets go of its vice-like grip and my paralysed brain kicks into gear. Riverdell is safe.

'Meet me at the salon first thing in the morning. Nine o'clock.'

'OK. Thank you.'

She's gone, and I've bought myself some time. But I'm rattled. The police are even closer than I thought. There's no choice now. I'll have to put my plan into action.

I go into the kitchen, my head a mess, to make a strong coffee. The plan itself is risky. Then there's *her*. She's broken now, and almost ready to join me. To be a proper part of my life. That's all I want. There's a familiarity, a comfort in having her around, like a favourite cardigan. But it's too dangerous now. I'll have to let go. Mother must be merciful.

It's Saturday night so only Jackie, one of the students, is

home. She's at the table, rolling a joint. Jackie's the perfect distraction.

'Hey, Melinda,' she says, in her thick Liverpudlian accent. 'Want some?'

'Just a coffee,' I reply, opening the fridge. 'Do you want one?'

She takes a huge drag on the joint. 'Yeah, please. Have to be black. I'm out of milk.'

Jackie has never bought milk. Or coffee. Or anything other than a takeaway. She's constantly stoned. She vaguely reminds me of a younger Shauna. I like her. 'It's OK, honey, I've got plenty. Sugar?'

She nods. Her brown hair is in thick dreadlocks, whether by accident or design I'm not sure, and her fingers are stained with yellow paint. She's studying art. One of her huge abstract canvases has been in the dingy hallway for months, practically blocking it, splatters in green and brown that look more like someone's thrown up than Jackson Pollock.

I find two mugs without a biology experiment growing in them while she blows smoke rings across the kitchen, and unlock my cupboard where a full jar of coffee and an unopened soya milk await.

'Heard about the girl who went missing?'

My heart thuds. So much for a distraction. Even Jackie wants to talk about it.

'Yeah, I saw it on the news,' I say casually.

'Had my parents on the phone. They're saying she was

last seen in Surbiton. Mum thinks a serial killer is on the loose.'

'That's parents for you.'

'I went round Thailand for two months and they weren't bothered.' She blows two big smoke rings and automatically passes me the joint. 'They're right wound up.'

'No thanks,' I reply, waving the joint away and placing her coffee on the table. Jackie takes a long, slow drag on the joint.

'How's the salon going?'

'Great.' Thank God she's changed the subject. I sip my coffee. 'Lots of rich footballers' wives wanting their nails done.'

'So, what do you think happened to the girl? It's been nearly a week now. She can't be alive.'

I have to stay calm. She's bound to talk about it. Everyone is. 'Let's hope you're wrong. Maybe she's just run away. Living on the streets somewhere. Or someone's helped her start a new life.'

'What I don't get,' Jackie says, warming to her theme now, 'is why the woman hasn't come forward. She must have been trying to help. Why else would she take Anna back to Surbiton, near where she came from? Women don't kill.'

She pauses for another drag on her joint. 'There's Myra Hindley, I suppose. And Rose West.'

How *dare* she compare me to those psychopaths? They killed for pleasure. Got their sexual kicks, too. I'm taking care of my girls. I'm *helping*. Taking away their pain.

Disgusted, I feel a surge of anger. But I can't lose it here, in my flat.

Jackie gazes into space. 'I ran away from home once,' she adds. 'Packed myself some Sandwich Spread sandwiches and a bag of crisps and made it as far as Lime Street station.'

'What did your mum and dad say?'

'They never knew. I got the bus home again.'

'Why?'

'Why did I run?'

I nod.

'I'd seen it in a film and thought it was cool. Got in trouble for bunking off school, though.' She began rolling a second joint. 'What about you, Mel? Ever run away?'

'No. Unless you count leaving Great Yarmouth at sixteen. I couldn't wait to get away from there, honey. Square peg, round hole.'

'Do you go back much?'

'Rarely. My father's there. In a home. Dementia. He has no idea who I am.'

Her hazy blue eyes look sad. 'Seeing your dad so… broken. That must be tough.'

'Yes.' I'm uncomfortable now. This isn't proving a distraction at all. I don't like sharing more than small talk about myself, and hippie Jackie, with her dreadlocks and her paint-splattered fingers and her talk of Rose West, has lured me in. I drain the rest of my coffee, even though it's too hot, scalding my throat. 'Better go,' I say. 'Work tomorrow.'

She senses my discomfort, nods and turns her attention to the joint. 'Course. See you later, Mel.' And as I close the kitchen door, she adds: 'If you ever want to, you know, talk. About your dad. I'm here.'

I'm touched. Properly touched. He hasn't got dementia. Nor is he in a home. He's now a wasted alcoholic, who hit the bottle when my mother died and I left, who spends his days in our now shabby terraced house, drinking until he wets himself on the sofa and spending night-time in the dark because he doesn't care enough to change the light bulbs. It's what he deserves. My mother would be horrified if she saw the mess. Despite everything, she kept the house spick and span. I've been back a handful of times, to gloat, to remind him – and myself – how far I've come. And because it's the only past I have.

'Thanks, Jackie.' I nod, closing the door. For a moment I see my mother's face, vacant and blind, and an overwhelming rage rips right through me. Death spared her.

Soozie's there at 9 a.m. Sunday morning, waiting for me outside the salon. I've had a fitful night's sleep and am really not in the mood, but I have to keep things normal. She takes a seat and I start to massage her hands.

'Sky's been having phone sex,' she announces. 'With Paul Eaves. Stepfather of the missing girl.'

It takes quite a lot to leave me speechless, but Sky and Paul Eaves have done it.

'What? When?' My mind races as I struggle to take this in.

'It's true. The police found their chats on his burner phone. Called himself Daniel.'

The YouTuber. Sleazy Paul Eaves posing as a teenage boy. It sickens me to my core. 'How is Sky?'

'In her room. Won't come out.' Soozie's eyes fill with tears. 'I keep trying to talk to her but she wants to be left alone.'

A thousand questions slice through my brain, as Soozie fills me in on the previous day's events. I can't bear to think of Sky – just a child behind her pout and her self-centredness – being lured in by a sick paedophile. God knows what he'd encouraged her to do or say. Or what videos she'd sent him. And what does this mean for me? Having the police sniffing round Soozie and Simon is terrible news. There's no reason for them to find out about Riverdell, but…

'Simon's gone berserk,' Soozie went on. 'He got back with a stinking hangover yesterday lunchtime to be told his daughter's been groomed by a paedo. And someone we *know*. It was all I could do to stop him driving round there and rugby-tackling Zoe. He says she must have known he was a pervert.'

'So this stepfather is in custody?' I must stay focused, in control. I need as much information out of Soozie as I can get.

'Yes. He'd arranged to meet Sky in Leicester Square exactly the time that Anna was there. That can't be a coincidence. There wasn't anything on the news when I left. Put Sky News on.'

I fiddle with the remote. If Paul Eaves was in Leicester Square, I hadn't seen him. They're talking about a delay in this year's vaccines, so I try ITV. It's on the local news.

'Police have arrested a forty-seven-year-old man from Kingston upon Thames in connection with child grooming.'

'He's got to be responsible for Anna. It's him, Mel. The bastard. The sleazy, paedo bastard.'

'At least he's in custody, Soozie. Can't hurt anyone else. And Sky's safe now.'

I rest Soozie's hands on a pink towel and pick up my phone to check social media. The #findanna hashtag is alight, and rumours that it's the stepdad are everywhere.

'I feel sick every time I think about him,' Soozie adds. 'Persuading Sky to watch YouPorn, and God knows what else. It's beyond disgusting.'

I touch her arm sympathetically. 'Maybe more girls will come forward once his identity is out there, honey?' I suggest. 'The more there are, the worse it is for him. And he deserves everything he gets.'

'I hope so. But what I really hope is they find Anna. Alive. Maybe she ran away because she knew what he was up to? Or maybe…' Soozie's voice dropped to a whisper, 'he did it to *her*.'

My thoughts wander to Anna in the cafe, as all of her anger and sadness and rage and disgust had tumbled out, her tears soaking into my shoulder. I'd done the right thing, taking her away from that bastard.

'Anyway, I've got a plan,' she goes on, tossing her streaked red hair over her shoulder. 'I'm sure Anna's mum, Zoe, knows the truth. And I'm going to get it out of her.'

'How? Won't the police do that?'

'She'll stand by him. I know her. Even if she's sure he's a paedo. Try and get him off the hook. She won't want the shame it will bring on the family, and on her. No one will believe she didn't know it was going on. But if I can get her to confess to me…'

'What makes you think she will?'

'She'll need someone to talk to. She always does. How can you live with a paedo and not know about it? Surely she must have seen him hunched over his computer, or looking at Anna in that way. I reckon she did, and she ignored it. But if she'd got her head out of her arse and put a stop to him…'

I think of my mother, changing my sheets without a word. Not a bastard word. The evidence was there, right there in her hands, but she said nothing. I think of my father, tucking me in at night with a 'see you in the morning', knowing that in a couple of hours, he'd be back. And how he had gone from touching and 'special kisses' to *that*.

The memories trigger a huge wave of fear and nausea and I walk over to the finger bowls by the sink, pretending to wash them. I take a deep breath. I have to focus on now.

'When will you call her, Soozie?'

'Not yet. The house is full of people. My friend lives opposite. Says cars haven't stopped coming and going. I'll try tomorrow.'

'But what if they release him?'

'They won't. I can't see he'll get bail. Surely grooming Sky is enough to keep him in custody, with his stepdaughter missing…'

She doesn't even mention Simon, and there's a sharpness, a determination in her eyes I've never seen before. 'Make sure you call me with an update, honey,' I say, as she strides out of the door. 'You've got to do it. Put that bastard behind bars, where he belongs.'

'And find Anna,' she adds. 'Oh, by the way, they wanted numbers for everyone Sky's seen lately. I gave them yours. It can't do any harm to chat to them. They might think of something we've missed. DCI Sue Fisher. You'll like her.'

Chapter Sixteen

Despite arriving home so late, Rob was up bright and early to leave the house at 8am, having placed a cup of tea on Sue's bedside table. She pretended to be asleep, but once the front door closed, Sue opened her eyes and stretched. Coping with his mood swings was like living on a perpetual roller coaster, blindfolded, with no idea what would happen next.

After that first time, when she was three months pregnant, he hadn't had an 'outburst' for a couple of years. Tom was a toddler when it happened again. He'd had a raging temperature, and Sue had finally settled him into her bed after an exhausting night of Calpol and cuddling when Rob came home late via the pub.

She knew straightaway he was drunk. Very drunk. It took him a while to open the front door, which he did while swearing loudly. Something about his mood reminded her of the past, of that night, and instinctively, she climbed into their bed beside the sleeping Tom and switched off the night light.

He strode into the bedroom and paused to look down at the pair, pacing round and round the bed, swearing, his breath fast. Sue's heart pounded so strongly in her chest she feared either she, or Rob, would wake Tom. All she knew was that she had to lie still. Very still.

It lasted for a couple of minutes, but to Sue it felt like forever. The fear swelled in her chest like a solid mass, pressing her ribcage outwards and her breath came in short, desperate gasps. He was so full of hatred, of rage that seemed to breed in his sick soul, and she had no idea where it came from.

Finally he took off his jacket, fell into bed fully clothed, and was snoring within seconds. It was over. Her chest tight, she unclenched her hands, silently swung her legs out of the bed and carefully lifted Tom over her shoulder, taking them both to the safety of his room, where she tucked him in carefully. Then she slumped to the floor beside a sleeping Tom, hugging her legs as she rocked back and forth, holding his teddy in her hand, silent tears streaming down her face, wondering what on earth she had done to make him resent them so.

It had happened countless times since. She sometimes fantasised about leaving him, escaping the toxic mess that left her riddled with anxiety and gasping for air. But she had been with him for so long that even the violence had a predictable comfort to it, and she feared life on the other side of the relationship more than she feared the known.

But today, with Rob out of the house, and Tom off to a chess tournament, she felt a release of the vice-like tension that made her shoulders hunch and her jaw clench. Eaves was safely behind bars, and the judge had allowed extra time to question him, so she wanted to leave him to stew for a few hours before resuming their interview.

'I brought you some toast.' Tom smiled, pushing open the bedroom door which Rob had left slightly ajar. 'You need to look after yourself, Mum.'

He set the plate down beside the teacup, and Sue pulled the duvet over her bruised arms, which Tom pretended not to notice. 'I've got that chess tournament,' he said, almost apologetically. 'Should finish about six. I'll be back straight afterwards.'

Sue smiled. 'I'm going to take it easy this morning. Got to go back in at lunchtime to question our main suspect.'

'Anna's stepdad? Do you think he did it?'

She sighed. 'No. And then sometimes yes. But my gut feeling is no.'

Tom smiled. 'When Garry Kasparov played chess against Deep Blue, a computer, he won. So sometimes it's not just about pure logic.'

Sue ruffled his hair. 'You're such a clever kid.' She grinned. 'Good luck today. How many matches is it?'

'Six. All rapidplay.' He pointed to the toast. 'Make sure you eat it. See you later, Mum.' Hearing the front door close, she picked up the toast and dunked it into her cold tea. The Nail Salon. Soozie had mentioned it and Sue figured an informal visit there couldn't do any harm. It was a great way to get the local gossip.

Sue ran a hot bath, the pipes creaking and the water spluttering as it always did, and poured in a slurp of Radox. Sliding into the water, the tops of her arms stung painfully at first, but once immersed they began to ease. Her shoulder-length brown hair swayed gently under the water as she stared up at the mottled avocado tiles, but all she could see was Paul Eaves' face, snot dripping from his nose, as she asked herself whether her gut instincts really could be right.

An hour later, dressed in black jeans, a loose, long-sleeved pale blue top and trainers, she turned off the A3 into Cobshott. It was barely 11am, and most of Cobshott was still having a collective lie-in, anaesthetised by a Saturday night of rich food (the men), skinny salads (the women) and too much wine (both) as they tried to blot out the sickening realisation that money can't buy happiness. Bells rang out from the tiny village church, but only a handful of people, all pensioners from the pricey residential home next door, were shuffling towards it. Sue slowed the car to examine the tiny group. Four women and two men, smartly dressed, whom, she guessed, had been put out to pasture by their wealthy local offspring, who had plenty of space to look after them but no desire to do it.

'Nails By Melinda' was squeezed between an estate

agent and a coffee shop – not a Costa or a Starbucks, Sue was pleased to notice. The tiny nail salon had its lights on and 'open' on the door. A colourful neon sign shouting 'NAILS' in the window seemed slightly out of keeping with the pretentious neighbourhood. Sue liked that. The owner clearly had the confidence to do it their way, and they would know all the goings-on in Cobshott, she was sure of it.

Sue turned off the high street onto a quiet road, where the back of the shops quickly gave way to Cobshott Woods on either side, and parked behind an old Mini.

'Hello,' the owner called out as Sue entered the nail salon. She had a pretty face, steel-blue eyes and very slim build, tiny waist, with a shoulder-length blonde bob. Red lipstick. Late twenties, at a guess. Like a young Debbie Harry. 'Welcome. I'm Melinda.'

'Hi.' She glanced around the tiny salon, beautifully decorated in pink and white. There were two stations to sit at, fluffy pink towels, and a big pink pedicure chair with foot spa, and background chillout music. 'I'd love a manicure, if you have time.'

'Of course. You're lucky to catch me. I had an early booking. I don't always open on a Sunday.'

'Must be nice to be your own boss.'

'I love it.' She took her hand. 'Now, what would you like?'

Sue looked at the price list behind her head. A straight manicure was twenty pounds. 'Just a manicure, I think. Do you take cards?'

'Cash only. Is that OK?

'Sure.' She took a note from her purse and laid it on the counter.

'Please choose a colour.' She gestured to the rows of nail varnish bottles behind her, 'and take a seat.'

There was the tiniest trace of an accent in her voice, but Sue couldn't place it. West Country? Norfolk? 'It's a lovely salon,' she chatted, handing over a bottle of pale-pink varnish before resting her fingers in a bowl of soothingly warm water.

'Thanks,' she replied. 'I've been here around five years now.'

'You must hear some tales in here.'

'Oh, you wouldn't believe it, honey. I'm pretty unshockable now. The tabloids came in once asking for dirt on Tiego Durie, the footballer, because his wife comes here. Their training ground is down the road.'

'What did you say?'

'That I didn't know her. I wouldn't sell out a client to the press. I'd be out of business.'

'Good for you.' She paused. 'So many girls get their nails done these days. Do you know Sky and Star Lightwater?'

'I do. And their mum, Soozie. They're often in here.' She reached for some trimmers and began to cut Sue's cuticles. 'Are they friends of yours?'

'Not exactly. What sort of girl is Sky?'

'Typical teenager really. Thinks the world shines out of her arse.' She smiled. 'Sorry to be so blunt.'

Sue laughed. 'Oh, don't worry on my account. Has she ever talked about boyfriends?'

'Lately it's been all Daniel this and Daniel that. A YouTuber, I think. But why do you want to know? Is she in trouble?'

'No, not at all.'

She squinted at Sue, and smiled. 'I know who you are. I've seen you on TV. You're that detective, the one trying to find the missing girl.'

'I am. But I'm not here officially. I just wanted a manicure. And a gossip.'

'Well, if it's gossip you're after, honey, you're in the right place.' She smiled, her eyes bright. 'So what's the latest on the girl? Anna, is it? The one with asthma? Hasn't she gone off with a mystery woman? I saw the drawing on the news.'

'That's right. Last seen at Surbiton station.'

'I heard her stepfather was involved. Some of my clients know him.'

'What have you heard?'

'Just rumours. Mums saying they didn't like the way he looked at their girls, especially when Anna had a pool party a couple of years ago. But they didn't mention it at the time. And there's been talk of him having a secret flat in town – Camden, I think.'

'Do you know where in Camden?'

'Overlooking the canal. One of my clients knew a girl in her late teens who had a brief affair with him. She was expecting some luxury apartment and it turned out to be an ex-council place squashed between the canal and a

Morrisons. Not quite the bolt-hole he promised. She was out of there like a shot, apparently.'

'Sounds lovely. Very convenient for the supermarket.'

'Hey, honey, I'm not knocking it. The flat, I mean. I grew up in Great Yarmouth and being squashed by a Morrisons would be a selling point. Proximity to a Wetherspoons would be most sought-after.'

Sue smiled. 'So what's Sky really like?'

'Typical teenager. Obsessed with Instagram. More confident than her sulky sister, Star. They're twins. Not much else to say. But if it's gossip you're after then you totally need to hear about the Starmers. On the Crown Estate. They got really into wife-swapping as a bit of fun, and it all went tits up when his wife left him for their neighbour. She still lives next door. Then there's Cleo – she's transgender, her wife has no idea. And as for the Berkhalls…'

Sue listened, transfixed, to all the neighbourhood gossip.

'There,' Melinda said proudly, taking her hands out from under the dryer. 'All done.'

'They're fabulous. Thank you.' Sue gestured to the twenty-pound note she'd put on the table.

'You're very welcome. Please do come again. And best of luck with the case. It must be so hard trying to get inside the mind of a serial killer.'

'It is. But we don't know Anna's dead.'

'No, of course not. I hope you find her. It can't be easy for her if she's on the streets. Rich girl like that.'

Sue nodded. 'Definitely not. Well, thanks again,' she said, strolling casually out of the salon.

Once outside, Sue paused.

Asthma.

Melinda said Anna had asthma. That was one detail the police hadn't released. Could she have heard about it through the Cobshott grapevine? It was possible. But the intense blue eyes. The pretty face. The height. Calling her 'honey', just as Juanita had described. Talking about a serial killer.

Sue realised she'd been staring straight into the eyes of Anna's abductor.

Chapter Seventeen

I recognise her before she even opens the door. The mousey, shoulder-length bob, the sharp nose, the pot belly, the cheap suit that has been all over the news. It's DCI Sue Fisher.

My heart is thudding, my chest in a vice, and I feel sweat pricking my face. I'd been expecting a phone call at some point, but not this. I grab a towel and dab my forehead, leaving a smear of foundation on it. I have to stay calm. Give nothing away. If she was here to arrest me she'd have brought the cavalry. Maybe she's just checking out the area, after what happened with Sky. I close the door to the salon's tiny kitchen area and turn to face the detective with a smile.

She beams as she walks in, asks for a manicure, and there's no hint of suspicion. Now I'm in uncharted territory, sailing into a gale-force storm, buffeted by the waves and with no real idea how to handle it. Images of the detective opening the door at Riverdell, finding her in that fetid room, surge into my brain. My secret life exposed to the world, splashed all over the tabloids as if I'm some kind of psychopath. They'll never understand. I'm doing this all out of *love*. I'm their *mother*.

But as Fisher takes a seat, an unexpected thrill rushes through me, calming my nerves and spiralling brain slightly. The one woman whose job is to find me is right here, I'm holding her hand, and she has no idea who I am.

I stick to the usual script. 'Choose a colour, honey.' She scans the rows of bottles forensically, and I can see exactly the type of person she is. Methodical. Determined. Doesn't give up easily. Passes by the bright neons and bold colours to go for a pale pink. I'm sensing an inner vulnerability that she shuts out with logic. Confident at work but not at home. Reading people is a gift I've had since I was a child. Maybe she can read people too – after all, my Google search told me she's put three rapists and one killer behind bars – but her passive, creased face suggests she's here for gossip. Background on the village, nothing more. I hope I'm right.

She makes small talk. And now she's asking about Sky. I relax slightly. This visit is all about Sky and as far as she goes with the questions, I know I'm in the clear.

My head is screaming at me to ask her about the case. She's been in all the papers, all over the TV, so surely it'll look suspicious if a gossip like me doesn't recognise her.

Sky News is on. The big story is still the hunt for the mystery woman. So I ask about that. Grab my chance to push Paul Eaves into the frame, inventing rumours that he'd leered at girls during a pool party. She's lapping up my every word. My confidence grows, and I can't resist throwing in a line about a flat in Camden. But my tongue is starting to run away with me, I'm jabbering nervously, so I turn our chat to the wife-swapping that's the talk of Cobshott and nothing to do with the case.

She's listening, I'm talking, probably too fast but my confidence is soaring. Her nails are done. I wonder how a forty-something woman like her gets inside the mind of a killer. So I ask. I want her to spill. How she uncovers motives. What kind of people make the best killers. Whether nailing someone for a crime turns her on. I've got a thousand questions. But she's not playing ball.

The wind chime by the door tinkles softly as she leaves, blending in with the salon's gentle music, but my mind is noisy, chaotic, unexpectedly buzzing with the thrill of the chase, uneasily mixed with resignation, an agonising grief that I'm going to have to leave this life I've made. And that won't be easy. Because while I'm soaking up every detail of my clients' lives as I paint and polish, or busying myself making up fresh beds at Riverdell ready for new lost souls to arrive, or curling up on the sofa in Camden, that agonising, black void inside me clamps shut for a while, and all the unbearable loneliness, the shame, the white-hot rage that threatens to tear me apart is crushed to its core by the promise of hope, of a future free from pain. Free from the past.

But now too many paths are leading here. Cobshott is now a place of interest. Even the salon. The Riverdell situation is too dangerous. I have no choice. I have to move on.

For a moment, I wonder about taking her with me. She's mine now, broken, sorry for what she did. I'm sure she'd come willingly. Maybe we could lie low together somewhere. Head for the seaside.

But even as I think it, I know deep down that it won't work. She's weak, and ill. The whole country is on missing girl alert, thanks to #findanna. We'll stand out in a crowd and life on the run won't be easy. What if she betrays me again? I'm not completely sure I trust her. I'm cornered. I can't set her free. She knows too much. And merciful Mother can't leave her behind to die, or kill her in cold blood.

My mind is made up. There's no choice. She'll have to be a sacrifice. Let go of the one to help the many. It's for the best. I reach under the counter for my MacBook, and open Tor, the browser that connects me to the dark web. It's a seedy, lawless place where you can find anything from the worst – or best, depending on your point of view – porn, drugs, weapons and hitmen. Best of all, it's anonymous. Untraceable.

There's no way back now. I open my undetectable email account, and write a new message.

To: Fixer72@Mail2Tor.com
From: Dreammaker91@Mail2Tor.com

She's ready.

Chapter Eighteen

Rob spotted her coming out of the salon on Cobshott high street. It was almost noon, and he'd just finished a gruelling rugby training session with the under-sixteens. Normally, he'd stay behind with the dads for a beer, but the late night was taking its toll and he just needed to go home for a fry-up and a lie-down.

A nail salon. She hadn't been to one of those in years, Rob thought, a jealous knot forming in his stomach. And she said she was having a lie-in. Why would she be getting her nails done in the middle of a case, with no weddings, no parties to go to? Not that he knew of, anyway. He drove past her as she rummaged in her bag, oblivious to his presence, and turned left, where he saw her little Fiat behind a Mini.

Rob parked his white van a few cars away on the same side, watching her from his wing mirror. She tried making a call, but whoever it was clearly didn't pick up, so she started texting, deep in thought.

It had to be Mike, he decided. That fat bastard she spent so much time with. Mike, with his jokes and his banter and his 'popping round' to play chess with Tom, who clearly saw him as far more of a father figure than he would ever be. She'd gone too far this time, the lying bitch. Way too far. He clenched his fist and punched the dashboard, splitting a knuckle, and stared at the trickle of bright blood as it dripped onto the seat, the visible, physical pain no match for the tormented spite inside.

Locking the van, he walked quickly down the quiet side street towards her and tapped on the window.

'Rob!' She was so startled that she dropped the phone into her lap, before leaning over to open the door, the sound of Fleetwood Mac's 'Rumours' on her car stereo. 'How was rugby? I've just been to—'

'I *know* where you've been,' he spat, climbing into the passenger seat and closing the door behind him. 'Look at them.' He grabbed her hand. 'Whore's nails. Fucking slut. All for that dickhead of a deputy, right?'

'Rob, I—'

His fingers clasped her hand tighter and tighter. 'Stop, Rob. You'll break my hand. I haven't—'

His eyes were wild, possessed, but Sue was trapped in the car, her seat belt pinning her down. 'You're taking the piss out of me,' he hissed. 'You and fucking lover-boy. Sitting here listening to love songs and texting him.'

Snatching the phone from her lap, he thrust her thumb

onto the home button, unlocking it. It opened on a new message to Mike, still unsent.

Need to meet. Urgent got… it read.

'Away from Rob? Day off? This is the last time you treat me like a fool, you bitch.'

His fist slammed into Sue's stomach and she let out a sharp cry. 'It's your fault,' he spat, punching her again. 'You're making me do this. If you treated me properly … if you were a proper wife who showed respect… For God's sake, Sue, you treat me like shit.'

Doubled over in pain, the seat belt pressing into her sore shoulder, Sue avoided his gaze, trying to make herself as small as possible. Fighting back, or antagonising him, was useless. But then the pain intensified so much that Sue begged him to stop.

'Let's hope you've learned your lesson,' he spat, throwing the iPhone into her lap. She glanced up at him to see that familiar triumph and guilt in his eyes, and she knew he was done. For now. But suddenly Rob's voice was distant, hollow, as if she was in a tunnel, and her vision blurred as she peered at him climbing out of the car. Her eyes unfocused, her skin clammy, her mind wandering and the pain intolerable, she began to panic as he slammed the door and walked away, but then she thought of Tom, sweet Tom, and how he'd laid the toast beside her that morning. Of Tom, his eyes shining, as he walked onto the school stage for his chess award. Of the day he was born, curled up on her tummy like a little mouse. And as blood poured out of her ruptured spleen, swelling her belly, Sue veered between terror and confusion, finally drifting into unconsciousness, remembering Tom's gentle kiss on her head while the leaves of Cobshott Woods swayed softly in the summer breeze.

Chapter Nineteen

My contact is usually quick to email back. But so far, nothing. It's now 1pm and I'm tense. Having made up my mind, I just want to get on with it. I don't want time to think about the details, or what Fixer72 has planned for her. I've told him I won't deal with paedophiles. He's arranged for her to be a live-in servant with a wealthy family in Eastern Europe. No one will know or care who she is. I'm selling her into slavery, and I know it. It's not the life I wanted for her. But the money I'll get will let me reinvent myself and start again, help more souls. This will mean so many more are saved. And from far, far worse.

I thought about asking Simon for a 'final payment' instead of letting her go. Getting him to stump up a few thousand in cash, in return for me handing over the keys to Riverdell. But I want that place left untouched as long as possible. My DNA will be all over it, though I shouldn't be on any police databases. Besides, there's still more than a year before I'm due to hand it back, and no reason for anyone to go there. That's plenty of time for me to disappear without trace.

I've closed the salon and I haven't eaten since last night, but being Sunday, the Cobshott sandwich bar is closed, though I rarely use it. Even a toasted cheese sandwich – sorry, a Croque Madame – is a tenner and everything comes with avocado. Everything. I'd love a comforting Yarmouth fish and chips, soaked in vinegar and crusted with salt. There's a little pub just at the end of the village high street which does a piss-poor version, all beer batter and poncy peas, but that runs the risk of bumping into clients having Sunday lunch with their husbands, the ones they spend their lives moaning about. Acting normal is what I should be doing, but I'm really not in the mood for their airhead chit-chat.

It's been almost a week since I met Anna, and I wish I'd never gone to Leicester Square. I never dreamed that by trying to help I'd have to say goodbye to all this. Now I'll have to reinvent myself again. Where shall I go? Ibiza? That would be a world away.

Shauna took me there for a few days once. The only time I've ever been abroad. She saved up for the flights and we stayed in her friend's tiny tumbledown beach house, a surviving relic from the early eighties before the big clubs and money-making yoga retreats took over, talking until dawn and watching the sunrise streak the sky with intense reds and oranges. Shauna made us picnics to eat on the beach, where the warm sea lapped against my toes, and afterwards we'd go back to the house, where white drapes swayed in the warm breeze and hippy knick-knacks covered every shelf. I was happy then, the happiest I've ever been, and could have stayed there forever. Safe. And loved. But her friend returned from her trip, our house-sitting was over and suddenly we were on that early morning easyJet flight into Gatwick, emerging into a chilly May day as we wheeled our cases past the flood of travellers going the other way. I begged her to go back. Use the money I had and move there, with me. But Shauna had her heart set on India. And she wanted to go alone.

I push the memory and the pain away, trying to think. I need to start again somewhere I've never been before. Ibiza is a pipe dream. It'll be easier to lie low in the UK, a town where I can blend in. No messy language problems, no work visas. No passport. Maybe up North, a million miles from the pretentious, window-dressed Cobshott, hiding its hollow emptiness behind curtainless, sterile Huf houses. Whitley Bay, perhaps. Or Sheffield. I've never been there.

My thoughts are interrupted by the wail of an ambulance zooming down the high street, followed by a sharp beep from my MacBook.

Fixer72 : Will collect her Tuesday night. Location TBC.

Tuesday? That's days away. I reply instantly.

Dreammaker91: Too long. Need earlier drop.

A pause. Then…

Fixer72: Got to lie low. So Tuesday. Do not let me down.

Dreammaker91 : OK.

Frustrated, I slam the MacBook shut. I need the deal done urgently, because part of me doesn't want to let her go, and it's clawing at me, eating away at my mind like a rat. She's learned her lesson, and as Mother, it's my job to protect her. Not do this. But I'm cornered now. Sacrificing her is for the best, I tell myself. The one for the many. And maybe, just maybe, if I get myself set up in a new home, one day I can buy her back.

I lock the salon door, eager to get home to change and then back to Riverdell to see if the antibiotics are working. But as I turn into the side street where I left the Mini, I see the ambulance just ahead of it, blue lights silently flashing, and two policewomen are standing by as a paramedic leans through the passenger door of an old blue Fiat.

One of my clients, Fi, and her eight-year-old daughter, Arabella, are hovering by the scene.

'Arabella saw her as we walked past,' Fi says tearfully. 'She asked if the lady was all right. Slumped in the driver's seat. I rang the police.'

'She's tachycardic,' shouts the paramedic. 'BP critically low. Going into shock. We need to get her out of the car right now.'

I don't know what I'm expecting – an elderly lady,

maybe – but as the paramedics and police half-lift, half-pull the casualty onto a stretcher resting on the pavement, I recognise her face. Her eyes are closed, and her skin almost white, too white against the dark hair. It's Sue Fisher.

Thoughts spiralling, I watch as they cut open her blue top. What could have happened? She seemed fine when she left the salon. Heart attack? Brain haemorrhage?

Most of her left abdomen is black and blue. Internal bleeding. I've seen that before.

'Ruptured spleen,' says the paramedic. 'Looks like she's sustained some hefty blows to the abdomen. We need to intubate and get her to A&E now.'

I'm nervous now, shifting uneasily from foot to foot. There's CCTV on the high street. They'll know she came to the salon. The net is closing. I can't imagine anyone attacking her on a sleepy Sunday in Cobshott and even if they did, why would they? Plenty of wealthy women with Fendi bags to snatch. This is personal.

The paramedic inserts a tube into Sue's throat, followed by a drip into her arm, while the second paramedic rhythmically squeezes the ventilation bag.

'Any ID on her?' asks one policewoman.

The other's face pales as she pulls a lanyard from Sue's handbag. 'She's one of us. DCI Sue Fisher from Kingston.'

'I know her,' replies the other. 'She's on the missing girl case. Call it in. They'll need Forensics here. Secure the area. This is a crime scene.'

A crime scene. Round the corner from the nail salon. Two minutes' drive from Riverdell. The police will be crawling all over Cobshott after this. It's going from bad to worse but a strange calm descends on me. If I'm going to ride this out, I need to take control. They've seen my face. They'll soon know she was in the nail salon. As the policewoman finishes unrolling 'do not cross' tape around the scene, I introduce myself. 'I'm Melinda Medford. I run the nail bar in the high street. I did this lady's nails an hour ago. She was alone and absolutely fine when she left.'

The policewoman flips open her notebook and jots down all the details. I give her my mobile number. 'Thanks, Ms Medford. I'll pass that on. We'll be in touch if we need any more information.'

She's on the stretcher now, the paramedic still squeezing air into her lungs as they slide her into the ambulance, which speeds off towards the A3 in a haze of noise and blue.

'I'm so sorry to ask, but would it be possible for me to move my car?' I ask, pointing to the taped-off area.

'I'm sorry.' The policewoman is abrupt now. 'We have a few checks that we need to make. A forensic team is en route. I can call your mobile as soon as it's possible.'

I nod, knowingly. 'I see. I'm guessing it wasn't a heart attack, then.'

'Like I say, Ms Medford, we'll be in touch as soon as the area is clear. If you could just move on…'

I cross the road and cut through the woods to the village station, where the electronic board shows the next train to Surbiton isn't until 2.20pm. Almost an hour. I can't bear to be in Cobshott for a second longer. I've got the keys to

Riverdell, but I don't want to draw any attention to it. So I walk back into the woods and head towards Esher, where I can catch a bus, forcing a smile as I pass the endless dog walkers and families out for a Sunday stroll. DCI Sue Fisher. Who could have done it? A vendetta against her from a previous case? She was in the fraud squad before taking on Homicide. Maybe she's rattled the wrong cages over the Anna one? Either way, even if she survives she'll be off this case for a while.

Above me, a small flock of birds streak across the cloudless sky, soaring free. I have to accept it. She will have to be sacrificed. My time at the nail salon is almost done.

Chapter Twenty

Mike sat at Sue's bedside, gently stroking her hand. 'I'll get the bastard who did this, boss,' he whispered. 'Don't you worry.'

Sue lay in the intensive care unit, a ventilator pumping air to and from her lungs, the thick blue and white tubes laid across her chest. Her face was paler than Mike had ever seen it, her eyes closed, her fingers resting on the crisp sheet. He'd never seen her nails painted before, so pink and pretty against the sterile white cotton. Apart from the beeping machines, the unit was eerily calm and quiet, and so cold, unlike any other hospital wards Mike had visited.

Ruptured spleen … low blood pressure … cardiac arrest in the ambulance … emergency surgery … signs of a violent attack … Mike could hear the doctor's words but struggled to take them in. She looked so utterly helpless, so vulnerable, so unlike the woman he'd come to know and love over the last four years.

'Was she…?' Mike's voice tailed off.

'There are no signs of sexual assault.'

'Th-thank God,' Mike stammered, sinking into a chair.

'From the evidence we have, the level of bruising and so forth, we think the attack happened in or near the car, quite quickly.'

Mike shook his head. It had to be linked to the disappearance of Anna Littlejohn-Eaves. Maybe Eaves was part of a bigger child sex ring. 'I can't think of anyone who would do this to her. We've put some slimy bastards away, but they're all still inside. And none of them were from gangs – all one-off fruitcakes.'

Dr Purani nodded. 'I heard she's a very accomplished detective.'

'Uniform tell me a witness said she'd been to a nail bar. She never does that. Someone must have followed her.'

'Do you mind if we step outside, DI Barley?'

He followed the doctor out of the ICU and into the shiny, overlit corridor to a small meeting room. 'I have to say,' Dr Purani said quietly, 'that I've seen quite a few cases of this over the years. Splenic rupture due to blunt trauma. And if I take out the ones from car crashes and drunken city centre punch-ups, all the others – without exception – were domestic violence.'

Mike stared at the doctor, confused. 'That's ridiculous. Sue's not a victim of domestic violence. I can guarantee you that. She'd never stand for it. She's a DCI! More balls than I've got. And she wasn't even at home.'

The doctor sighed. 'Look, I'm not telling you how to do

your job, DI Barley. I concede this could have been a random attack. And this won't be easy for you to hear. But her shoulders have recent bruising on them, finger marks, suggesting she's been held down or shaken. She has four newly broken ribs – probably from today's attack – and six healed ones. There are also two healed, long scars on her upper thigh, which have been made by something jagged, possibly broken glass. If I saw these injuries on a child, social services would have the parents in custody like *that*.' He snapped his fingers. 'And that's without the cigarette burns on the top of her inner thighs, which are probably a couple of years old.'

Mike didn't reply. He couldn't. He tried to speak but no words came out. Sue? Abused? It was nonsense. She was feisty, the first to head into danger if it meant catching a rapist or a killer.

'But … but Sue's worked with a lot of victims of domestic abuse,' he spluttered. 'And helped put quite a few abusers behind bars. Mostly men, but a woman too. She wouldn't stand for it. She knows how their minds work. The control, the put-downs, she's an expert on it…'

His voice tailed off. Sue was an expert. Could it really be because she was a victim herself? It was almost impossible for Mike to take in. And then there was Tom. He'd become close to the lad over the years, knew he absolutely adored his mum. Tom would never let anyone hurt her. Tom would have told him…

The doctor laid his hand gently on Mike's arm, and brought him a paper cup of water.

'Rob? Her husband?' he whispered, his voice hoarse. 'I just can't believe he would do this. He's the life and soul of any gathering. Always laughing and joking.'

'They often are.' Dr Purani sighed.

'And they have a son. Tom. He's fourteen. He'd never, ever let anyone hurt her.'

'Children don't always react to abuse in ways we expect. They can become quiet, withdrawn, zoned out, and blame themselves when they're too frightened to step in. Or,' he paused, 'he could be being subjected to violence too.'

'Oh my god.' It couldn't be true, but if it was, why hadn't he seen it? 'I play chess with Tom every week. He's never mentioned anything. And Sue would never let that happen. I know her.'

'Just to be safe, I will need to report my concerns to social services as well.'

'Christ. They won't take him into care, will they? Sue would be devastated.'

'He's fourteen. They'll talk to him. It's about keeping him safe. Where is Tom now?'

'I don't know. I tried calling him, but his mobile is off. Rob is on his way here. I sent a squad car to pick him up from their house as soon as I heard. He sounded desperate. Crying down the phone.'

The doctor nodded. 'If he's a typical abuser, he'll be in the "sorry" phase by now. No immediate threat. He'll trust that Sue will lie to cover for him, just as she must have done before. Tom too, if he knows. But he may verbally threaten them.'

Suddenly Mike remembered Sue turning up to work, maybe three years earlier, with a bright-red cornea. 'She did come in with a burst blood vessel in her eye once. Said she walked into a door.'

'It's usually doors. Or coat hooks. Never their partner's finger or fist. Look, I'll tell him he can see her for a couple of minutes with a nurse present, no more, because she needs complete rest. After that, whatever you do is up to you. All I can do is share my concerns. Obviously it will be up to her if she wants to press charges. Unless she's in no fit state to do so…'

Mike took a deep breath. 'The one person I need to talk to is the one I can't.' He had to ask it, even though he couldn't bear to hear the answer. 'Is she … going to be all right? Still Sue?'

'Let's take it one step at a time, DI Barley. We don't believe she was starved of oxygen. The paramedics defibrillated her quickly. She's had emergency surgery. She's heavily sedated. She just needs time. Hopefully we can get her off the ventilator in a day or two, and you can talk.'

Mike nodded. 'Thank you.' Dr Purani pointed to an armed officer by the entrance to the intensive care unit. 'We'll have someone stationed there 24/7. Just in case. Until we find out what happened.'

'Of course. You can't be too careful.'

The doors at the end of the corridor burst open then, making Mike jump, and Rob hurtled through them. 'Where's Sue?' he gasped, completely out of breath.

Mike stared at Rob, seeing him through a new lens. The brutish, rugby-playing shoulders. The huge hands. The emotional distance from Tom. Taking other people's kids on rugby tours while showing no interest in his own son's love of chess. Rob played such a small part in Tom's life that he rarely even mentioned him. But broken bones, bursting someone's spleen in public ... surely it couldn't have been him? Surely it had to be a random attack? Mike had come across domestic violence so often as a copper, both male and female victims, and it was classless, just as likely behind the John Lewis curtains as the grubby nets, though probably more hidden. Surely Rob wouldn't attack her in a public place? He would have waited for her to get home…

'Are you all right, sir?' Dr Purani asked.

'Yes. Yes I am,' Rob puffed. 'I ran up the stairs. I'm Sue's husband. How is she?'

'Sue's still in intensive care,' Dr Purani replied, his face expressionless.

'Is she going to be all right?'

'We hope so. She's in good hands here.' Again, there was no hint of suspicion in the doctor's voice.

'What happened? Is it to do with the case?'

'She has sustained injuries to her abdomen. Most likely from repeated punches.' Mike had to hand it to him. The doctor was simply stating facts, and far more calmly than he would be able to do.

'I've told her that job is too dangerous. So many times. Can I see her?'

'Only very briefly, I'm afraid. If you press the buzzer you can access the waiting area. I'll join you shortly.'

'Thank you. And thanks for getting me here so quickly, Mike.'

It was all Mike could do to be civil. 'Have you told Tom?'

'Tom? No, I … I came straight here.'

'Where is he?'

Rob paused. 'I don't actually know. Chess, maybe? He plays a lot of tournaments.'

'Don't worry. I'll find him.'

Rob nodded and disappeared through the doors.

'He didn't ask where it happened,' Mike said.

'And blaming her for taking the job,' Dr Purani said. 'Classic.'

Chapter Twenty-One

Tanya was my first. Seven months ago. I approached her in an alleyway near Victoria Coach Station, fresh off the National Express. She was way more streetwise than Anna. Tanya wasn't clutching her rucksack like a comfort blanket. Very short dark hair. Sequinned mini skirt over black tights – it was a freezing January lunchtime – fluffy waist-length jacket, cheap skyscraper heels and red lips. Blood red.

I was nervous. I'd been dreaming of this for months and now, finally, with Riverdell in place, I was going to make it happen. I decided to start by helping a street sex worker, someone who'd had a really rough childhood and had nothing left to sell but themselves. They could stay at Riverdell, live there rent-free. Find a job locally. Get on their feet. Have a genuinely fresh start. And maybe, if I made it wonderful enough, they'd stay with me forever. Be part of my perfect family. Be *safe*.

I'd been scouting the scene on and off for weeks, working out which ones had pimps, frustrated yet glad to see they all looked out for each other. And then I got lucky. I saw her climb off the coach. She hadn't worked this area before. A newbie. Perfect.

'You OK, honey?' I asked, sweet Sally's face full of concern, steely blue eyes hidden by brown contact lenses.

'You lookin' for fun? I do women and men. Whatever you like.'

'Oh, no, I'm a street pastor. Keep an eye on the girls, make sure they're all right. You're new, aren't you?'

She eyed me suspiciously. 'Yeah. I'm from Middlesbrough, like.'

'I thought so. Let me buy you a cuppa. I can give you the low-down on the streets here. There's a few pimps you'll want to avoid.'

'No, ta.' She began to walk away. 'Look, leave me alone. I'm working.'

'How much do you charge? At least let me make sure you're not being ripped off.'

'You're a pig, aren't you?' She glanced around nervously, checking the street.

'No, love, I'm not with the police. Look.' I pulled out a business card, freshly printed on my computer, complete with photo. I'd even laminated it. 'Sally Croft. Counsellor and street pastor.'

She looked at the card. 'Tenner for a handjob. Fifteen for a blowie. Twenty if it's bareback. Thirty for a fuck.'

I pulled five ten-pound notes from my pocket. 'Here's

fifty quid. That should give you a couple of hours off. Let's get that coffee.' I point to a greasy spoon by the coach station. 'Just there.'

She was suspicious. Someone who had never trusted a soul, and never would. 'I'd prefer a voddie,' she replied, quickly pocketing the cash.

'I've got some,' I smiled, taking a hip flask from my bag. 'Smirnoff. We'll order orange juice and slip it in.'

'OK. Just a quickie. I need to work.'

We took a seat in the dingy cafe, jostling with tourists and travellers waiting for their coaches, huge rucksacks and cases spilling over almost every inch of floor space. I bought us two orange juices and a bacon buttie which she devoured almost instantly with a huge slug of vodka. I bought her another. With a full belly and a temporarily numbed mind, she began to open up. Tanya. Eighteen. Or so she said. Her life story tore at my heart, and I soaked up every agonising second of it.

'Me ma was on smack. And me da.'

'Did she get off it?'

'She OD'd. I found her. Still had her works in her arm.'

'I'm so sorry.'

'Don't be. Useless fucker.'

'When was this?'

'Last week. In her squat. She'd been dead for days.'

I tipped another shot of vodka into her orange juice. She was devastated. Behind the bullshit, she was in pieces. I'd never heard anything like it. This was a girl I could really help. She needed me.

'Her skin was black. Probably all the shit she put in it.' She drained her glass. 'I used to go and see me ma, like. Make sure she had fags and some food in.'

'What about your father?'

'Dunno where he is. I lived with me nan.'

'Does your nan know you're in London?'

'Yeah. Told her I was gonna see friends. She wanted me to go back for the funeral. I ain't. Just a load of smacked-out junkies who only give a shit about their next fix. Be tryin' to rob everyone.'

I drained my drink and leaned across the table. 'Look, Tanya, I haven't been entirely straight with you.'

'I know. What do you think I am, a fuckin' idiot? That ID card is a fake. You just lonely? Or want a bit of action now?'

'I do keep an eye on the girls on the street. But I do it for a very important client. She'd rather remain anonymous.'

'Client?'

'Yes. Very rich.'

'And?'

'She likes to help people who've had a difficult start in life.'

'I told you. I do women.'

'It's not like that. No sex, no strings. Just the chance of a fresh start. Money. A job. She has a big house in Surrey. You can stay there rent-free until you get on your feet.'

'Where's that?'

'Not far. Maybe a forty-five minute drive.'

'What is she, religious? Runnin' some kind of weird cult? You'll be gettin' me to drink the Kool-Aid next.'

I smiled gently. 'Not at all. Like I said, she's very wealthy. And she had a tough start, too. So she wants to help people like her.'

I picked up my bag. 'Look, if you're not interested, I can find another girl…'

'No!' She grabbed my arm. 'I'll go. Just for tonight, like. See the place.'

'I'll pick you up at 8pm. There's a road near Temple Underground, Temple Place. Come out of the Tube and walk along the road until you're on the corner of Arundel St. I'll be in a Range Rover.'

I wasn't sure she'd show up. But she did.

Chapter Twenty-Two

Tom stood outside the ICU unit, his chest tight, his head dizzy.

'Your mum needed a little help to breathe, so you'll see some big tubes near her face, but don't worry,' Dr Purani said gently. 'They're just making sure she has enough oxygen. And there are quite a few machines around her, checking she's stable. Monitoring her, really. That's all.'

Beside him, Mike placed his arm tenderly around Tom's shoulder. 'It's probably best if you just see Mum for a few minutes, Son. She's tired after the surgery. We can come back a bit later. She might be more awake then.'

Tom nodded. 'You'll need to wear these,' Dr Purani added, handing him a plastic gown, mask, gloves and shoe covers. 'It's just because some of the patients are very poorly.'

'D-does she look ... I mean, can you see...'

Mike shook his head. 'Her injuries are on her tummy, and a few on her arms, so she looks just like Mum. It's just all the wires and tubes that are scary. But they're only temporary.'

Once he'd put on the protective gear – his hands sweating, legs trembling – Tom followed Dr Purani into the ICU ward.

'Oh my god.'

The sight of his mum in the bed, as the beeping machines sliced through the unnatural, cold silence, welled up an anger so intense, so overwhelming, that Tom wanted to run screaming from the room. A wave of dizziness swamped him and, instinctively, he took a step backwards.

'It's OK,' Dr Purani whispered. 'Take some deep breaths. Count with me. Inhale … and exhale. That's right. It's bound to be shocking, seeing her like this. Come and hold her hand.'

His breathing controlled, Tom's dizziness began to subside. 'What about the machines? What if I accidentally lean on something? I don't want to hurt her.'

'You won't.'

Taking a seat beside her, Tom slid his blue-gloved hand into Sue's, and huge tears swelled his eyelids. 'Oh, Mum,' he whispered. 'Who did this to you?'

Could it be his dad, Tom wondered. That didn't make sense. His outbursts were always at home. Occasionally on holiday. But always in private. And his dad had been coaching rugby. It had to be linked to the missing girl. Or maybe one of her old cases with a grudge, turning up after they saw her on TV. Whoever it was, Mike had to find them.

Lost in his own thoughts, he heard Dr Purani's voice, distant and echoing. 'Let's leave Mum for some rest, now,' the doctor whispered. 'Mike's going to take you for a cup of tea.'

They took the lift in silence to the ground floor, following the signs to the cafe, which turned out to be a Costa. Mike bought him a panini and a cappuccino. 'Mum would have something to say about this,' he said thickly, forcing down a bite of panini. 'She hates Costa. And Starbucks.'

Mike smiled. 'I know.'

'She had pink nails. Mum never does her nails.'

'We think she'd been to a nail bar in Cobshott. That's where the car was parked when she was found. Uniform took a statement from the salon's owner, who said she was fine when she left. That ties in with the attack being in the car. But I'll go and see the owner myself first thing. Double check.'

'I did tell her to go and pamper herself.' A thick tear swelled and dripped down his cheek. 'If only I hadn't.'

'Don't be silly. It's not your fault.'

'You have to find them, Mike. Whoever did this.' He took a sip of coffee. 'Do you think she was followed? By someone linked to the case?'

'It's likely. Though we can't rule out that it was a random attack. Wrong place, wrong time.' He paused. 'Try and eat something, Son.'

Tom took a bite of panini. 'Where's my dad?'

'He went off somewhere. Said he'd meet us here in half an hour. Look, Tom … there are some people from social services who want to talk to you. For some, um, background on your mum.'

'Social services?'

'It's just routine.'

Tom fiddled with the half-eaten panini on his plate. This attack was in broad daylight, in a village. It couldn't be his dad. Had to be linked to her work. Nothing to do with the 'episodes' at home. They were different. Private. And he would never say a word about them without speaking to his mum first. What if they took him into care? She'd chosen to keep the abuse hidden for so long, and if he revealed it, everyone at her work would know. Everyone. And so would the world, when it went to court. She wouldn't be feisty DCI Fisher, she'd be that policewoman who let her husband beat her up. They'd be *that* family. Her reputation would be ruined. And he'd be the son who stood by and did nothing, the pathetic fourteen-year-old who couldn't – no, *wouldn't* – protect her. He was so used to hiding her secret, hiding the fact that he knew what went on, that the idea of revealing it to anyone terrified him. Especially Mike, the father he'd never had. Mike would be disgusted that he'd stood by in silence, Tom was sure of it.

'OK. But there's nothing to say.'

Mike eyed him carefully. 'I don't know who did this, Son. But if it's possible it was someone you know, now is the time to speak up.'

Tom shook his head firmly. 'I can't think of anyone.'

'Of course. Well, as I say, it's just routine.' He paused. 'Look, are you happy about staying at home tonight? I know it'll be upsetting without your mum there.'

'I'm fine.'

They finished their drinks in an uneasy silence, interrupted by Rob's arrival. 'Thanks for picking up Tom,' he said, with his trademark grin.

'It's fine,' Mike's voice was icy. 'He was at chess, weren't you, Son.'

'How is she?'

'The same,' Mike replied. He could hardly bear to look at Rob. 'Are you two going to stay at the hospital tonight? I could go to your place and pick up a change of clothes, and anything else you need.'

Rob and Tom nodded. 'I'm staying,' Tom said. 'But I don't need anything.'

'Nor do I,' Rob added. He patted a bag over his shoulder. 'I've got my laptop. But thanks again.'

Mike stood up. It was clear both of them wanted him to go. 'I'll be on my mobile all night if you need me. Please ring if there's any change. Anything at all.'

'I will,' Tom replied.

He glanced over his shoulder as he left the cafe, father and son sitting in silence, both clinging to the familiar facade of happy families that had been their mask for so long. If Rob was the attacker, Mike promised himself that he'd make the bastard pay for every single moment of pain and fear that he'd put Sue through. Even if it meant being banged up himself.

~

The shed door was secured with two huge padlocks. Leaving the hospital, Mike had gone straight to Sue's house and climbed over the back fence. He'd heard talk about this 'shed' from both Sue and Tom once too often. Rob was up to something, he knew it.

Maybe Forensics would find something, though Rob's DNA being in his wife's car wouldn't be enough – the defence could easily argue you'd expect to find it there. But the bastard clearly needed locking up, and if he couldn't get him on the attack, he'd have to find something else. Privately. He didn't want to involve any of the team down at the station until he had to. Not while Sue was unconscious, anyway.

Being a locksmith, Rob had secured the shed with steel hinges and master padlocks so thick that Mike's bolt-cutters barely made a dent. The tiny, opaque window was barred. But Mike had arrested enough burglars to know exactly how to get in, and fast. Taking a hairgrip from a pack in his pocket – hastily bought at the Shell garage en route, to a raised eyebrow from the spotty youth on the till – he bent it over and pushed it into the lock, fiddling with a second hairgrip to release each of its four pins.

As the second lock clicked open, Mike paused. Before his divorce had sent him into the ex-council flat, he'd spend an inordinate amount of time pottering in his own garden shed, listening to Radio 4 with a weak tea in a chipped mug. Though he'd never admit it, he had a well-thumbed copy of *Penthouse* stashed up there too. Maybe that's all Rob did? Pottered and wanked. Harmlessly. Like millions of other middle-aged men around the country. But he had to know for sure.

Opening the door a little, he snapped on the light. The neighbours were used to seeing a glow from the shed through the trees at all hours, so they wouldn't be suspicious.

Mike wasn't sure what to expect inside. Greasy workbenches, perhaps. Oily rags. Ancient tins of paint that had long solidified. Rusting bicycles. But this shed was immaculate. Every tool was in its place on a rack, in ascending order, smallest to largest. Bottles and tins were neatly stacked on shelves. Even odds and ends were placed in labelled boxes. A long workbench rang the full length of the shed, opposite the tiny window, and on it stood a huge Airfix model of a warship, which Rob had almost finished. Six tiny tins of paint and two small brushes were lined up beside it, ready for use.

Five other finished models – two warplanes, a racing car, and two old ships, one of which Mike recognised as HMS *Victory* – were displayed along the workbench. 'So this is what he does in his spare time,' Mike whispered to himself, marvelling at the precision, the attention to detail, on each of the models. Each must have taken weeks to make.

With everything labelled, checking the rest of the shed

was easy, and to his surprise, not a porn magazine in sight. An old armchair sat in one corner, with a small fridge beside it, which hummed in the silence. Inside were six cans of Stella, a half-empty bottle of vodka, and a KitKat.

Mike sank into the chair, the day's events catching up with him. The shed was clean. Rob was a wife-beater, and he'd get the bastard somehow for that, but there was nothing illegal here. He felt a sudden pang of sadness that Rob had never involved Tom with any of his hobbies, or even shown them to him.

Snapping off the light, Mike tiptoed out of the shed and began to close the door behind him. That's when he had a sudden thought. The armchair.

He slipped back into the shed and closed the door behind him. Tipping the chair backwards, Mike couldn't see anything unusual at first. Then he spotted it. An almost invisible small pouch neatly hand-sewn into the fabric underneath. His heart raced as he slid in his hand. Inside was a burner phone.

The message was still on the screen. Typed but not sent.

114b Onslow Avenue, Mayfair. 9pm. Tuesday.

An affair. That made sense. Shagging a woman behind Sue's back, feeding off the power it gave him. The control.

Taking a photo of the message, and being careful not to send it, Mike replaced the phone in the pouch.

He padlocked the door behind him, leaving no trace of his visit.

So, 9pm Tuesday. Mike smiled. Whatever happened, he wouldn't be bringing him in for questioning before then. Rob would be in for a hell of a shock when he showed up.

Chapter Twenty-Three

He's not answering his emails, and I'm starting to feel panicky. What if he's backed out? I'll have to run, and I can't just leave her behind.

I first made contact with Fixer72 months ago, just another stranger in the cesspool of the dark web. I'd decided early on that if one of my children rejected the life I had to offer – opening presents by the fire on Christmas morning, a doting mother always ready to listen, living in luxury with everything I never had – then they'd have to be taught a lesson. Spend time in the basement. And if that didn't work, I wanted a fallback, someone ready to take the problem child off my hands. I couldn't risk one ruining our perfect world, and I'd make money to help others who'd be *grateful*.

The trouble is, there's still a part of me that doesn't want to let her go. She's become familiar, a stable part of my life. We have our routine. I wash her, care for her, feed her, dress her. I've even *educated* her. I wish I had more time. But I don't, and ten grand is a lot of cash. That's how much this Eastern European family will pay for her, apparently. Fixer72 is just the middle man. He's probably getting twenty.

I'm stressed, jittery. The longer I don't hear from Fixer72, the more desperate I am for the deal to be done. And now a detective, DI Mike Barley, is coming to the salon tomorrow morning. He rang the mobile number I gave the police. Said it was a 'routine inquiry' because I may have been the last person to see her before the attacker. Barley may be right. But the last thing I need is a full grilling by an experienced detective. My tongue ran away with me last time. I need to be in full control.

I open Tor and check my emails before I've even stripped away Beverley's heels and makeup. Nothing from Fixer72. If he can't take her, there's no time to find someone else who will. I'm claustrophobic, cornered, raging at myself for trusting him, and fling the laptop at the coffee table, watching in horror as cracks splinter across the screen.

That's when the email pops up.

Fixer72 : Confirmed. Drop Tuesday, 9pm.

Finally. It's sorted, and the sense of relief is overwhelming. But I'm struggling to read the details. The screen is flickering and the message is obscured by the web of cracks. It looks like '114b Onslow Avenue, Mayfair. Park in residents' bay'. I try to type a reply, but the laptop is wrecked. It's hopeless. Ten grand and my new life is at stake. He's given me a burner phone number for emergencies. Well, this is an emergency.

My burner phone is hidden inside a coffee tin on my shelf. I click through my contacts. Fixer72's number is there.

I type a new message: *Confirming Tuesday. Need to re-send address. Email currently down. Use text.*

He doesn't reply straightaway, but no matter. He will. The deal is set. My panic subsides, and I know I have to let her go. Reinvent myself somewhere new with my ten grand, and, one day, find a *good* girl to join my family. A girl who deserves it.

It's 8.30am and I'm at the salon in plenty of time for DI Mike Barley, cancelling each of my four Monday morning regulars with a text.

> *Sorry, honey, but no can do today. You'll never BELIEVE it. The policewoman who was beaten up yesterday was a walk-in. So I have to talk to the cops, tell them everything I know. Catch up soon. HUGS xxx*

They'll have heard on the grapevine, anyway, and I need my text to be typically Mel, nothing out of the ordinary. After a sleepless night, I'm so done with this place. I'll be gone from here on Thursday, wiping Cobshott and its ghastly, vapid inhabitants off my shoes like dog shit.

I flip the sign on the door to 'closed', place fresh pink towels by each chair, and settle back to wait. Today, I'm serving gossipy Mel, Cobshott's favourite best friend, with a glittery gold iPhone, left face up on the sofa so he knows I've got nothing to hide. Inside, I'm jittery, but focused.

Barley turns up at 9am, bang on time, and he's exactly what I expect. Old, overweight and doubtless divorced – no wedding ring in sight – probably with a couple of kids he never sees who eat up his salary in child maintenance. Huge bags under his eyes, big black crumpled ones slumped on top of his cheeks. Clearly had a sleepless night, too, worrying about his boss. He wants to know who did it. So do I.

'Welcome,' I say, opening the salon door. 'Please, come in. I hope I can help, honey. We don't get this sort of thing in Cobshott. So whatever I can do…'

Mike grunts in agreement and we sit on the small pink sofa in the waiting area.

'How is your colleague?' I say, eyes full of concern. 'DCI Fisher, is it?'

'In intensive care.' He clears his throat. 'So anything you can tell me, anything at all, could be helpful.'

'Of course.' I pause. 'Silly me, I haven't even offered you refreshments. Would you like a herbal tea? I've got vitamin water, organic juice…'

'No, no, thank you. Take me through yesterday. DCI Fisher arrived about 11am?'

'Yes, that's right. She was a walk-in. Most of my clients are regulars, but you know, I do offer a service without an appointment if I'm free.'

'And you always open on a Sunday?'

Nosey sod. I can tell he's going to be trouble, and I'm feeling pretty strung out. I keep my breathing steady and calm. 'Not always. But one of my regulars had called to ask for an early manicure, so I did. I like to keep them happy.'

'Can you remember what she talked about?'

I pause. This is another chance to dump stepfather Paul Eaves in it. But I need to pace myself. 'She asked about one of my clients, Soozie Lightwater, and particularly her daughter, Sky. I don't know why. There wasn't much to tell.' I lower my voice. 'Bit of an airhead. Loves Instagram. Been going out with a YouTuber. That's all I know.'

Barley is listening to me, intently, but his eyes keep darting around the salon. It's making me uneasy. 'I hear all kinds of gossip in here. Your colleague said she was on the #findanna case and I said rumour is that her stepfather did it. A few mums weren't keen on how he looked at their kids. That was pretty much it. She paid cash, and left. About midday.'

He nods. 'These mums. I'll need names.'

I smile. 'That's more than my life's worth, honey. I'm their confidante. It's only gossip. What happens in the salon stays in the salon. It's like therapy.'

'Then I'll need a full list of your clients.'

'Of course.' I smile. 'I register them all on this iPad. You can see them all on here. Shall I email it to you now?' I swipe open the screen.

'Email would be great. Thank you. But by the way, you do realise that if a therapist suspects someone is in danger, they're duty-bound to tell us?'

I need to play ball. 'I know, officer. I'd always report a crime. What I hear is just gossip. I don't know if there's any truth in it. I've lost count of the number of clients who are constantly having funeral fantasies about their philandering husbands. You'd be arresting half of Cobshott if I called you every time that happened.'

As if on cue, the door bursts open and Soozie sweeps in, sniffing, clearly at least two lines of coke down. 'Darling, I just heard on the grapevine you were the last person to see that policewoman…' she gabbles, stopping in her tracks at the sight of the detective. 'DI Barley. I'm sorry. I wasn't expecting…'

I know Soozie. DI Barley is *exactly* who she was expecting. She's heard that I'm talking to the police and she can't resist sticking her oar in. But having her here is sending my stress levels through the roof. I can control a two-way conversation. Throw a coked-up Soozie into the mix and anything could happen.

'Mrs Lightwater.' They shake hands.

'You two know each other?' I chatter, feigning surprise.

'Yes,' Soozie replies. 'Sky got into a bit of, er, trouble recently. Nothing serious. DI Barley helped me sort it out.'

Barley looks bemused. He's smart. I need to be careful.

I'm pretty sure he knows Soozie is a coke-head, and that she has already told me exactly what Sky was up to.

'So is it true?' Years spent dealing with bolshie celebrities have made Soozie utterly shameless, with or without drugs. 'That you did the policewoman's nails?'

'Yes. And as I'm telling DI Barley, she didn't say much. Had her nails done and left. I wish I could be more help.'

'Have you heard anything, Mrs Lightwater?' Barley says. 'Unofficially? On the grapevine?'

'Everyone's convinced there's a lunatic on the loose,' she replies. 'First Anna goes missing, then the detective hunting for her is put in a coma. Those two things must be related. A couple of friends have employed private security guards to patrol the perimeter of their houses. One can't be too careful.'

Barley nods, and shuts his notebook. 'Well, thank you for your time.' He hands me a card. 'If you think of anything else, you can reach me on this mobile. Any time. And don't worry. I will find the person who did this.'

Soozie grabs his arm. 'You know that business with Sky?' She reaches into her cavernous Fendi bag. 'I thought you might find this useful.'

'What is it?'

She pauses. So dramatic.

'Paul Eaves' laptop.'

'It … it can't be,' Barley splutters. 'We've already got it.'

'This is his *other* laptop. The one he didn't want you to find.'

I can't believe my luck. Whatever is on that laptop is bound to incriminate Eaves. And it will buy me more time.

Barley is so stunned he almost drops it. 'This is evidence, Mrs Lightwater. You should have called us straight away. How long have you had it? His defence will have a field day if other people could have accessed it.'

Soozie's bottom lip, already sausage-like from too much filler, pouts even more.

'Paul Eaves?' I say. 'Isn't he the missing girl's stepfather? Oh my God, Soozie, where did you get it? That's genius.'

She brightens. 'I went to see his wife Zoe last night. Took a bottle of Grey Goose. Her favourite. Turned on the charm and the sympathy. She was already pissed, has shut herself away since they took him and has no idea that Sky is involved.'

I play dumb. 'What's Sky got to do with it?'

'Eaves was messaging her. Sexy stuff. The pervert. Anyway, several more vodkas down, she told me Paul has a laptop. One she's hidden from the police. He kept it under a floorboard in the corner of his study and has no idea she knows about it.'

'OMG, Soozie…'

'I know. She only found out it was there a few weeks ago when the plumber came to fix their underfloor heating. Zoe's completely convinced herself he's been doing dodgy deals at work on it. Big-time fraud. And that it's all on this laptop so it could drop him right in the shit.'

'And you persuaded her to give it to you?' I coax. 'For

safe-keeping? Honestly, DI Barley, Soozie's brilliant. You'd never have found it.'

She nods. 'I hope this can help find Anna. And prove he's a fucking demented paedo. Zoe's in total denial. She insists it's all dodgy "work" stuff. Poor, deluded cow.'

Barley nods. 'Have you looked on it?'

'God, no,' Soozie squeals. She has.

Barley gives her a withering glare.

'OK, I *tried* to look. But it's all password-protected. I couldn't get in. Zoe said she'd tried too.'

He takes the laptop. 'I'll get this to the lab right away. Thank you, Mrs Lightwater. I'll need you to come to the station and give a statement about how you came across this.'

'Sure.' Soozie clearly has nothing else to do. 'I'll come now.'

Barley turns to me and shakes my hand. 'Thanks, Ms Medford. If I need anything else, I'll be in touch.'

The door closes, and I sink down onto the sofa, drained. At least Barley didn't suspect me, I'm sure of it. And thank God for Soozie. That laptop should keep them busy while I make my escape.

The one person I'm going to really miss is Cleo. I adore my Thursday afternoons with her. Sometimes I dream that Cleo has left her wife and we're together, a happy couple, living by the sea in Ibiza, in a beach shack just like the one Shauna took me to. Long walks along the sand, a cocktail in a bar with friends. New friends. Accepted, and loved.

Maybe in time Cleo will join me. But for now, I have to stay focused on the plan.

Tomorrow is a big day. I need to move her, without any fuss. No looking back, no thinking of what could have been. No regrets. A quick injection of Camden's finest heroin should do it. Then I can move on, start again and, in time, find more lost souls to help.

Chapter Twenty-Four

Mike hurried up the steps of Green Park tube into the warm, pink Monday night sunset, sweating profusely underneath his light jacket. Trying to dress like a tourist hadn't been easy. He'd finally squeezed into a pair of old chinos, belly sagging over the waistband – last worn the night his ex-wife said she'd met someone 'who actually loves me' – donned a pair of sunglasses, and dug out his old Canon camera, which he slung around his neck. Earlier that afternoon, they'd charged Eaves with child grooming, and he'd been remanded in custody, so he could focus on finding out what Rob Fisher was up to.

Clutching a brand-new A–Z, Mike stood on the corner of Onslow Avenue and Stratton Street, where a stream of taxis dropped and collected the wealthy from the Mayfair Hotel. He needed to check out the area, ready for Fisher's 'date' tomorrow. Although it was Monday, the area was busy with tourists, and Mike found it easy to disappear into the crowd. Onslow Avenue, however, was a different beast. Rows of tall, cream-coloured, terraced Georgian houses lined each side of the street, with black railings in front of them. Plenty of empty parking spaces, as they were all residents' bays. Only a couple of people were hurrying down it, clearly using it as a cut-through to the Tube.

Pulling out his iPhone, he located number 114, about halfway down on the left. Fisher was at the hospital, so there was definitely no risk of bumping into him, but the flat could belong to one of his mates, and the last thing Mike wanted was to arouse any suspicions at all.

He ambled down the street, stopping briefly outside number 110 where he pored over his A–Z. Number 114 was easily visible. One black front door. Bells for three flats, including a basement. A locked postbox attached to the railings beside him read '110a. Basement Flat'. So 114b had to be the ground floor.

He walked on, slowly, eyes appearing to gaze at the map. The ground-floor curtains were open, and a steady light glowed from what appeared to be a table lamp. Everything about the property dripped wealth, from the thick velvet floor-to-ceiling drapes in the tall front windows, to the elaborate cornicing around the ceiling and the leather Chesterfield sofa. Behind it hung a large, old-fashioned painting of a hunt, with white jodhpurs, black hats and red jackets streaking across a countryside landscape. This was the sort of apartment you'd find politicians in, he thought, not locksmiths from Kingston with a bit on the side who could easily check into the local Travelodge. Maybe he was trying to impress. Maybe she was wealthy. Maybe the owners were on holiday and Fisher had access through work. That was a possibility. He did a lot of work for lettings agencies, and emergency call-outs.

Reaching the corner, Mike walked around the block and stopped again by the Mayfair Hotel. Onslow Avenue was one-way to cars. That was a blessing. If he stationed himself in the crowds there tomorrow night he'd see Fisher go past. And he would definitely be driving. The risk of being seen on public transport with his floozie in tow was too great. All Mike needed was a photo of the woman, enough to prove to Sue what was going on. He wouldn't show it to her unless he had to. But if she refused to give evidence against the bastard, still trying to protect him, perhaps knowing that other women were also at risk, might do it.

Sky hadn't left her room since Saturday, and Soozie was worried. Really worried. With Paul Eaves now charged with child grooming and remanded in custody at HMP Parkside, his name and photo were all over the news.

'Can I come in?' she said softly, knocking on the bedroom door.

'No.' Sky's voice was flat, expressionless.

'Miquita's made us some hot chocolate. With soy milk, of course. Look, I just want to talk. To tell you the police now have Paul Eaves' laptop. His secret one. They found it this morning. So I hope they will be able to send him to prison for a very long time. None of this is your fault. It'll be forgotten soon.'

Sky said nothing. She sat on her bed, clutching her teddy, her hair matted and her scrubbed face puffy, black-rimmed eyes staring blankly ahead. Beside her, messages, emails and Instagram notifications silently flashed up on her phone every few seconds. One after another after another.

Saw a video of you on the dark web. Oh, Daniel, oh, ohhhhhhh.

Sky, are you OK? It's Jen from school. Call me. I heard what happened. I'm worried.

You're a porn star, girl! Check out Sky Lightwater on Tor. You've got your own channel.

At first they were people from school. Then 'Friends' on Facebook. She'd blocked them. Realised she had no idea who most of them were. All ages. All over the world. Social media had been her life, her breezy Instagram 'likes' the root of her self-esteem. Now it had turned into a whirling cesspool, sucking her deeper and deeper into its darkness, to a place where the pretty teenager was just seen as a paedophile's plaything, someone to laugh at or drool over.

Her mother's footsteps padded softly towards the stairs.

'I've left your hot chocolate outside the door,' she called. 'Come down when you're ready. We can watch Netflix.'

This would never be forgotten, Sky decided. Never. Those videos Paul had persuaded her to send him. Videos of her touching herself, playing with sex toys, watching YouPorn, they were on the dark web now. For ever. And everyone knew it.

Her mind numb, Sky put her teddy in her dressing gown pocket, swung her legs over the edge of the bed and stood up, unsteadily. Her favourite pink chiffon scarf lay over the beside chair and she picked it up, tenderly tying it around her neck. The chair wasn't heavy, but she'd barely eaten since Saturday, so she dragged it into her walk-in wardrobe. Sky took off her dressing gown, folded it neatly and placed it on the floor, before climbing onto the chair and reaching up to the knob on the top cupboard.

Soozie didn't hear the thud as Sky kicked the chair sideways, or the merciful crack as her neck snapped. There was no struggle, no convulsions as she gasped for air. It was Star who found her twin sister an hour later, her face blue, her eyes staring, her swollen tongue lolling and her legs soiled. Screaming, she grasped Sky's limp body and tried to lift her down.

'Help me, Mummy!' she screamed as Soozie stood frozen in the doorway. 'Please...'

It was Star who grabbed a blanket and wrapped it around her sister, trying to protect her dignity. It was Star who dialled 999. And it was Star who dragged the chair across the room and cradled Sky in her arms until the police arrived, as Soozie stood in the doorway, numb, her eyes staring straight into her daughter's dead ones.

There was no more news from the hospital. Sue was still on the ventilator, showing no signs of waking up. 'We just have to be patient,' Dr Purani said, as Mike sat at her bedside, late on Tuesday afternoon. 'We've reduced the sedation, but she's still unconscious. Sometimes our bodies do shut down after a major trauma. Give her time.'

Mike nodded. 'It's just so hard, you know…'

'It must be.' Dr Purani paused. 'What's happening with her husband? Is he going to be arrested? He's been sitting with her on and off and of course we can't refuse to let him in unless…'

'The investigation is underway,' Mike replied. 'Social services interviewed Tom, but he insisted everything is fine. Rob's DNA is in the car and on her clothes, but that's not enough – they're married so you'd expect that. Forensics found a trace of his blood on the passenger dashboard, but he says that's from a nosebleed. But don't worry. He won't get away with it.'

There was more than enough to bring Rob in, at least for questioning. But Mike wanted to wait. He had to find out what Rob was up to, and if photos from 114b Onslow Avenue tonight would persuade Sue or Tom to speak out, the wait would be worth it.

His phone vibrated and Mike pulled it from his pocket

to see DCI Lauren Brown's name on the screen, a high-flying young detective covering for Sue. She was early thirties, public school educated, with a forensically sharp mind and a reputation for 'taking no shit', as Sue put it. She'd also been incredibly sympathetic and kind to him after Sue's attack. 'I've got to take this,' he told Dr Purani, hurrying out of ICU and into the empty corridor.

'Paul Eaves' laptop.' Lauren's voice was grim. 'It's chock-full of inappropriate photos of Anna. A few of Sky. A couple of videos of Anna, too, stripping off. Sick bastard. And he's downloaded hundreds of images and videos of teenage orgies. Girls with older men. Nasty stuff. We're still going through them but in one grainy shot there's a glimpse of a girl who could possibly be Anna. IT are trying to enhance it so we can see her face more clearly.'

'My god. Have you been to see Eaves?'

'Went straight up to Parkside. I knew you were at the hospital and Chief Biller said we should get right on it, so he came with me.'

'Biller wanting a bit of the glory…'

'Exactly. Anyway, Eaves is still claiming he has no idea where Anna is. When I showed him the video and pointed out the glimpse of the girl, he completely freaked out. Started slamming his fists into the wall and mumbling. There was blood everywhere. Even his lawyer looked scared. They had to restrain him and call the resident psych. The chief got me and his brief straight out of the room.'

'Was he faking?'

'Hard to say. I don't think so. His eyes were wild.

Drooling at the mouth. I couldn't understand what he was saying.'

'Could you make out any of it?'

'No. He was rambling. Mostly along the line of "I didn't hurt her."'

'What did the psych say?'

'I didn't speak to them. Eventually the chief went back in and came out saying we must suspend all interviews with Eaves until the psych says he's fit to be questioned. The chief is worried he'll get off on diminished responsibility. That wouldn't look good on his watch. We can charge him later. He's not going anywhere.'

'What about Anna?'

'I'm checking with the CPS to see if there's enough to charge him with involvement in Anna's disappearance as well. Maybe he took her to an orgy that went wrong.'

Mike sighed. 'Christ. Nothing surprises me anymore. But if he did, surely there's still a chance she's still alive.'

'Exactly. It's possible. I'm so frustrated we can't speak to him. But we've got to play this right. I've got the team going over all the data again – phone, social media, his car's movements, to see if we can pinpoint any possible locations.' Lauren paused. 'How is she, Mike?'

'The same. The doctor says her body's just shut itself down. To rest. But he's hopeful she'll just wake up.'

Lauren sighed. 'We're all thinking of her. Are you sure you're happy to stay on the case, with all this going on?'

'Definitely. It's what Sue would want. Listen, Lauren,

keep me posted. I've got to go into town tonight. Personal stuff. The ex-wife. But I'll be on text and email.'

'That's fine, Mike. It'll take the CPS a while to wade through all this, probably a couple of days at least. Hope it goes OK tonight. Take the night off. See you tomorrow, bright and early. With any luck, we can have another crack at Eaves then.'

Chapter Twenty-Five

Soozie pushes open the door of the nail bar and shuffles in, still wearing yesterday's clothes. I hardly recognise her. I've had so many texts from clients telling me what's happened, and it's all over social media. She clearly hasn't eaten or slept since Sky was found. Black circles of eyeliner and exhaustion ring her eyes, and old makeup is smeared down her puffy cheeks. Her familiar Chanel perfume is replaced by sweat. She's beyond crying, in that zombifying zone where the brain starts to shut down. I know this pain. Her body is rigid, numb.

'I'm so sorry,' I say, taking her hand and leading her to the pink sofa. I mean it. Soozie didn't deserve this. Nor did Sky.

'She was being trolled,' Soozie says blankly. 'On social. Apparently the Paul Eaves thing was everywhere.'

'What about Star? How is she?'

'Checked in to the Priory and on suicide watch. I can't lose them both. Simon's in pieces. He can't get out of bed.'

Confident, dramatic, PR Soozie has gone. She sits on the sofa staring into space, her speech slow, huge pauses between each sentence as she drifts in and out of a temazepam-induced haze.

'So where is Sky now?' I say gently.

'The morgue. They're doing a post-mortem today. Going to cut my baby girl open…'

An agonising wail echoes around the salon and my thoughts drift to when they did a post-mortem on my mother. Barbiturate overdose. My father found her dead when he woke up. I heard him screaming and I stood in the doorway staring at her, numbed, her blue eyes staring as vacantly into space as they had done in life. Her skin was ice-cold, the coldest thing I had ever touched, her thin frame curled up like a baby. I crouched beside her as my father called for an ambulance, and brushed a piece of hair from her face. Her eyes were clouded just like Smokey's, and she'd no longer have to blind herself to what he did. She was free. I wasn't. It was the most selfish thing she'd ever done.

'How about some tea?' I suggest.

Soozie shakes her head.

'I'm sure that laptop will put him away for a very long time.'

Soozie doesn't reply.

We sit in silence as Soozie rocks back and forth. Her pain is palpable, filling the entire salon, and it's triggering ghastly waves of guilt. If I hadn't taken Anna, Sky would still be alive.

I just want Soozie to go. She's distracting me, making me remember. It's my last day at the salon and I've only come to pick up a few things, say my private goodbye to the business that I built. I'm so done with Cobshott now, its people and everything that has happened here. Riverdell was supposed to be a sanctuary but it's become a hell, a millstone I need to be free of. So has Soozie. The guilt is replaced by a cold, silent rage rising in my throat. This isn't on *me*. It wasn't taking Anna that killed Sky. It's Soozie's vapid, pointless world, filled with designer labels and social media and too much money, where you tell your innermost hopes and fears to a stranger doing your nails rather than to those you love. The world she brought them into. Where success and clothes and cars and mansions and having who or what you want is valued over love. That's all her girls had ever known. It wasn't their fault they were so foolish, so hollow. I feel the darkness rising. She should have been a better *mother*.

I glance at my Fitbit. 'I'm sorry, Soozie, but my phone is ringing and I have to take this call. Would you mind…'

She stares at me, bewildered.

'Sorry, honey,' I say, glancing towards the door. I see my mother's eyes again. She has to leave. Now. There's a void opening up inside me, a blackness, a rage, which I won't be able to control.

'C-can I wait?'

'Sorry,' I say, more abruptly than I mean to, pressing my

phone to my ear, pretending to chat. 'Hi. I'll be with you in a minute. A client's just leaving.'

Soozie picks up her bag. 'It's just I-I don't have anywhere to…' she mumbles.

'Just coming. Yes. Oh, yes. I couldn't agree more.' I turn to her and give her a hug. 'I'm so sorry, Soozie. But I'll see you soon.'

She ambles away, leaving a faint smell of sweat in her wake, and I sigh, relieved, as the rage subsides and I flip the sign on the door to 'closed'. The Nail Salon is closed for ever. Soozie was my final customer.

I turn the Range Rover into the Crown Estate, driving past the perfect Huf houses, the new builds, the ornamental hedges, the fountains, and park in Riverdell's garage for the last time. My belongings from the Surbiton flat are neatly packed into a black suitcase in the boot. The second, wheeled case is brand new. It's for her.

I've gone full Beverley with the big red wig, black stilettos, skin-tight black jeans, hastily pulled on in the salon's kitchen. I'm early, maybe too early. But this could get messy and I can't be late. My mind is in the zone, the black void has closed again, and I'm totally focused on what I have to do now, so much so that the state of the room barely bothers me. She's sitting up on the bed, looking a little better. I'm really going to miss her.

'Do I get chocolate?'

'Not today. But I have wonderful news. You're going home. First you need to drink this.'

Her green eyes shine with hope and confusion. 'H-home?'

I place a plastic water bottle on the bed, filled with a couple of inches of orange juice. 'Drink it, honey.'

She unscrews the lid and swallows all the juice.

'Good girl. Now I need to sort out some things upstairs—'

'Don't go! Please. You said…'

'It's all right. We'll be leaving soon. Today, I promise. I'll be back in a minute.'

I lock the panic room and take a last look around Riverdell while I wait for the big dose of diazepam in the juice to kick in. Past the bathrooms with their gold taps, into my bedroom with its soulless soft cream walls and hideously ornate gold mirrors, into Anna's pretty pink one. Her rucksack is still by the bed, and the room immaculate. How different things could have been.

The stairs are my favourite part, wide and sweeping, with gold rails, the kind of stairs you make an entrance down. I remember Anna padding softly up them to the bedroom where she spent her first night, and me making pancakes, sweet ones, with maple syrup. 'Get some rest,' I'd told her. 'And in the morning we'll make some calls, so you can make a fresh start.'

'I can't find my phone,' she'd said. 'I really should let Mum know I'm OK.'

'It's probably in the car,' I'd told her. 'Don't worry about it. We'll ring her later.'

She never made the call.

The diazepam has worked and she's slumped on the bed, dozing. I can't allow myself to think about what might have been. I've already prepared the heroin. Just a little bump, I can't have her overdosing. Enough to knock her out for the journey. And I need to make her beautiful again. Not just for the money, but because Mother is proud.

I swap my heels for flat pumps and pull some white decorating coveralls over my clothes, tugging on a pair of latex gloves and a clean face mask from the salon. She's so thin that the vein pops up within seconds when I tie an elastic band around her arm, and the needle slides in easily. Releasing the band, I step back and watch as the heroin surges through her veins. Her eyes open suddenly and she sits up, eyes glazed, a rather sweet, strange smile on her face.

'I'm going to take you home soon,' I say softly. 'All you need to do is sleep.'

I don't know if she hears me. Her eyelids are heavy and she lolls backwards on the bed, orange vomit pooling in her mouth. I've overdone it. I'm panicking now. She can't die. Dropping the needle on the floor, I push her onto her side, and thump her on the back. The sick spurts from her mouth onto the pillow. Thank God. So much for the diazepam. I'll have to hope the heroin will do it. And that she doesn't choke on the journey. I rest her head on my lap and stroke her matted hair. For a moment I'm filled with love for my rebellious daughter.

'One day,' I whisper, 'you'll come home again. To my new home. But not now, my darling.' Tears begin to fall as I grieve for the life we could have had, and as they soak into my mask they're replaced by a white-hot fury, a rage against her for forcing me to do this, and at myself. I throw her back onto the bed and take out the scissors, ready to cut off her filthy clothes, but instead I jab them into my thigh, over and over, until the pain obliterates everything and I'm numb again.

Unchaining her is simple. I'm back in the zone now, and cut off her ragged clothes before carrying her upstairs to the main bathroom. Even though she's skinny, she's still heavy, and she's making a mess everywhere but I don't care. I'm not coming back. My leg is bleeding, soaking the coveralls, and it leaves a deep red trail on the white carpet. I put her on the bathroom floor and pull down my coveralls and trousers. This has to be done. I flinch as I clean my leg wound and pull it together with steri strips from the bathroom cabinet, covered with a large dressing. Stupid, stupid. I have to stay in control. Focus on the plan.

I've already run a bath and I lower her into it, the smell of Molton Brown and her an unholy mix which makes me retch. She stirs, slightly, every now and then, but rubbing her with a flannel removes most of the dirt and she looks much better. I take off my filthy coveralls, lay her back on the bed and dress her in black trousers, a grey T-shirt and pumps. Her hair is wet, so I pat it with a towel and pull it into a ponytail. The perfect housemaid.

The big fabric suitcase is waiting in the basement and she fits in with surprising ease. My leg is throbbing and there's a drop of blood coming through the dressing, but I don't have time to deal with it. I put her face down, just in case she's sick, zip it up tightly, click the padlock shut and lay her carefully in the back of the Range Rover.

That's when I hear it. The intercom.

They press it once, setting off buzzers around the whole house. For fuck's sake, it'll wake her up. I check the camera. Two men, in uniform, standing by the gates. Security guards. Must be the ones the neighbours employed after the detective was attacked.

My heart is racing so fast it's making me light-headed. I sit on the bed and take deep breaths. Perhaps it's a scam. They're checking to see if the house is empty before burgling it. Either way, I can't risk them pressing that buzzer again.

I touch the intercom button. 'Yes?'

'Sorry to disturb. We're private security for next door. Golden House.'

'I don't need any security, thank you.'

'It's not a sales call, madam. We were patrolling the perimeter and we think you may have a dead animal in the wooded area of your garden. There's a strong smell of it when the wind is in a certain direction. Maybe a stray dog or a deer has got in. Just wanted to let you know.'

'Thank you. I'll have one of the staff check it out.'

They turn and walk away. I need to get out of Cobshott. Now. I run up to the bedroom and touch-up Beverley's makeup, then head straight down to the basement, past the fetid panic room, and into the Range Rover. As the garage doors close behind me, I check my rear-view mirror. Goodbye, Riverdell. It's been a blast.

Chapter Twenty-Six

For a side street, Onslow Avenue had a lot of coming and goings, Mike thought, as he sipped his takeaway Costa and lurked near the entrance to the Mayfair Hotel. He always had a good supply of coffee on a stakeout, usually in a flask, which he'd share with Sue as they sat in the warmth of their car, swapping stories and chatting about Tom. How his chess was going. What he planned to do after GCSEs. Mike couldn't believe she'd never even alluded to what was really going on at home. There had been so many times when she could have confided in him, revealed the real Rob Fisher, and it broke his heart that she hadn't. He could have *helped*.

Clutching a small bunch of flowers, Mike checked his watch nervously from time to time, as if waiting for someone. So far, no one had gone in or out of number 114. He had the perfect diagonal view of the front door from his vantage point until a delivery van pulled up on the corner, forcing him to move slightly closer than he was comfortable with.

8.15pm.

8.30pm.

He'd been here for over an hour now and there was no sign of Fisher or his bit on the side, but there was still plenty of time. Maybe Fisher had already arrived. The sunset sent a warm glow across the rooftops and the light was fading when a black Mercedes pulled up. Diplomatic plates. A uniformed driver climbed out and opened the rear door. Two men stepped out. One was grey-haired, mid-fifties, dressed in a suit. The second was younger, maybe late thirties, also smartly dressed, carrying a briefcase. As they walked up the steps, the front door opened. Mike couldn't see who let them in, and the moment the door closed behind them, the Mercedes drove off.

All three flats were registered to overseas owners, in the Cayman Islands. Probably a couple, living in one of the other flats, Mike figured. Finishing his coffee, a pair of headlights swept past the hotel and turned into Onslow Avenue. A dark, sporty BMW. It parked further down the street. It had to be her. Mid-thirties, long hair, heels. But she opened the boot, took out two large Harrods bags and a small dog, and disappeared into a house at the far end.

The Range Rover purred past Mike, its tinted windows concealing the interior. He watched it park almost outside 114 and a redhead opened the driver's door. Late twenties, Mike guessed, snapping away on his iPhone, but it was hard to tell. Skinny jeans and high heels. Strong, too, as she lifted a huge, clearly heavy suitcase out of the boot and carried it up the steps. What was that all about? Were they planning to run away together? Had her husband found out about their affair and kicked her out?

This time, the door didn't open straight away. She pressed the buzzer, and spoke into the intercom. It had to be her. Rob must have arrived earlier. The door opened and she disappeared inside. He sighed. He'd have to try and photograph them together as they left.

Wishing he hadn't had such a large coffee, his bladder at bursting point, Mike slipped into the grand Mayfair Hotel, where a large group of Japanese tourists and their luggage were checking in. The loos were the best he'd ever had on a stakeout – normally he'd be diving into a McDonalds or a pub – with marble sinks and an attendant to hand you a fresh towel. Also the most expensive, Mike sighed to himself, dropping a pound coin into a small glass bowl labelled 'tips'.

The Range Rover had vanished by the time he'd returned to his post. He stared up and down the street in disbelief. Four minutes. That's all he'd been gone. Had a second driver been in the car? Had she picked up Fisher and gone somewhere? But if so, why lug that massive case inside? Maybe they'd gone for dinner. Maybe they were coming back. Or maybe she was nothing to do with Rob Fisher at all. Furious with himself, Mike shoved the flowers in a bin, cursing his rookie mistake.

That's when he saw Fisher, coming out of one of the apartments on Onslow Avenue, directly opposite. Mike bent down behind a waiting black cab, fiddling with his shoelace. What on earth was going on? He'd triple-checked the address. Fisher stood on the street corner, hesitating. He, too, was watching and waiting.

An hour passed. Fisher stayed in position, lurking in the shadows. The Range Rover didn't come back. People came and went from the Mayfair Hotel and Mike began to feel very conspicuous. From what he could see, all the curtains were drawn, and there was only light coming from the ground floor flat, at the front at least. Everywhere else was in darkness. There was a tiny crack in the curtains, and the dull glow seemed to be coming from the rear of the house. Finally, Fisher spoke briefly into his phone before walking off towards the tube.

Mike was thoroughly confused, hungry and incredibly thirsty, having munched his way through the Crunchie and bag of Mini Cheddars in his pocket. He had no idea what Fisher was up to. And being on a stakeout on his own felt wrong. He missed Sue's banter, her quick mind. Losing the Range Rover would never have happened on her watch.

Finally, the black diplomatic Mercedes returned, double-parking outside. Seconds later, the two men he'd seen earlier came out, the older one now carrying the briefcase, and sped off.

Mike waited another half an hour, then took one last, frustrated walk up the street, noticing that all the lights in number 114 were now off, before hurrying to Green Park station, where he endured sitting next to a drunk girl eating a pasty on his way back to Waterloo. Whatever Fisher was up to, he couldn't stall any longer. Sue was still unconscious, and as the days passed, even though he could hardly bear to admit it, her chances of a full recovery lessened. Tom would be devastated, and so would Sue, when the truth came out. But with no other suspects in the frame, tomorrow he'd have to bring Rob in for questioning over Sue's injuries. Cruel to be kind.

As he came up the escalator onto the wide station concourse, his phone buzzed. Two missed calls from the hospital. And a message from Tom.

It's MUM! She's AWAKE!

Chapter Twenty-Seven

I'm driving up the A4, past Hammersmith, and the traffic is flowing nicely. There's no sound from the boot, and I'm praying she's OK. Through Kensington, past the vast stone edifice of the Natural History museum towards Harrods and on to Park Lane, where I take temporary refuge in an underground car park, to wait. I open the suitcase for a minute or two to give her some air. She's sleeping, curled like a baby. It's barely 8.30pm, and he's going to text me when they are ready for the drop. Half an hour. I've brought my iPad as a distraction, and I pop in my headphones to drift away on a sea of Goldberg Variations. I don't want to wake her.

Fixer72 is just the middleman. He finds people what they need. Anything from drugs to people. Even kidneys. I'd asked for £15k. He came back, offering half that. We'd settled on £10k. Cash. Untraceable notes, on delivery. And a guarantee she'd be placed with a family where, in time, I could buy her back.

I climb in the back of the car and listen to her breathing through the case. She's snoring now.

My burner phone beeps.

Fixer72: Ready. Password is Philomena. Give that at the door.

It's almost nine. I lock the car, pay cash for my parking at the pay station, and drive up the ramp into Park Lane, where the sun is setting over the trees in Hyde Park. I'm nervous, palms sticking to the wheel, feeling way out of my depth. Beverley's steely reflection stares back at me from my rear-view mirror as I drive down Onslow Avenue. There's a space right outside and I take it, hauling the case out of the boot and up the steps.

There are three buzzers. I press 'B'.

'Who is it?'

'Philomena.'

The front door opens and a blond man beckons me inside. Thirties, handsome. His accent is hard to place. Polish, perhaps? Definitely Eastern European. Is he Fixer72? We've never met.

I wheel the case inside and he closes the front door. He's holding a gun. My legs are turning to jelly.

'This way.'

The key is in the lock of flat B and he opens it, gesturing for me to go inside. There's a front room straight ahead with a huge painting on the wall, but he follows me down a long passage to a dimly-lit room at the back of the house, my heels clicking on the tiled floor. It's like *Downton Abbey* in here, all Chesterfield sofas and period paintings, except there's a huge olive-skinned bodyguard inside, dressed in black, with an earpiece in, pointing a gun at me. I'm properly scared, and a trickle of urine leaks into my jeans. I should have kept her. I should never have got involved. I could be back at Riverdell now, with her, cooking a veggie meal. Just the two of us. Or I could have risked it and taken her with me, on the run.

'Open the case.'

I lay it flat, crouch down and fiddle with the lock, my hands trembling. She's stirring now, but only slightly. Sliding the zip all the way round, I open it. She's curled like a foetus, and apart from wetting herself, no harm done.

'Cash is on the table,' he says, gesturing towards it with the gun. 'Take it and go.'

It's in bundles of fifty-pound notes, beside a small back holdall. I just want out of there. But I keep my composure, flick through several of the bundles, and sweep them into the bag.

'Good doing business with you,' I say. No one replies. My nerves are in shreds, my black jeans wet and sticking to my legs, but Beverley doesn't show it. I turn on my stiletto heel and stride back down the passage, where a second bodyguard is waiting by the door, also with an earpiece in and gun pointing directly at me.

He opens the door just enough for me to pass, thick city

air rushing into the hallway. Suddenly I'm out, the door is closed and I'm in the Range Rover, the holdall beside me.

I'm breathing fast, too fast, and I feel dizzy. She's gone, and I'm missing her already. I tell myself over and over that I'm free again. In time, I can always replace her. Or bring her back.

Chapter Twenty-Eight

Mike burst through the hospital's main doors, puffing as he ran up the stairs to the intensive care unit. An armed policeman was still stationed outside the door, and he raised his gun at Mike as he emerged from the stairwell at the end of the corridor. 'Stop!' he shouted.

'I'm DI Mike Barley. Put that down.'

'Sorry, sir.' He lowered his gun. 'Didn't recognise you for a moment.'

He pressed the ICU buzzer. 'DCI Fisher is awake.'

'That's wonderful news, sir. Her son arrived about an hour ago.'

The night nurse came to the door and Mike held up his badge. 'DI Mike Barley,' he said. 'I had a message from Sue's son. She's woken up?'

Nodding, she unlocked the door and beckoned him into the relatives' room. 'Wait here,' she said. 'I'll fetch Dr Purani. He's in his civvies. We bleeped him.'

'Has Sue said anything?'

'She's still on the ventilator, so she's heavily sedated. And very weak. But she's opened her eyes several times. Her son is with her.'

She bustled away and moments later, Dr Purani strode into the room. 'The signs are hopeful, DI Barley. She seems to recognise Tom. They're only brief moments of awareness, but she's answered a couple of simple yes or no questions by squeezing his hand.'

'Can I see her?'

'Briefly. But please don't ask any questions or say anything that might upset her. I know you want to. But we need her to be a lot more stable and off the ventilator for that.'

'Of course. Did you contact her husband?'

'We tried to. Her son answered the home phone. Said his dad was out. I rang again when Tom arrived and left a message for him on the home answerphone.' He smiled. 'Somehow I've temporarily mislaid his mobile.'

'Thank you.'

'Come through, I'll take you to her now.'

Tom sat beside the bed, holding his mum's hand. Sue's eyes were closed. He smiled at Mike. 'I asked her if she can hear me and she squeezed my hand,' he whispered. 'She knows me. I could see it in her eyes.'

'That's wonderful, Son,' Mike replied, placing a fatherly arm around Tom's shoulders. He took Sue's other hand. 'I'm here, boss,' he whispered. 'Everything's fine. It's all under control. We'll have you up dancing in a day or two. I'll take you horse riding.'

Sue's eyelids flickered and Mike felt a tiny squeeze. A thick tear balanced on his lower lid. 'Someone must have cut onions in here.' He smiled, wiping it away with his finger. 'Come on, Son, your mum needs to rest. Let's get you home.'

Mike had too much on his mind to go home and sleep, so after dropping Tom off he went to the office. DCI Lauren Brown would be in early, and hopefully they could question Paul Eaves again over Anna. What the doctor had reported about her injuries should have been filed immediately – but his friendship with Sue meant more to him than that. As for Rob, he hadn't been at home. He'd deal with him later.

Mike checked over the file, and clicked on a random sample of pictures Eaves had downloaded on his laptop. Everything was categorised, and even the file names made him nauseous.

Over the years, especially during his time on the Child Safeguarding Unit, he'd had to watch a few sickening videos, and it never got any easier. After one particularly harrowing case, he'd become quite withdrawn, flinching whenever his wife touched him. The GP diagnosed post-traumatic stress and offered him tablets. He hadn't taken them. Or accepted the counselling on offer at work. Mike was old school, a man who saw admitting mental health issues as a weakness. He struggled on, withdrawn, irritable, as weeks turned into months, until the day his wife announced she was leaving. It was his fault, and he knew it, so he let her guilt him into giving her the house while he holed up in an ex-council place. Sue had been a rock throughout it, always on the end of the phone when he was too broken to get out of bed, covering for him if he turned up still pissed from the night before. Now he knew that, all that time, Sue had been coping with her own secret horror.

Whatever Paul Eaves had downloaded, he needed to see it before the interview. Carrying the laptop into a quiet room and plugging in his headphones, he opened the file.

There was no preamble. The whole horror was filmed on a headcam, looking down.

As the camera briefly panned upwards. Mike jabbed the pause button. There, on the wall, was a huge painting of a hunt, with men in white jodhpurs and red jackets.

It was 114b Onslow Avenue.

'Use extreme caution,' DCI Lauren Brown barked into her headset. 'There may be a child or children in there. Do you hear me? Minors. *Extreme* caution.'

'Roger that.'

Mike and Lauren were sitting in the station's control room, watching a monitor in a police van parked in Stratton Street, around the corner from Onslow Avenue, alongside an ambulance. He'd told Chief Biller he'd had a very reliable tip-off and within minutes armed police were ready to raid the flat.

'Ready, chief?'

'Ready.'

'Go go go.'

Eyes glued to the monitor, Mike watched as armed police leapt out of the vans, a tumble of bulletproof vests and helmets, smashing through the front door with a battering ram. Three shots rang out.

'One armed suspect down in hallway. Entering Flat B now. Living room ... clear.'

Two more shots, this time from outside. 'Armed suspect down. Garden.'

A different voice. 'Rest of house clear. Other flats empty.'

Then another. 'It's OK. We've got her. Rear bedroom. Need paramedic *now*.'

The firearms officer's headcam panned round, showing a large, swarthy man dressed in black, face up in the hallway, a gun lolling in his hand. Stepping over him, the officer ran to the back of the flat, into a large living room with open French doors where two policemen were giving CPR to a dark-haired man on the ground.

'In here.'

The chaos of the previous minute had gone, replaced by an eerie silence. Four armed officers stood in the room, their weapons lowered. She was tied up, crouched in the corner of the room, eyes glazed.

'It's OK, Anna,' the lead officer said, placing a blanket over her thin body. 'It's the police. You're safe now.'

'For God's sake, cut her free,' Lauren snapped into her headset.

He pulled a penknife from his pocket and cut the cable ties binding her hands and feet.

She recoiled as he touched her, whimpering, as if every pore in her body hurt, her pupils pinpricks. Infected welts on her wrists and ankles oozed pus. As the cable ties released, she tried to scramble towards the door, but the officer held on to her.

'My name's John. We're here to take you home, Anna.'

Her strength gone, she stopped struggling and began to cry, clinging to him. As his camera swept the room, Mike saw three syringes on the bedside table. Two were used, but the third contained a brown liquid.

'Heroin,' Mike whispered.

'Where are those paramedics?' Lauren shouted.

Two women, dressed in green overalls, ran into the bedroom. 'I'm Niamh, a doctor,' said one, crouching down beside her. 'This is Rosie. We're here to take you to hospital, Anna.'

The girl lifted her huge, black-rimmed green eyes. 'Who's Anna?' she croaked, in a thick Mancunian accent. 'I'm Cindy.'

Chapter Twenty-Nine

I'm sitting in the flat in Camden picking at fish and chips from Poppies, my favourite takeaway. I ditched the Range Rover in Chiswick, leaving it in a random residents' bay, then walked to Hammersmith and took the tube to Embankment, crossing the river for a late-night stroll along the Thames, trying to quieten the adrenaline still surging through my veins.

That's where I first met Cindy. My number two. Sitting on a bench somewhere between the Festival Hall and the Oxo Tower. A Thursday evening. I'd spent the afternoon with Cleo in the Premier Inn and taken the train back to London with her. Waited in her seedy hotel room round the back of Waterloo while she turned into Charles again, and waved her off as she went back to her wife, before walking along the South Bank.

Cindy wasn't planned. I was dressed as me.

'Want some?' I said, offering her my bag of crisps.

She took a handful, so I gave her the bag. 'You look like you need it. Sleeping rough?'

'Yeah.'

'I did that when she first came to London. I run a business now. A nail bar. So you won't be stuck in this shit forever.'

We sat in silence for a minute or two as she munched the crisps.

'Been four months now.' I recognised the accent straightaway. Manchester. Not the posh bit.

'So where are you sleeping?'

'Hostels, sometimes. The Sally Army let me have a B&B for a couple of nights but I didn't feel safe there. How did you get off the streets?'

'Luck. I met someone who offered me a place to stay.' I took out my phone and showed her a photo of Riverdell. 'She's called Beverley. Loaded. Likes to do her bit for the homeless. She knows how it feels. So why are you sleeping rough?'

'Didn't like the children's home. Ran away a few times. Usually Liverpool. Thought I'd try London. But I sent a message to me ma, telling her I'm all right. On that missing persons' website. She'd put a picture of me on there.'

'Why don't you go and live with your mum?'

'Social say she can't look after me properly.' She spat on the ground. 'But I've tried two foster families and they were just shits.'

I liked her spirit. I had to make this work.

'Here's twenty quid,' I said, taking it from my wallet.

'I've been in your situation. I know what it's like. So I want to help.'

Cindy snatched the money out of my hand and pocketed it. 'Ta.'

'Don't spend it on drugs. Or booze. Get some food.'

'I don't do drugs. Saw what they did to my brother. He was in the home with me.'

'Where is he now?'

'Dunno. Last time I saw him he was living rough in Manchester. Tried to pimp me out to his dealer in exchange for a fix.'

'I'll be here this time next Thursday,' I said. 'With more money.'

'OK.'

I walked off towards Waterloo, leaving her on the bench. As I glanced back, she reached in her bag and took out a can of Special Brew.

We met on the bench five times. That's when I invited her to Riverdell. Gave her a one-way ticket to Surbiton, a bag of clean clothes and told her Beverley would collect her from the back of the station in a Range Rover. Cindy looked like any other Surrey kid getting picked up by mummy. I even let her take a dip in the indoor pool. We had fun trying on glamorous designer outfits from Riverdell's wardrobes, watched Netflix in the cinema room and cooked a huge bowl of pasta together.

I must have dozed off during one of the movies, and when I woke up she'd gone.

I found her trying to open the electric front door, with

cash from my handbag and my jewellery in her pockets. She was even wearing my fucking fur coat.

'I was gonna come back…' she began. 'Just going for some fags.'

She wasn't coming back and I knew it. She'd used me. She'd lied. I'd invited her to be part of my family and she'd *betrayed* me. Just like my father and my bastard mother. Just like Tanya. Except Tanya had stayed a week before trying to leave.

That familiar, blinding rage surged, so fast and so devastating that I couldn't stop it. I picked up the lamp by the front door and smashed it over her head. She slumped to the floor, eyes closed, blood dripping from her head onto the white fur.

I crouched down beside her, the surge subsiding as I gazed at the wound on her forehead, numb. She was still breathing. She knew all about me, about Riverdell, so I couldn't let her go. Minutes passed, maybe an hour, and still I gazed at her. What had I done? She was family now, whether I liked it or not. *My* girl. I swaddled her head with the fur and carried her down to the soundproof panic room.

That's when she stirred. Her eyes flickered open and met mine before closing again, unexpectedly slicing through my frozen soul.

She'd survived for a reason. Maybe she was sorry. Maybe she could still be part of my family. Maybe my role, as Mother, was to teach her some respect.

When Cindy finally woke I'd dressed her wound and was sitting there, watching, an anxious parent.

'W-where am I?'

'Riverdell. This is your home.'

'You hit me.'

'That's right. You were stealing my money. And my coat. So you'll have to stay down here until you learn to be grateful.'

She tried to move, and realising she was tied to the bed, began to panic. And when she saw the bath, she screamed.

'Come on, Cindy. You'll hurt yourself.' She screamed again, railing against the world, and when it stopped she began begging, pleading to be let go.

'Calm yourself, my love.' I stroked her head. 'Just rest.'

'What do you want from me?'

'What any parent wants. Love and respect.' I laid her back on the bed. 'You're safe here. Now sleep.'

Some days I told her about myself, my childhood, what life was like for me in Norfolk, how what happened to me meant I understood her pain. Sometimes, if I didn't feel like talking, I brought music for us to listen to. At first she just lay on the bed, staring at the wall, refusing to speak, picking at her food or kicking the plate over, like a toddler. Once I got the padlock and chains in place – drugging her with diazepam was easy – she could reach the toilet and move about the room a little.

She didn't say much. But as the weeks passed, her wound healed and she'd ask me to bring her treats. She read the books I brought and talked about them a little. I played her favourite, Billie Eilish, and introduced her to Bach. Debussy, too. I looked forward to seeing her, even though the room was fetid, waiting for the moment I felt she could be trusted, and I could move her back upstairs. It was so close. If only time hadn't run out.

I scrunch up my fish and chips paper and throw it into the bin, ignoring a surge of jealousy that Cindy is with another family now. One more night in Camden, I decide. I've checked the cash in the holdall. Exactly ten grand. There is honour amongst thieves.

Slipping on a pair of flip-flops, I walk down Jamestown Road, past the chattering classes in the vegan restaurant longing for a steak, to the high street. Leather-jacketed crowds are gathered outside the Electric Ballroom, waiting for a gig, swigging vodka and eating street food, as a girl vomits into the gutter and a skinny homeless guy takes a dump in a doorway. The smell of weed hangs in the air like an unseen fog. I need to clear my head, ready to move on in the morning. My last night in Camden, and it doesn't disappoint. It's been my sanctuary for so long, hiding amongst life's flotsam and jetsam. I'm going to really miss it.

Chapter Thirty

Mike sat in the corridor outside the ICU on Wednesday afternoon, mulling over the previous night's events. A report just in from the Met's call centre showed an anonymous member of the public had reported suspicious activity at 114b Onslow Avenue around 10pm that evening. They'd called from an unregistered mobile, close to the location. Was that Rob? How the hell was he mixed up in all this?

He was lost in thought when Dr Purani walked out. 'How is she?' Mike said, jumping to his feet.

'Do you mean Sue or Cindy?'

'Both. Well, Cindy. Like I said, there's a chance the other missing girl is alive. Cindy could be our only hope of finding her.'

'Physically she's in bad shape. Mentally even worse. We're pumping in fluids and IV antibiotics. Her kidneys are severely infected. She's malnourished, dehydrated, has a multitude of other infections. I'm keen to sedate her more, but the heroin has slowed her heart rate so much that I have to wait.'

'We've got uniform trying to contact her family in Manchester right now. She went missing from care five months ago, when she was fourteen.'

'And you think she might know the missing girl, Anna?'

'I can't be sure. But it's possible.'

Dr Purani sighed. 'Two minutes. That's all. If it could help save another life…'

'Thank you. *Thank you.*'

'You'll need to wear the usual overalls. But don't put on the mask. She completely freaks out if anyone wears one. Maybe your female colleague should go in? Though to be honest, she's terrified of everyone.'

Mike paused. He wanted to talk to Cindy himself. If Rob was somehow involved, he wanted to be the first to know. But Cindy had been through enough. 'Good idea. I'll call Lauren.'

Cindy lay in the hospital bed, green eyes staring straight ahead, her tiny wrists neatly bandaged, IV lines taped to both stick-like arms. Now that her face was washed, Lauren could see clearly how thin she was, her cheeks sunken, skin spotty and rough. There was a huge bruise on her forehead, as if she'd been hit or headbutted the wall.

'I'm Lauren,' she said gently. 'A policewoman. Cindy, we will find the people who did this to you.'

No response. Cindy just stared into space.

'We think the people who did this to you took another girl,' she added. 'Did you see a girl when you were held?'

Her cloudy eyes suddenly locked on to Lauren's and Cindy began to scream, letting out a howl of such raw, agonising terror that she would never forget it for the rest of her life. Alarms sounded and Cindy began to convulse, saliva frothing in her mouth.

'Out!' barked Dr Purani, running into the cubicle with three nurses. 'Diazepam IV five milligrams. Watch those oxygen levels…'

Reeling, Lauren retreated to the corridor, slumping onto the chair where Mike was waiting.

'My God, Mike.' She ran her hand through her short brown hair. 'Whatever Cindy saw, it scared the hell out of her.'

Paul Eaves lay on his bunk in his cell at Parkside, thinking of his wife, Zoe. There was no way back from what he had done. He no longer cared about his own life, but the shame he had brought on her was unimaginable. The Tillingham Estate would shun her, her family wouldn't want to know, and she'd be utterly alone. He'd tried to contact her, using the wing's payphone, but she wouldn't pick up. And worst of all, the pain that ripped him wide open, was Anna. Where was she?

Eaves glanced around his cell. At least he was on remand with other inmates who were in for sex-related crimes, on a separate floor from the rest of the prison. Below Eaves, his cell-mate, Jones, was watching *Can't Pay? We'll Take It Away*, snorting with derision every time a bailiff turned up. They were sharing a tiny space but had barely spoken since he arrived, apart from exchanging names. Privacy was non-existent. The curtain around the steel toilet in the corner had long since disappeared. He wasn't even allowed a family photo.

The cell door clattered open. Exercise time, outside in the yard. Later it would be association time, two hours where he could queue for the payphone and try to avoid having to talk to other inmates. Two hours of hell, as every single one of them knew who he was from the news and social media. Some gave him a knowing, congratulatory look. They wanted to talk about it, hear every detail, revel in his stories, share their own tales. Some asked him where Anna was. Some ignored him, keeping themselves to themselves. So far, he'd said nothing.

'Fuckin' typical,' Jones snapped at the TV, turning it off. Eaves had no idea what he was talking about. He climbed off his bunk and followed the line of prisoners shuffling down the metal staircase from the fourth floor towards the yard.

The catcalls started as soon as they reached the third floor – the 'threes'. General prisoners were locked in their cells, but they could hear the inmates clattering down from above them.

'Nonces.'

'Perverts.'

'We'll get you, you sick fuckers.'

No one replied. They picked up their pace and hurried down past the 'twos'. He didn't see the lifer's cell door open, just the burly man rush towards him and the glint of a blade as it sliced through his neck. For a split second, Eaves felt a rush of agonising pain and terror. Then the blackness closed in and he collapsed to the floor, blood pouring from his severed artery. Dropping the homemade blade on the floor, the lifer didn't struggle as two officers pushed him down onto the ground.

'Got one, lads!' he yelled, to cheers and whoops from the cells.

Paul Eaves lifeless body lay on the cold concrete, his eyes staring upwards, as a pool of blood edged outwards around him.

Mike and Lauren were on their way to HMP Parkside when the call from the prison governor, Judith Waugh, came through.

'I'm sorry to tell you that Paul Eaves is dead,' she said, her tone matter-of-fact. 'He was being moved through B wing when Michael Shaw – yes, him – attacked him.'

'Christ. Eaves was the one person who could help us

find the missing girl.' Mike was seething. 'How the hell did Shaw get access to him?'

'I'm aware of that, DI Barley. I can only offer my sincere apologies. I've already begun an investigation. It would appear he called to an officer, indicating his cell-mate was unconscious. Two officers entered the cell shortly before Eaves passed it.'

'I'm guessing the cell-mate made a miraculous recovery,' Mike snapped. 'We'll be there in about seven minutes.'

There was little more that the governor could tell them. The lifer – Michael Shaw – was a notorious gangland killer serving a minimum of thirty years for the torture and murder of two associates. He'd be almost eighty by the time he was let out, and everyone knew no parole board would ever grant his release.

Nothing to lose, Mike mused.

'Do you think he targeted Eaves in particular?' he asked the governor once they arrived.

'Probably,' Judith replied. 'He's very high profile. Earned himself plenty of goodwill from the other men. Known to hate paedophiles. My officer says Shaw ran past a line of men, as if he was specifically looking for Eaves. We'll have to release a statement saying a man has died. I can't pretend there aren't mobiles in this prison. Word will already be out there.'

Mike nodded. 'I'll visit his wife in person to break the news. We've had close contact over her missing daughter.'

'Of course. This will be devasting news for her. Time is of the essence. Would you like to see Shaw now?'

Shaw sat in the prison's interview room, handcuffed, with Eaves' blood still on his sweatshirt. Beside him, a duty solicitor flicked casually through a file and yawned.

'So, Michael, I'll ask you again,' Lauren said calmly. 'Did you know the man you stabbed?'

'No comment.' He leaned back in his chair and smiled, revealing a row of even, nicotine-stained false teeth.

'Come on, Michael. You stabbed him because he's charged with disgusting child sex crimes, didn't you?'

'No comment.' More smiling.

Twenty minutes later, charged with Eaves' murder, Shaw was taken to a solitary cell, having grinned his way through continual 'no comments'.

'He definitely targeted Eaves,' Lauren said, as they drove back to the police station. 'Could Eaves have been silenced to order? Any links to Onslow Gardens? Maybe this is all connected?'

Mike shook his head. Was there a connection? Rob Fisher and Paul Eaves knew each other from the rugby club, but he wasn't going to reveal that.

'Anything from the Onslow flat owner?'

'Not much,' Mike replied. 'They're absolutely horrified.

Only use it a few times a year. A management firm has the keys. We're checking them out.'

He'd already checked. Rob Fisher, locksmith, was on their payroll.

It only seemed like yesterday that Mike was arriving at Zoe's house to ask about her missing daughter, with Sue beside him. The news from the hospital was encouraging – Sue was becoming more aware, and they'd try taking her off the ventilator in the next day or two. But as he parked in the driveway, unannounced, with Kim, the Family Liaison Officer, he was most worried about the situation with Rob. The bastard deserved to die for what he'd done. And he could hold the key to finding Anna. But if he reported it, Mike feared the shitstorm that would rain down on Sue and Tom would be something from which they might never recover. No. He'd find his own way to deal with Rob.

'Have you found her?' Zoe asked, running out of the front door before they'd even got out of the car. She was even thinner than when they'd first met, her face drawn and her streaked-blonde hair unwashed and greasy.

'Let's go inside, Ms Littlejohn,' Mike said, his tone gentle, the Family Liaison Officer beside him.

'Oh my god.' Zoe lifted her hand to her mouth, her face ashen.

Kim led her into the living room, where her

housekeeper, Zelda, was chopping vegetables. Seeing Zoe's face, she dropped the knife and put her arms around her.

'Please sit down, Ms Littlejohn.'

'Is she…?'

'I'm afraid we haven't found Anna yet,' Mike said. 'But there has been an incident at Parkside Prison.' He paused. 'I'm sorry to tell you that your husband is dead.'

Zoe gasped, clinging on to Zelda, who helped her to the sofa.

'W-why wasn't he on suicide watch?' she stammered.

'He didn't take his own life, Ms Littlejohn. Another inmate attacked him.'

'Murder?' Zoe couldn't take it in.

'I'm so sorry.'

Silent tears streaked down her face and she clung to her housekeeper.

'Did they kill him because they think he's a … a … paedophile?'

'A prisoner serving life, Michael Shaw, will appear in court in the morning charged with Paul's murder,' Mike said gently. 'We don't yet know his motive.'

'But Paul should have been *protected*,' Zoe wailed. 'All these lies put him at risk. What did they do to him?'

'I'm afraid Paul was stabbed. There has clearly been a failure in the prison's duty of care.'

'Failure?' she spat, her shock turning to anger. 'Of course there's been a failure. He should never have been arrested in the first place. So there will be no trial? About the ridiculous allegations?'

'No.'

'But without a trial we'll never be able to clear his name,' she sobbed. 'And what about Anna? We have to find her.'

There was no point in adding to Zoe's distress by telling her about the laptop. 'We do have a few new leads,' Mike replied. 'I can't go into detail, but they are things we need to chase up right now. Kim can stay with you for a few hours, and arrange for you to see your husband, if you'd like to.'

Zoe stood up, opened a kitchen cupboard and took out a bottle of vodka, poured a huge glug into a teacup and knocked it back, before pouring another one. 'No one's ever going to believe he's innocent now,' she said. 'I just want to find my baby girl and leave all this behind. All of it. Move to the seaside where no one knows us. *No one*.'

'We'll be in touch, Ms Littlejohn,' Mike said gently. 'I'm sorry for your loss.'

He dialled Lauren's number as he walked to the car. 'The team have been going through calls to the hotline,' she told him. 'Plenty of nutters claiming they did it. But we've also been checking out Simon Lightwater, following Sky's death. He's clean. Only thing that's come up is he's the registered owner of a mansion on the Crown Estate in Cobshott. I've looked back through the notes and I don't think they've ever mentioned it.'

Mike sighed. 'Probably just a handy nest egg. I bet he's got offshore bank accounts, too.'

'Yeah. You could be right. But strange they didn't mention the place. Why hide it?'

He paused. What was it Soozie had said, when he'd

gone to talk to her about Sky? Eaves had looked down on them because *'we're not rich enough to own a place on the Crown Estate'*.

'The wife doesn't know about it, Lauren. I'm sure of it. Maybe he's got a mistress in there. Who knows? Let's check it out. What's the address?'

'Riverdell. They don't have numbers, just names.'

He rolled his eyes. 'Just to make it that little bit trickier to find. Meet me at the Lightwater house on Cobshott Drive. I'll be there in an hour. We need to talk to them about this.'

The sun was setting, and Soozie was in bed, with Simon beside her, when Mike hammered loudly on their front door. Neither of them had dressed or eaten for almost two days, but their grief had brought them closer than they had been for years. Each instinctively knew the pain of the other, without the need for words, a soul-tearing agony that no one else could even imagine. For the first time in years they'd even held each other in bed, desperate for comfort, the future stretching out in front of them like a cold wasteland, knowing that Sky's death was a toxic, jagged wound that would never heal.

'Only the police knock like that,' Simon murmured, his head under the duvet.

Instinctively, Soozie swept her untouched cocaine pick-me-up, still in its little resealable plastic bag, into the bedside cabinet. 'I don't give a fuck what they've got to say,' she sighed. 'Probably come to tell us Eaves is dead. So what? Nothing can bring Sky back.'

She'd thought of nothing but her daughter, spending most of her time in Sky's room, lying on her bed or cuddling her clothes to breathe in the scent of her, and for those few seconds Soozie was alive again. Only Star kept her going. Star would be home from the Priory in a few weeks, and she had to be strong for her.

Pulling on her dressing gown, she heard Miquita's voice, followed by the housekeeper softly padding up the stairs. 'Miss Lightwater,' she said gently through the door. 'The police are here.'

Soozie took a deep breath. 'I'll come down, Miquita. Thank you. Please offer them something to drink.'

She went into the bathroom and washed her face with water, something she hadn't done for years, drying it roughly on a towel. The lined reflection that stared back at her had aged beyond recognition, her streaked hair ragged and her eyes swollen from crying.

The detectives were in the kitchen, where Miquita was pouring hot water into a large teapot.

'Mrs Lightwater.' Mike shook her hand. 'This is DCI Lauren Brown. I expect you've seen the news about Paul Eaves.'

'Yeah. He deserved it.'

'There's an inquiry into what happened,' he said gently. 'But, of course, there won't now be a trial.'

'I don't care. I've got justice. He's rotting in the ground. Or the morgue.'

'How's Star doing?' Lauren asked.

'She's going to be in the Priory for a few weeks. They've said it's best if we don't visit for a few days. Let her settle in. But she texted me. Said they're looking after her.' Soozie paused. 'I'm so sorry about your colleague, DI Barley. How is she?'

'On the mend, thankfully,' Mike replied. 'Though still in intensive care.'

'Have you found Anna?'

'Not yet,' Mike replied. 'We're actually here to ask about your house on the Crown Estate.'

'What house?'

'Riverdell.'

'But we don't have a house on the Crown Estate.' Soozie was puzzled.

'Actually, we do,' Simon said quickly, ambling into the room, his vacant eyes suddenly sharp. 'I bought it for you. Just recently. It was going to be a … a … present.'

'Simon, you're telling me we've got another *house*?'

'It was a good deal. I had to act fast. You've always said you want to live there.'

'So you just went ahead and bought us another house?' Her eyes narrowed suspiciously. 'With what money?'

'We need to take a look around it, Mr Lightwater,' Lauren said. 'Just as a routine inquiry.'

Soozie's dead eyes were alive now, alert, inquisitive.

The little colour that was in Simon's face completely drained from it, as Soozie stared at him, incredulous. 'I-I don't go there,' Simon said. 'A business associate uses it.'

Mike flipped open his notebook. 'What's their name?'

Simon paused. 'Beverley.'

'Surname?'

'I-I don't know.'

The anger, despair and sadness that consumed Soozie boiled over and she slammed her fist on the worktop. He'd betrayed her. 'You've installed one of your *floozies* in a house on the Crown Estate?'

'No, no, it's not like that. I hardly know this woman.'

Soozie glared at him. 'And you really expect me to believe that? When she's living in your fucking secret *house*.'

'W-we have an agreement,' Simon stammered. 'She uses the house for a year or so, and I don't interfere. The Range Rover, too. Said it was for business. All I have is a mobile number.'

'So she's renting it from you?' Lauren said. 'We've accessed your bank account and can see you're paying all the bills for Riverdell, but there's no rent coming in.'

'It's going into an offshore one,' he said quickly. Too quickly for Mike's liking. 'Look, if we're going round there I need to notify her.' Simon's voice was colder now, more controlled. 'Anyway, you'll need a warrant.'

'We don't.' Lauren checked her watch. 'This is a missing persons' and a murder inquiry. We can have armed officers on standby near the house if we think this is connected. So you can either give us the keys, or we can smash our way in.'

Simon paled. 'Riverdell's got nothing to do with any

missing girls. Or your colleague. I don't have the keys. Beverley said she would change all the locks.'

Soozie's voice was cold and controlled. 'So you've got an offshore account I don't know about. You've bought a house, another car, and you've given it to a *woman* who has changed the locks. Even if I believed that pile of horse shit, don't you realise that woman can just squat in it? You'll never get her out. I *know* you, Simon. You're way too smart to do that. So why don't you give us all a fucking *break* and tell us what's going on. Start talking, Simon. *Now.*'

'I don't know anything about the missing girl. Nothing at all. This Beverley was blackmailing me.' He looked at Soozie. 'I'm so sorry. I was briefly seeing someone else.'

'Who?'

'Someone at work. She meant nothing. But this Beverley contacted me and said she'd tell you unless I let her use Riverdell.'

'How did she know about Riverdell?' Soozie snapped.

'I don't know. She must have seen me taking Mia there.'

'Mia? Your *secretary*?'

'I-I'm so sorry, Soozie. It was just a fling.'

'In a *multi-million-pound house* on the Crown Estate. Which you said we couldn't afford. Showing off, were you?'

'I really did buy it for us. For the future. As an investment.'

'Bollocks.'

'So this Beverley sent you a text message?' Mike asked.

'Yes. Three of them. I can show them to you. Here.' He scrolled through his phone. 'Threatening to tell Soozie.

Then I called her and we met, once, on the South Bank. I can check my diary and give you the exact time and date. We agreed she'd use the house for a year, maybe eighteen months. Use the Range Rover there too. For free. Ask Mia. I told her about it at the time.'

'So you don't have an offshore account? We will check.'

'I do.'

Soozie looked murderous.

'But this Beverley didn't know about it.'

Mike took out his mobile and composed a text. *DC Green, I need a check on a phone number. Now.* He added in the number.

'And you haven't been back to Riverdell?' Lauren asked.

'No. I drove past a couple of times and the place looked fine. No riotous parties.'

'So where have you been fucking Mia then?' Soozie spat. 'And what's this offshore account for? Nice little nest egg for the two of you?'

Simon didn't reply. He slumped onto one of the kitchen bar stools, staring at the floor. 'It was for the girls,' he whispered. 'For their eighteenth birthday. You can check. Their names are on the bank account. And it's in my will.'

'So you didn't trust me to give it to them? Had it all ready for when you binned me off and set up shop with Mia?'

Mike's phone beeped with a text message.

Number is an unregistered pay-as-you-go, boss. A burner.

'Christ, Simon,' Soozie spat. 'What are you involved in?'

'We'll need to take you in for questioning, Mr Lightwater,' Lauren said. 'You can either come now, voluntarily, or I can arrest you. Also now. Your choice.'

'I'll come.' Simon was ashen. 'Of course I'll come. Search everything, take my phone. Contact this Beverley. I have nothing else to hide.'

'Would you mind coming too, Mrs Lightwater?' Lauren added. 'We'll need a statement. It's best if we do it now. We can escort you both upstairs to get dressed. You'll need to travel in separate squad cars.'

Soozie nodded.

They changed and sat side by side in heavy silence in the living room until they heard the crunch of the squad cars on the gravel drive.

'I'm sorry, Soozie,' Simon said, as two officers led them to the cars.

'I'm done with you, Simon. *Done*. Mia's welcome to you. And don't bother coming back here. Now it'll be my turn to change the locks.'

As the cars sped off, Mike turned to Lauren. 'I still think this has nothing to do with Anna. My money's on this Beverley being another spurned mistress. Or some financial scam Simon's got himself caught up in.'

Lauren nodded. 'I know what you mean. But he seemed like he was telling the truth. Let's leave him to stew while we check out this Riverdell.'

~

Night had fallen as Mike and Lauren parked outside Riverdell's electric gates. The house was hidden behind trees, and a faint light glowed from it.

'Nice place,' Lauren said. 'Stone lions on the entrance. Classy. New-money heaven. Almost certainly gold taps inside, too.'

Mike scanned the gates. 'Wonder what this Beverley is up to? It's pretty secluded. She could be running anything from here.'

'That's why I've brought the cavalry,' Lauren replied, gesturing to a van of armed officers parked down the street. 'I doubt we'll need it. She'll probably answer the door in her lingerie and in half an hour we'll be on our way home with chapter and verse. I'll end up having to justify all this to the chief. But if she's mixed up in drugs or some other high-end deal…'

Mike nodded. He pressed the buzzer. No reply.

'We'll have to force it,' Lauren said. 'Going to be a lot of paperwork on this one. At least Simon's given us permission to enter.'

Lauren barked into her microphone. 'To confirm, we're not sure what the house is being used for. Could be any kind of illegal activity, or nothing at all. Use extreme caution.'

Moments later, the waiting police van, with six officers inside, smashed through the gates, careering up the tiled driveway with Mike and Lauren driving in behind them. The security lights on the front of the house snapped on. Both the van and the car turned off their engines, and three of the armed officers silently fanned out around the house.

A warm light glowed through from one of the downstairs rooms, through a gap in the thick cream curtains.

'The gardens are clear, ma'am.'

'Good. Go in.'

'Armed police! Stand back.'

It took several seconds to ram the double front door. The armed officers fanned out, ready to search each room with Mike and Lauren behind them.

'That smell,' Lauren said. 'It's faint, but it's here. Death.'

'Down here,' an officer shouted. 'Basement.'

There was the sound of retching and two officers ran back up the stairs, one vomiting copiously on the hall floor. As Mike reached the stairs, the smell was so powerful that he took out a handkerchief and tied it around his mouth.

The panic room door had been left open, revealing a sight so sickening that Mike had to fight the urge to vomit. A body was liquefying in the bath, so decomposed that it was impossible to tell if it was a man or a woman, the skeleton showing through the patches of missing skin. Two fat flies buzzed around it.

He turned his eyes away from the body to the filthy bed, covered in excrement and flies, chains and handcuffs scattered on it, the remnants of a recent meal on a plate on the floor.

Mike prayed that this wasn't where Cindy had been kept.

'Code one. Riverdell, Crown Estate, Cobshott. Backup needed now,' he snapped into his radio.

'En route.'

He stopped Lauren as she walked in through the basement door. 'You'll need a strong stomach for this, boss.'

She nodded. 'Go up to the top floor, Mike. There's another one.'

Chapter Thirty-One

I'm on a coach heading, ultimately, to the seaside. Somewhere up North. Whitley Bay, perhaps. You can't beat a thousand acres of sky, the wide, empty beaches, the cafes which give you a cuppa with your two quid egg and chips. Like Norfolk, but without the memories. I want somewhere a world away from Cobshott's pretentiousness, where a sandwich is two thin slices of white bread with a slice of cheddar cheese between them, and watery ketchup comes in a greasy plastic bottle shaped like a tomato.

I've left the iPhone in a bin outside Camden Morrisons, after texting all my clients to say I'm going to be away for a few weeks due to a 'family emergency', removing the pay-as-you-go sim card. My wig is long and pale brown, and my clothes a baggy T-shirt, pale-blue tracksuit and trainers. The traffic is light and the coach rumbles on, up the M1, rocking me in and out of a fitful sleep. My eyes flicker open and I shift uncomfortably. The coach seat is making me itch.

My first stop is Sheffield, where I plan to disappear for a while. I play Debussy's Clair de Lune on my old iPod, longing to float away into the piano-filled soundscape, but I can't settle. I was focused, sharp while I had the plan. Now I feel fuzzy, uncentred, frightened, with the days stretching out in front of me like a mysterious, mist-covered void.

At the front of the coach is a silent TV with subtitles, but the whirl of adverts makes me car sick, so I close my eyes, nausea still picking at my throat, as the surge of adrenaline from the past few days begins to subside. I left without saying a proper goodbye to Cleo, and I miss her. I'm missing my salon, too, my life, my Riverdell. There was a predictability about my days, about my Thursday afternoons with Cleo, even about that fetid room, that's gone. But I have to keep going, to set up a new life and, once I'm on my feet, go back for Cindy.

The nine o'clock news comes on. That's when I see it. Riverdell. White-suited forensic teams are going in and out and there's a reporter at the gates. Police cars and officers everywhere. 'Reports are coming in of bodies found in Cobshott, Surrey. Police are holding a forty-seven-year-old man in custody.'

They've found them. My whole world, my life, is going to be exposed. I thought it would be weeks, even months, before they discovered Riverdell. Maybe years if I'd kept stringing Simon Lightwater along. I thought I'd have *time*.

I'm beyond terrified now, panicking as unwanted emotions and thoughts slice every which way through my head. Think, Mel. The man in custody must be Simon. He's going to take the rap for now. They're not looking for you. And no one will link it to the nail bar. Why would they? Even if they do, you're long gone.

Anna. All of this comes back to that one, stupid, split second in Leicester Square, when I decided to help her.

I think back to Anna's first night at Riverdell. After dinner I showed her the apartment – a huge bedroom and bathroom originally designed for a live-in nanny – on the top floor. I'd bought pink curtains, a pink duvet cover, cushions, cuddly toys, books and board games, turning it into the cosy, safe space I dreamed of having as a child. She didn't seem as impressed as I was expecting. Said it was like her bedroom back home. Cindy had been far more awestruck at first. Tanya, too. I should have realised she was rich, and that her family would come looking for her. But even if I had, it would have been too late then to let her go.

After Cindy had tried to escape, I'd made sure the apartment was secure. I'd sealed all the windows and fitted special locks on the door. Anna climbed straight into bed, and as I pottered about the room, folding towels and tidying up the cuddly toys, she fell into an exhausted sleep.

'We'll call your parents in the morning,' I'd told her. 'And you can stay here as long as you like.'

Her rucksack was on the floor, her phone by the bed. I took both, and silently locked her in.

'I can't find my rucksack,' she'd said thickly, her mouth full of pancake, as I brought her breakfast in bed next morning. 'I've got to take my inhalers. Both of them. And my phone was by the bed.'

'Don't worry,' I'd replied. 'I've put the phone on to charge for you downstairs. It was totally flat.'

'Thank you.' She jumped out of bed, smiling, a sense of relief on her face. 'You've done more than enough for me, Sally. I'll get it.'

Her fingers clasped the door handle. I saw the panic in her eyes then, a desperate, primal urge to run, to escape. 'Why is the door locked?' I didn't reply. Anna was wheezing now, her breath rasping. 'I need to call Mum. She'll be worried. Looking for me. I need to—'

She was really short of breath, and tried to scream but no sound came out. Her voice tailed off and her breath came in shorter and shorter gasps as she rattled the door handle, then sunk to the floor. 'Can't breathe…' she wheezed. 'Call an ambulance…'

Her lips were turning blue. 'Ambulance…' She gasped. 'Help me … want my mum…'

I was her mother now. And she was dying in front of me.

Too weak to move or speak, her whole face turning blue, she reached out a hand, begging. I unlocked the door and ran downstairs, digging through the rucksack to find the inhaler. But by the time I came back she was semi-conscious. I held it to her lips, jabbing the top, but it made no difference and her unfocused eyes tried to fix on mine, green on blue, as they closed.

She died right there in my arms. Dear, sweet Karen, who

would have been a wonderful daughter. Who would have lived at Riverdell as a happy family with me, with girls and boys I'd hadn't rescued yet. I hugged her still-warm body and my tears soaked her softly curled hair, willing her to come back to me.

She was still warm when I laid her body on the bed, staring at her for hours, watching her eyes cloud over. Just like Smokey's, making me numb. She wasn't Karen anymore. Karen had gone. There was a strange comfort in that, because I knew this corpse in front of me was just an empty shell, and after Tanya, I had to be ready for what would happen. So I wrapped her in plastic sheeting from the garage and put her in the blanket box at the end of the bed. A makeshift coffin. Locked the door, and put towels around it. The guilt that I couldn't save her has been clawing at my mind ever since.

I gaze up at the subtitles on the coach's TV screen. 'Unconfirmed reports are that one is the missing schoolgirl Anna Littlejohn-Eaves. Police are refusing to comment on whether there are links to the earlier raid on a flat in Onslow Avenue, Mayfair, where a fifteen-year-old girl was rescued from a suspected child sex ring.'

A child sex ring. Cindy. Fixer72 promised me she'd be safe. That's the only reason I let her go. I *loved* her. Everything I did for her was out of kindness, helping her become the loving daughter I knew she could be. The one she *wanted* to be. Moving her on was only ever a last resort. What had they *done* to her in that place?

I was going to go back for her one day. Now I've lost her too.

The scissor wound on my leg is throbbing and I'm sweaty, nauseous, flooded with anxiety. Why was I so *stupid?* What horrors did they inflict on her after I left? And now I'm not safe anymore. She'll tell them all about me. I'd shared so much of my past with Cindy that they'd be sure to track me down. My fingers are on my leg, kneading the ripped flesh, sending spikes of pain through my body, hating every fibre of myself. Blood is soaking into my tracksuit trousers, the pain barely numbing the torrent of fear, of shame, of fury.

Outside, the darkening sky screams by, streaked with mauve and deep, dusky brown. I sold Cindy into the kind of life I wanted to keep her safe from. I have failed as a mother. There is no worse crime than that.

Chapter Thirty-Two

Sue was off the ventilator, and sleepy, with Tom holding her hand.

'The sedation is wearing off,' Dr Purani told him, placing a cup of water by the bed. 'When she wakes up, she can have a tiny sip. Just a sip, though. And call me as soon as she does.'

'Has someone told my dad?' Tom asked. 'I still can't get hold of him.'

'I'll check with the nurses. Let me know when she opens her eyes.'

Sue looked so peaceful, and Tom wished she could stay like that forever. The case was all over the news, and he was terrified that whoever had attacked her would come after her again. His dad couldn't have done this. Maybe now he'd stop hurting her. Maybe now he'd realise she just needed to be loved.

Her eyelids flickered and opened slightly, before closing again.

'Dr Purani,' he called. 'Mum's opened her eyes.'

They sat by Sue as her eyelids flickered a few more times, before opening fully, her blue eyes hazy at first, then focused.

'You're in the hospital,' Dr Purani said softly. 'Everything's fine. Tom is here.'

Sue nodded, smiled, and drifted back to sleep.

'Should I give her the water?' Tom asked.

'Not yet. Let her wake up a bit more. It won't be long.'

Simon Lightwater was sitting opposite Mike and Lauren in the interview room, face ashen, looking at a photo of the basement at Riverdell.

'Jesus Christ.'

'I'm going to ask you again,' Lauren said. 'Who is she? How did this young woman end up in the bath?'

'I didn't even know Riverdell had a panic room. I've never been in it. Mia and I only used the upstairs. Maybe the living room a couple of times. Wh-who is it?'

'And what about this?' She pushed a photo of Anna's white body, wrapped in plastic, across the table.

'My god.'

His solicitor interjected. 'I think my client needs a break.'

'No!' Simon snapped. 'And I'm not hiding behind "no

comment" because I've got nothing to hide. Who are these poor people? Why are they in my house?'

'We believe this is Anna Littlejohn-Eaves. How did you meet her, Simon?'

'I've told you a thousand times, I don't know her. She was a friend of the twins' at primary school, but I only know that because they told me recently. You need to find this Beverley.'

Back at their desks, Mike and Lauren mulled over his replies.

'Do you believe him?' Mike asked.

'I don't know. Mia says he told her he was being blackmailed, that's why they couldn't use Riverdell anymore. The team are checking his description of Beverley against our database, but nothing so far.'

'How about Lightwater's DNA? Or Eaves's?'

'None in the basement so far, nor in the top apartment bedroom where Anna was found. It's in the master bedroom, where Cindy's ragged clothes were found, but his DNA isn't on them. None of Paul Eaves' anywhere either. They're double-checking unidentified DNA on the clothes, and in the basement, kitchen and top room.' Lauren paused. 'And Cindy was definitely chained on that bed. Most likely for months.'

'The poor girl.' Mike was ashen. He'd worked on some gruesome crimes before, but this was beyond horrific.

'Blood traces in the kitchen had been cleaned, but Forensics picked them up, suggesting the girl in the bath was hit there. There is a deep cavity in her skull so we suspect she died from a blow to the head. We're checking the missing persons' records, but it's going to be tough, given the state of her.'

'So Lightwater could be telling the truth,' Mike mused. 'His contactless card shows he did travel to the Southbank area on the day and time he said he met this Beverley. And his laptop doesn't have anything other than soft porn on it. Plus a lot of photos of Mia.'

Lauren nodded. 'We've got about fifteen hours before we have to charge him or release him. What about the neighbours?'

'One said they saw a Range Rover going in and out occasionally – we still can't find the car – and that their private security guards had recently reported a "dead animal" smell near the boundary with Riverdell. Rang the intercom and reported it to the person who answered. Forensics suspect it was wafting from the house.'

Mike's phone buzzed with an incoming text. 'It's Sue!' he said, brightening. 'She's off the ventilator. And talking.'

Sue's eyelids were too heavy to open. She'd seen Tom sitting beside her, and smiled, before drifting back into an unwanted doze. Memories floated into her mind. Trapped in the car, as Rob smashed his fist into her. Tom playing chess. The missing girl, the one they had to find. And the nail bar. The woman with the steel-blue eyes.

She forced herself awake.

'Mum,' Tom smiled.

'M-mike,' she croaked, her throat dry and sore. 'Get Mike.'

'Here, have a sip of water,' Tom said, holding the plastic cup to her lips.

'M-mike' she repeated, he eyelids heavy again.

'I'll text him. Get him to come straight in.'

It took Mike twenty minutes to drive to the hospital, running every red light on the empty, early morning roads. 'What's she said?' he puffed, sitting down beside Tom.

'She asked for you. Nothing else. Have you seen Dad? He wasn't at home last night when I came up here. I'm getting worried.'

'I haven't, Son. I'll find him for you.'

Mike took Sue's hand. 'I'm here, Sue,' he said. 'Don't you worry about anything. Especially work.'

She opened her eyes. 'The girl ... Anna...'

'It's all under control. We've got a suspect in custody. Don't even think about the case.'

'The woman who took her ... owns the nail salon.' Her eyes, straining to stay awake, focused on Tom.

'The nail salon in Cobshott? Where you went?'

Sue nodded. 'She's the one.' Her eyelids closed again.

'I know who she's talking about,' Mike said to Tom. 'Melinda Medford. Stay here with your mum. I'll be back.'

Chapter Thirty-Three

It's late at night when the coach pulls into Sheffield Interchange, and I sit on a bench for hours, dazed, blurred, unsure what to do or where to go, hating myself, loathing the world. I'm homeless again, right back where I started when I left Yarmouth – alone, unwanted and unloved.

Dawn creeps in early, rousing me from my fitful doze, briefly brightening the sky before thick rain clouds wash in, greying out the green park and soaking into my sweaty tracksuit. I can't think about Cindy. Or Anna. Or Tanya. I can't think about Riverdell and the life I've left. The past is blackened, smouldering. I have to think of the future.

Rubbing my eyes, I emerge from the park, blinking, into the rain-soaked street, my long brown wig itchy and matted, taking refuge in a cheap cafe. Egg, chips and a cuppa. I don't want them, but I have to order something. The place is dingy, my mug is cracked, and everything is coated with a slimy layer of grease, even the air. A thin young man, his skin pock-marked and his stripy apron grimy, plonks my plate in front of me.

'Ketchup's over there.' He gestures to a table laden with half-empty bottles of tomato sauce, vinegar and salt.

'Thanks.'

He walks away and I glance around the cafe. Cheap Formica tables, hard chairs, and net curtains covering the lower half of the windows. Above them I can see the sky, heavy and grey. It's so early that there's hardly anyone here, just a shabby middle-aged man in dirty fingerless gloves clutching his mug of tea, and a young girl in jeans and a hairy oversized sweater – a junkie, I'd say – making her way through a fry-up as if she hasn't eaten for days. This isn't a place where people come to talk. It's anonymous. A shelter from the shit that life has rained down. Where tea and toast and baked beans and a dry seat are a brief anaesthetic, before being cast out into the cold world yet again.

I pick at the egg and chips as a young man enters, quite smartly dressed for this kind of place, and takes a seat at the table beside mine, smoothing out his *Daily Star*.

'HOUSE OF HORRORS' screams the headline. 'Two bodies found at mansion in hunt for missing Anna AND link to child sex ring.' There's a photo of Riverdell.

The egg and chips rises up in my throat and I know I'm going to vomit. Doubled over, I feel a gentle hand on my back as I'm copiously sick on the floor. 'You OK, love,' says a voice. It's the junkie. The one with the hairy sweater.

'Yeah, yeah, I'm sorry…'

I stagger to my feet and pull a twenty-pound note from my pocket. 'Sorry,' I say again, dropping it onto the table, as the young waiter with the pock-marked face emerges with a mop and bucket. My chest is being squeezed, crushed like I'm in a vice. I have to get out of here. Clattering through the chairs, I yank open the door, out into the rain. I knew they wouldn't understand. I never touched the girls. They were my daughters. I'd never, ever have done *that*.

The nausea passes and I stand up, my feet soaking, my wig wet through. Across the road is a newspaper kiosk. I stumble towards it, every headline burning my eyes. It's the front page of every single paper. Fumbling in my pocket, I pull out a pound coin and buy a copy of *The Sun*.

'Grim business, love,' says the seller, nodding at the headline.

I can't reply. Can't even nod. I fold the paper under my arm and walk aimlessly along the street until I reach an empty bus shelter. I don't want to unfold it. But I have to see what it says.

Two bodies. Not yet formally identified. One dead in a bath, the other in a blanket box. A torture chamber in the basement where a third girl is thought to have been held, a fifteen-year-old recently saved from a child sex ring. I hear a howl, a primal, desperate scream, and realise it is coming from me.

Chapter Thirty-Four

Mike and Lauren arrived in Cobshott just after sunrise. The Nail Salon was locked up, and a pile of flyers on the mat suggested it had been closed for a couple of days.

Wearing gloves, Mike picked the lock and walked inside. The place was immaculate. Neatly folded pink towels, spotless nail stations. Even the bottles of varnish in rows along the wall were perfectly grouped in shades, from pale to dark.

'So this is the only address we have for her?' Lauren asked.

'Yep. The owner lives in Spain. We're trying to contact them. Her car's the Mini parked round the corner.'

'What about previous addresses?'

'That's where we're struggling. Sue said Medford spoke about growing up in Great Yarmouth. There are several Medfords in the area. Local force checking them out. She's not showing up on any electoral rolls. She did everything by cash and prepaid card. A ghost.'

'Anything from the iPhone number Soozie gave us?'

'Unregistered pay-as-you-go. It's frequently switched on in the Surbiton/Tolworth area. Last used in Camden, around the Lock. We can't be more specific than that.'

Lauren peered into the sterilizer, where rows of implements were neatly stacked. 'She's methodical. Organized. What time is the public appeal going out?'

'We've got a media release ready with Medford's name, a photo supplied by Soozie Lightwater and a hotline number. Told people not to approach her. Let's get Forensics in here. We need her DNA.' Mike paused. 'But what's the connection between her and the Lightwaters? Could Medford be Simon Lightwater's mystery woman? Beverley?'

'It's possible.'

'But what about Soozie Lightwater? Is she involved?'

Lauren shrugged. 'We can't rule it out. But she looked like one hell of a spurned wife to me. I don't believe she knew about Riverdell, nor his mistress. Or the brand-new Range Rover he had parked there. We've picked that up in Hammersmith. Forensics are going over it now.'

Mike nodded. 'Look, Lauren, I need to pop back to the hospital. Take Tom home. I'll be back in an hour.'

'Sure. I'll be here.'

~

Tom was sitting beside his mum, who was sleeping. 'She hasn't said anything else. The nurse says it's good that she rests. Have you found the suspect? And where's Dad?'

'Come outside,' Mike said gently. 'I need to talk to you.'

They took a seat in one of the empty relatives' rooms. Mike took a deep breath. 'For your own safety, I want you to stay at my place.'

'Why?'

'Your mum's been attacked, and we now know it's linked to the case. This woman is a killer. She may know where you live. She may know your mum's woken up. So I'll be stationing extra armed guards outside the ICU. We'll catch her, Tom. It's only temporary.'

Tom's face paled. 'OK. But my school stuff is at home. I need my books. I've got so much holiday work to do for my GCSEs.'

'I'll get that brought to you.'

'And Dad? Will Dad join me? He's still not answering my calls.'

'I'll find him, Son. Let's get you to my place. I'll phone the school, explain you won't be in today. I've got Netflix. And unlimited Wi-Fi.'

Melinda Medford was long gone, Mike was sure of it. He didn't believe she posed any threat to Sue. But Rob Fisher was another matter. After dropping Tom, he called by Sue's house and let himself into the shed. The burner phone was still there, under the armchair. Mike pocketed it. He had to find out what Rob Fisher was up to.

Back in the office, Lauren began wading through the paperwork from a deluge of hotline calls following the release of Melinda Medford's details and photo.

'Jesus, Mike, we're never going to trace Medford from this. Practically every woman in Cobshott was a customer. All ringing up wanting to chat, but not telling us anything new. I've got a sighting in Glasgow, three in Cornwall, about sixteen on various Tube lines, four on London buses and one woman claiming she's her long-lost daughter. And what about this one? Art student from Surbiton claiming she lives in their shared house.' She paused. 'The student says she has two cars – a Mini and a four-wheel drive, possibly a Range Rover…'

They looked at each other.

'Call her.'

The house was a typical student rental, in a Victorian terrace with straggly overgrown grass, overflowing bins, and tablecloths pinned up as curtains. A single, shadeless bulb hung in the grubby narrow hallway, casting a harsh light on what Mike felt sure were giant paintings of vomit.

'Mel's room is in the basement,' Jackie drawled in her thick Liverpudlian accent, her paint-splattered clothes and dreadlocks reeking of dope. She was clearly stoned.

'How long has she lived here?' Mike asked.

'A few years. Moved in a couple of months after me.'

'And you're sure she's not here now?

'Nah. I checked. Gave her a knock.'

'So she might be in? Mike, we'd better get armed response in here…'

'Nah.' Jackie looked uncomfortable. 'She's definitely gone. I went in this morning. Just in case she was dead, like. I've done it before.'

'Checked on her being dead?' Lauren asked.

She looked sheepish. 'Borrowed some of her cash. She's got stacks of it about. In envelopes. Her clients don't use cards. I will pay her back. I was only, you know, *loaning* it. Needed some, er, tea.'

'So you have a key?'

'Two.' She held up a Yale and a deadlock. 'From the previous tenant. And it looks like she's moved out. She hadn't even used the deadlock this time.'

Turning the key, his firearm ready, Mike pushed open the door. The room was tiny, painted a drab beige, with a single bed, a sink, and a fold-down table with a chair. Utterly soulless. A few shirts, trousers and dresses hung in the open closet, and a half-empty mug of coffee was on the table. 'Did she ever talk about anywhere else? Anywhere she might have stayed?' Mike asked.

'Only the nail bar. She didn't talk much. Said she was from Great Yarmouth. And that her dad has dementia. I felt sorry for her.' She lowered her voice. 'Mel used to dress up. As different people.'

'Can you describe them?'

'One was a redhead. Huge hair. Very glam. Like someone off *Drag Race*. Big heels. Sometimes I saw her getting out of a big four-wheel drive parked round the corner dressed like it. I only knew for sure it was her cause I'd seen all of her wigs in the room. We made eye contact a few times. I pretended not to recognise her.'

Mike and Lauren exchanged a glance. The Range Rover. It had to be Beverley.

'What about the others she posed as?' Lauren said.

'One made her look older. And fatter. Brown hair. Frumpy. She had a skinny student look as well. Short hair, Vans and jeans. I didn't see any others, but she had stacks of different wigs. They've all gone. And most of the clothes.'

'Like this?' Mike flicked through his phone and showed her the CCTV picture of Anna and a mystery woman on the train.

'Yeah. That could be her. I didn't put two-and-two together when you first released this. I'm sorry, man. She just looked like, you know, *anyone*.'

Mike sighed. 'We'll need you to help our artist draw a sketch of them.'

Jackie smiled. 'No need. I painted them myself. From memory. Hang on.' She disappeared into her room and came back with two small canvases. 'Here they are.'

Mike wasn't holding out much hope, expecting an abstract splatter. But they were good portraits. He recognised her straightaway. The woman he'd seen going into Onslow Avenue. The one with the suitcase.

'I painted them 'cause I find her fascinating,' Jackie drawled. 'She's such a character. Or lots of characters.'

'Can we take these?' Lauren asked. 'We will return them.'

'Sure. I saw her picture on TV and thought I'd better call. Said she might be dangerous. She always seemed so nice though.'

'And you're sure you didn't see her with a girl here?' Lauren added.

'Definitely not. She was always alone. No one ever came to visit. Kept herself to herself, like. Only ever spoke to me, and that wasn't often. Am I safe here? Is she coming back?'

'We doubt it. But we'll have officers outside, in case.'

'That's her!' Simon Lightwater gasped, as Mike showed him a photo of the painting across the interview table. 'Beverley. That's the woman who blackmailed me. Have you found her? And why the fuck is she in a painting?'

Mike pushed a photo of Melinda Medford in front of him. 'What about this woman?'

'No idea. Who is she?'

'This is Melinda Medford.'

'Who?'

'Runs the nail bar in Cobshott.'

'Mel? Soozie's always on about her. I've never met her, but I'm sure she can give you the low-down. They're good mates. What's she got to do with it?'

In the corridor, Mike and Lauren discussed their options. 'Simon's more use to us out there,' Lauren insisted. 'We'll get the team to tail him. Voice intercept on his calls. The works. Unless he's squeaky clean, we'll get him.'

'Thanks for your help, Simon,' Lauren said, striding back into the interview room. 'You can go.'

'Go?' His eyes blazed. 'Having fucked up my entire life, have you finally realised I'm telling the truth?'

'We're releasing you pending further inquiries,' she replied coldly. 'Here's your phone. Obviously Riverdell is off-limits at present as it's a crime scene. We'll let you know when you can access it again.'

'Access it? I'm not going near the fucking place. Ever. Where's Soozie?'

'Mrs Lightwater made her statement and has, I believe, gone home.'

Simon switched on his iPhone. Ten missed calls from Mia. Soozie wouldn't speak to him, he knew that. Mia would have to be his lifeline.

Chapter Thirty-Five

I've been walking for hours, my clothes soaked through, my hood up and my head down, because I don't know what else to do. My name is all over the news – I've seen it on TV screens in shop windows. Wanted for questioning in the Riverdell case. I'm too dangerous to approach, apparently. They're talking about me as if I'm a cold-blooded serial killer, stalking the streets. It breaks my heart. Everything I've ever done has been out of *love*.

Cleo will have seen it. She loves me. She'll know they've got it all wrong. And she won't have been to the police. She wouldn't betray me, and she wouldn't risk her secret life coming out. I have to talk to her, to explain. There's a phone box on the corner. I dial her mobile.

'Charles Longcross.' She's in the office.

'Cleo. It's me. Mel.'

There's a pause. A stunned silence. She's formal, of course. I'm expecting that.

'Hello, sir.' She pauses. I can sense the fear in her voice. 'Yes, of course, the project is well underway. How can I help?'

'I know you won't believe what you're seeing on the news. They've got it all wrong, honey. That's why I've had to go away for a bit.'

'Of course. I understand. Where are you?'

'A phone box. I don't know where. I don't have my mobile anymore. Or email. Unless I can get to an internet cafe. Listen, Cleo, wait for me. Please. I'm going to find somewhere new to live. Somewhere we can be together. Whenever you want to be. It'll take me some time.'

'I'll make sure I do that.' She pauses. 'It would be useful to have an idea of the location, sir. Perhaps we could meet to discuss? What's the best number to call you back on?'

Her voice is unsteady, panicky. She's trying to trap me, find out where I am.

I hang up.

Cleo. My gorgeous Cleo. Now she's betrayed me, too. The rage begins to swell inside me, pressing behind my ribs, urging me on. I pull my wet coat around my chest, turn around, clench my fists into a ball and walk towards the town centre.

Chapter Thirty-Six

Sue was out of the ICU and in a private room at the hospital, an armed guard still stationed outside it, tucking into an unexpectedly tasty lasagne. 'Medford must have realised I knew it was her,' she said thickly. 'She came after me when I left and punched me in the street. You wouldn't have found her DNA in the car.'

'Forensics are working on her flat and the nail bar. We'll have it soon.'

'I didn't realise how badly I was injured. I got in the car, tried to text you and must have blacked out.' Sue shovelled a huge fork-load of pasta into her mouth. 'God, Mike, I am so *hungry*. Is Tom still at yours?'

'Yep. I think it's best, while Medford is on the loose.'

'What about Rob? I've called him but it goes straight to voicemail.'

'I'm sure he'll be in soon.'

Sue nodded. 'How's the girl you found? The one who was in care?'

'Cindy. They've transferred to a local hospital in Manchester. Her mum has been to see her. Physically, she's on the mend. Mentally, well ... everyone's doing what they can. She's not talking at all, but she's our best hope. It's going to take a long time.'

'And the other girl? Any idea who she is?'

'No clue. No DNA matches. We're trawling dental records. But her teeth were quite decayed. It's possible she never even went to a dentist.'

Sue scraped the last of the lasagne off the plate and opened her tub of orange juice. 'Let's go through it one more time,' Mike said. 'Was there anything else that Medford said in the nail bar? Anything you can remember?'

'It's still hazy.' Mike overlooked the fact Sue seemed to have a crystal clear memory of the attack by her car. 'She talked non-stop. Most of it gossip. About families in Cobshott.' She paused, frustrated. 'I can't remember the details.'

'Don't worry. Dr Purani said it'll gradually come back.'

'She did mention Camden,' she added. 'Paul Eaves' secret flat there. Where he took his mistresses. I'm guessing you've already checked that.'

'Camden?'

'I'm sure it was Camden. Said it was between Morrisons and the canal. I remember that because apparently he was known to joke about it. Ex-council. Not the sort of place you'd expect to find a city banker.'

Mike leapt to his feet. 'We didn't know about that, Sue. Medford's phone was often located in Camden. By the lock. It's not Eaves' place. It's *hers*.'

~

Mike sat in Morrisons' cafe, eating his way through a fry-up. There was only one ex-council block between the store and the canal, comprising about thirty flats. All were under surveillance. No one could go in or out without Mike knowing about it.

Raiding the whole block was impossible. Most of the flats were illegally sub-let, so no one really knew who lived there. Kids, refugee families, hippies, elderly couples – the whole thing would be a PR nightmare if they went in heavy-handed, or so Chief Biller told him. So he had to wait, at least for now.

'Let's try door-to-door,' Lauren had suggested. 'We know this Medford is a loner. At least we can rule some of them out. Then raid the others.'

They'd narrowed it down to six flats, where the occupants didn't answer. An armed unit would be there within the hour. Mike doubted Medford was there. She'd be long gone. But they had to be sure.

The first three flats were a non-starter. Two were completely empty, and the third littered with crack pipes and dozing addicts. Even the fourth didn't look hopeful. It clearly belonged to a hippy, with the smell of joss sticks, peace flags, tatty CND posters and tie-dyed throws everywhere. On the low, scratched coffee table was the remains of a fish and chips takeaway, an empty can of Diet Coke and two CD cases – Fleetwood Mac and Debussy. Dog-eared books on meditation and India lined the shelves.

But there was something else. Mike didn't notice it at first. A trace of a sickly, acrid smell, just as Lauren lifted an eiderdown over a box-shape in the corner of the room and saw the chest freezer.

'Christ.'

They paused, neither of them wanting to open it, preparing for the horror that might be inside.

Chapter Thirty-Seven

I've checked into a cheap hotel on the other side of town, a single, ensuite room with a tiny window, a cheap, thin duvet, nicotine-stained walls and grimy shower. The kind of place where no one asks any questions. There I think of Cleo and our afternoons at The Fairmont Hotel, looking out over fields and horses. Maybe I was wrong. Maybe she wasn't trying to catch me out. But I can't risk calling her again. I know I've lost her. I've lost everything. But every time the agonising loneliness threatens to overwhelm me, and I reach for the six packets of paracetamol ready by the bed, anger begins to burn. It starts deep in my belly, boring its way through every vein, every pore. I didn't deserve this. Any of it. I've been labelled a serial killer, a paedophile. Some newspapers even called me a psychopath. I have to keep going, to start again, to create a life and a new family. I just need time.

Cleo is the only person I've loved since Shauna, who

was everything to me – my rescuer, my mother, my life, right there in Camden. But she was a free spirit, and I knew as the months went on, our friendship was starting to make her claustrophobic. I didn't like her seeing friends, going out without me. Sometimes I'd hang out in the record shop where she worked, just to be near her. Our cuddling did lead to sex a few times, not passionate but warm and gentle, our bodies and minds so close that it felt so natural to become one. She was my first. My father didn't count.

But after we began sleeping together, the more I tried to show her love, the more distant she became. Suddenly, all she ever talked about was India. She'd heard about an ashram where she could stay for free, meditate, and find herself. I said I'd go with her, but she was evasive. Said maybe I could join her in a few months, once she'd settled in. That was a lie, and I knew it.

Then she bought her plane ticket, one way, and we both knew she wasn't coming back. She had goodbye drinks with a couple of mates in the World's End pub. And that night, our last together in the flat, I did it. The swift hammer blow from behind. This was merciful. I did it out of love. Just like I did with Tanya, in Riverdell's kitchen. I couldn't let her go. I couldn't allow that unbearable loneliness to shatter my soul, so agonisingly reconstructed from a million little pieces. And as I cradled Shauna's dead body in my arms, tears of happiness and sorrow dripping onto her wrinkled face, what I felt most was relief. At least now she would never, ever leave me.

Lying on the floor, with her in my arms, her grey

dreadlocks draped gently over my chest, I closed her eyes so I wouldn't see them cloud over and I could tell myself she was sleeping. I cried until there were no more tears, until the numbness came, and the rising sun sliced red through the window. Guilt began to claw at my soul but I forced it away, deep inside. I should phone an undertaker. I should call the police and report what I've done. That's what I'll do, I told myself. But not yet. I want to keep Shauna for a few more days. I'm not ready to let her go, and it won't make any difference to what happens to me. The days turned into weeks, then months, then years, and still I couldn't bear to let her go.

Tanya was different. She'd stayed with me for a week before she tried to sneak away. I didn't want to keep her. She wasn't *family*. She was an ungrateful *liar*. I just needed to get rid of her body. I only put her in the bath because I didn't know what else to do, never thinking I'd need to use the panic room for Cindy, the disobedient child I'm missing so much.

Warm summer rain is falling, streaking down the hotel room window. I focus on one fat raindrop and trace its path. I've lost Cindy. And Cleo. Now I've had to leave Camden, and Shauna. Starting again isn't going to be easy.

Chapter Thirty-Eight

White-suited forensic officers silently went about their work, as Mike and Lauren waited outside the flat.

'Forties. Female.' The lead forensic officer said. 'Looks like she's been taken out from time to time and placed on the sofa in a sitting position. There's evidence she's slightly thawed and then refrozen, though that could partly be down to the freezer's defrost cycle. She seems to be intact. Injury to the back of the head which was probably the cause of death. A hammer blow, possibly.'

'How long has she been in there?' Mike asked.

'Difficult to say. I'll know a lot more once we get back to the lab. Depends on how robust this freezer is, too, and if there have been any long power cuts. But potentially anywhere up to a few years.'

'God,' Mike said. 'Keep us posted.'

In the hallway, Lauren was looking over her notes.

'The neighbours aren't much use,' Lauren said. 'Probably illegal immigrants. Terrified of the police. But an elderly gent in the nearby pub, the Good Mixer, says an older lady with grey dreadlocks used to live there. Worked in a record shop on Inverness Street. He recalls her name was Shauna, possibly O'Mara. She went to "live in India" some years ago and no one has heard from her since.'

They stood in silence for a moment. Thick grey dreadlocks were frozen over the dead woman's face.

'I'll go and tell Sue,' Mike said. 'We'd never have found Shauna O'Mara without her.'

Mike couldn't put it off any longer. Once he'd filled in Sue on the entire case, and Shauna O'Mara, he had to bring it up.

Sue was sitting in an armchair in the hospital room, looking much brighter, her mind racing. 'We've got to find Medford before she kills again. Or skips the country. Can you bring me the file? I'm stuck here doing sod all, Mike. I might spot something everyone's missed.'

'Sure. We've got alerts on all the ports and airports. Posters everywhere. She's a master of disguise. They're working on the DNA, so we might get a match on the database. Riverdell and the flat were plastered with it.'

'What about tracing her family in Yarmouth?

'Uniform are going door-to-door with her photo. But she's a ghost, Sue. We don't even know her real name.'

He paused. 'I'll bring you the file. But there's something else I need to talk to you about. It's...sensitive. About Rob.'

'What? For god's sake, Mike, spit it out.'

'When you had your scans they found a lot of old injuries, Sue,' he said gently. 'Healed ones. Broken ribs. The doctor said they were consistent with long-term, sustained physical abuse.'

He wasn't sure what to expect. A denial, perhaps. Claiming she'd been clumsy. An accident. But he wasn't prepared for the shame that filled her eyes.

'D-does Tom know?'

'No. Social services have asked him a few questions. They're satisfied he's safe, and as far as they're concerned – and everyone else – you were attacked by Medford.' He paused. 'It was Rob, wasn't it, who did this?'

'Yes.'

A single tear trickled slowly down Sue's cheek. There was so much to say, but now was not the time. Mike took her in his arms, like a bear gently holding her cub, rocking her back and forth, as Sue wept – for Tom, for herself, even for Rob, and began to let go of the secret, the shame, pain she'd held inside for so many years.

Mike was still holding her in his arms when the call came.

'That was Forensics. Medford's DNA. It's male.'

Chapter Thirty-Nine

I've made it to Brighton. Staying up North wasn't safe, after I stupidly made that call to Cleo, and the posters of me say I may have links to Yarmouth. So the South Coast it is. There's a small, boutique hotel just off the seafront. It's pricey, but it'll do for a week or two. I need a little luxury. And I need to keep moving.

It's easy to be anonymous here. No one cares who you love, what you wear. Or who you are. All I knew, growing up, was that I didn't want to be 'Loner Mark' or 'Bonkers Baker' as the kids at school yelled, pushing me against the wall, sneering. Withdrawn, shy. Depressed, when I look back. Traumatised.

Only my friend Liza understood. She was another silent soul, friendless, a misfit, bullied for being fat, enduring a hateful bitch of a mother who'd longed for a son and constantly put her down in public. Sometimes Liza joked that we should swap places. If only she knew. The torment she endured was visible, the emotional scars raw and oozing, while mine was unseen, unspoken. I couldn't tell her, because I didn't know how, and even if I did, maybe, just maybe, she'd be so disgusted that I'd lose her too. Yet she sensed a sadness in me, and our inner pain bonded us together, safely hidden behind homework and a love of Snow Patrol, while secretly all that fear and shame ate away at my soul. We dreamed of moving to London, renting a flat, and *being* someone. Because we knew who we were wasn't enough.

The night after my mother's funeral, I packed a bag and found the strength to tell my father I was leaving. He stared at me, blankly, and said simply: 'Why?'

Of all the words he ever spoke, or whispered, that single one was the cruellest.

I never did go back for Liza. I promised I would. Said I'd settle into life in Camden and bring her to join me. But somehow Liza was part of what I'd left behind. It had to be a completely new start. And I made sure that whenever I did go back to see my father, I bragged about my happy new life in London. Most of the time he was too pissed to notice. But I like to think it hurt him.

I sink back onto the pillow-strewn, soft hotel bed, and think of Liza. I googled her once, and found a wedding photo in the local paper. Liza, still huge, marrying some guy I'd never heard of, back in Yarmouth. I hope she's happy. She deserves that.

A shaft of sunlight streams through the window, making the air sparkle like stars. My leg is on fire, so I down a couple of the paracetamol and two of the antibiotics I'd bought for Cindy. Maybe a walk would help.

They'll have found my DNA at Riverdell so they'll know I'm male. And they'll probably be expecting me to be disguised as a woman, so I won't do that. Dressed in a short blond man's wig, skinny jeans and Vans, I step out into the warm street. Ahead, the pier is a whirl of colour, mixed with the smell of doughnuts and candy floss, chips and stale beer. The boards are springy underfoot, leading me past the tiny henna tattoo parlour, the gypsy fortune-teller, to the funfair at the end, where sticky-faced children stand outside the ghost train, mesmerised, listening to the teenage squeals.

I open a can of coke and walk back up the pier, along the seafront and down the slope, past the pubs packed with revellers spilling onto the stony beach as seagulls screech and soar overhead. I crunch my way to the shoreline, find a spot and sit down, gazing out across the grey-blue water to infinity, as the waves gently lap at my toes. Beside me, a small child crunches on a stick of pink Brighton rock, but her mother stares only at her phone. So much colour, so much beauty in the world, and she can't see it.

The pain in my leg is easing now, so I stay and watch the sunset, streaking it with Ibizan reds and golds. A thick tear swells in my eye, but I won't let it fall. The past is pain. The future is fear. Crushing the coke can in my hand, I take a final look at the blackening sea and head for the hotel. I've never felt so alone.

Chapter Forty

Rob was slumped in the train carriage, a half-empty bottle of vodka beside him in a carrier bag. 'We're at Waterloo, sir,' the guard said, tapping him on the shoulder. 'All change.'

His eyes glazed, Rob nodded, stood up and stumbled off the train. Through London's Waterloo station, where the shiny concourse was packed with weary late-night commuters, wishing they hadn't stayed for another drink. Down the steps and out into the cool night air, where the bars and restaurants, still open, gave the city its warm glow.

The voicemail message from Mike had been brief. 'We need to talk. I know about Onslow Avenue.' Rob hadn't returned the call. Mike detested him, he knew it, and would do anything to put him away. He'd never believe the truth.

It had started with an emergency call-out. 3am. A tenant on the very top floor of number 113, directly opposite, had locked themselves out. Rob had finished the job and as he went back to his car he noticed a burly blond man, dressed in black, smoking on the steps of number 114. He'd done a couple of jobs in there too over the years, as they had the same management company. Usually the tenants were politicians, often from overseas, using it as their London base. But something about this man didn't seem right.

'Tuesday then. 9pm. 114b Onslow. For the drop.'

The man speaking had an earpiece. And round his waist was a gun. Head down, Rob had shuffled past without a word. Was he a bodyguard? Possibly. But Rob's hunch was something illegal was going on in there. Drugs, perhaps.

He'd thought of calling the management company. Or telling Sue. But why should she get all the glory? For once in his life, he wanted to be the one who foiled a crime. It excited him. Gave him a thrill, a purpose in his cold, closeted world. He usually spent his nights poring over his Airfix models, perfecting every last detail to blot out the burning jealousy of his own son, and of Mike, which gnawed at his every waking moment. This was a new distraction. He bought a burner phone and read up on crimes. Typed in the address and time, planning to send it anonymously to the police as a tip-off. But what could he say? He had no evidence, no idea what was going on. Just an address, a time and a hunch. So he'd returned on Tuesday to watch the flat from the hallway opposite. Nothing much had happened, so he didn't bother to report it.

Hours later, he'd seen the reports of the police raid, and the horror they had found inside. His hunch was right. But now Mike Barley thought he was involved in a child sex ring. The burner phone was missing. Barley must have it. The address was on the screen. He'd have told Sue. Mike would do anything to get him out of the way, he was sure of it, using that phone to prove a connection. And if Sue thought he was a paedophile, she'd make sure he went down for years, even if it wrecked her own career.

Taking a swig of vodka, he walked onto Waterloo bridge, car headlights blurring as they passed him. Tears began to trickle down his face. *She'd* made him a monster. He'd almost killed her. He hadn't meant to do it. He *loved* her. It wasn't his fault that she loved Tom, and Mike, so much more. He'd tried so hard to give her everything. *She* was the one to blame. She'd brought all this on herself.

Rob had heard what happened to Paul Eaves in prison. No. He'd do this his way.

He didn't see the passer-by running towards him as he climbed over the rail, or hear her shout 'no!' as he jumped. The cold brown water bit into his skin and for a moment he gasped for air, arms flailing, as his body instinctively fought to live. But the River Thames swallowed him up, the currents sucking him deeper into its depths, suffocating and filling his lungs.

It was two days before they found him. Rob Fisher, bloated and blackened, washed up on the riverbank in East London.

Three weeks later, Soozie and Simon Lightwater sat beside each other in the front pew of Cobshott church, a pink coffin resting on a stand in front of them. The church was packed, and screens had been set up to relay the service to the crowds gathered outside, where journalists and live TV cameras waited eagerly to mull over every detail, from Soozie's black veil to the giant spray of sunflowers on top of Sky's coffin. The story of the wealthy young girl who took her own life after being groomed by a paedophile and bullied on social media had completely captured the public's imagination. In death, Sky finally had the attention that she'd craved in life. She was even trending on Twitter.

Sue sat in the back row, alongside Mike. She was surprised they'd been invited, especially after Simon's arrest, but Soozie had phoned personally and asked them to attend. 'If you hadn't caught Eaves,' Soozie said, 'Sky could have been drawn in even further. Or ended up like those other poor girls. We are both so thankful for that.'

It was Sue's second funeral in a month. The first was the day she laid Rob to rest, still a blur, a haze of 'sorry for your loss', sherry, and guests saying what a wonderful man he was. Tom crying. Wandering back to the house together, emotionally lost. Mike making them dinner. And, after Tom was asleep, going down to the shed, as if being inside it brought her closer to him, gazing in disbelief at the intricate models he'd secretly built.

The service over, Simon took his place by his daughter's

coffin, joining the other pallbearers as they carried her out to the cemetery. Crowds parted to allow them through, and people who had never met Sky shed tears as they watched on their phones, their laptops, their televisions. She was buried with her favourite teddy and a sealed note from her sister.

Sue and Mike stood a respectful distance back from the grave, allowing friends and family to move in front, but as the mourners began to move away, Soozie saw them and walked over, lifting her veil over her face. 'I'm so sorry about your husband, DCI Fisher.'

'Thank you.'

'And thank you for coming. If it wasn't for you…' Soozie paused. 'How are the injuries?'

'On the mend. Tired. But I want to get back to work. Take my mind off things. Sitting at home doesn't do me any good. Medford's still on the run. And I will catch him.'

Soozie nodded. 'I never guessed Medford was a man, let alone a killer. Medford seemed so, you know, *sweet*. Harmless. Caring. I can't imagine how someone like that could kill, hold a young girl prisoner, *torture* them, and go about their day acting as if nothing had happened. Shows how well we really know people.'

She paused. 'I know what you mean about work. I'm going back to PR. This time for a charity. Helping families whose children have gone missing. And Star and I are moving to London when she leaves the Priory. We're going to rent a flat while we decide where to settle. I can't stay here.'

'How is Star?' Sue asked.

'Doing really well. Zoe Littlejohn is in the Priory too. Checked in straight after Anna's funeral. They're helping her come to terms with what Eaves did. I've visited her a few times. She wants to help out at the charity when she's well. We've both lost a daughter, and we both want something good to come out of this mess.'

Soozie glanced over at her husband, still beside the grave. 'Simon's with Mia. And she's welcome to him.'

She looked deep into Sue's eyes. 'It's the guilt,' she said. 'When someone you love takes their own life. That's the worst thing. Not realising how depressed they secretly were. I can't stop blaming myself.'

'I know,' replied Sue. 'Me neither.'

The Medford case had fallen off the front page and despite reports of sightings of 'The Nail Salon killer' all over the country, he was still at large. As the weeks passed, with no leads on his true identity, and no photos, only the paintings of him in disguise, to go by, Chief Biller said he needed to start diverting resources elsewhere. Sue didn't agree. Medford was a sadistic killer, the most dangerous she had ever met, and even though she was back at work focusing on other cases, she would not rest until Medford was caught.

It was the weekend, and Mike had taken Tom down to Dorset on a walking and fishing trip. They'd sent her selfies of them on the South West Coastal Path, tucking into pasties on windswept cliffs against a dramatic backdrop of the wide, blue-grey ocean. Mike had been her rock, always ready to listen when she wanted to rail against the world, and to hold her when the sadness dragged her into despair. It was Mike who broke the news about Rob's suicide, Mike who held her and Tom's hands at the funeral, and Mike who had helped her get back to work again.

The house still felt so empty without Rob in it. But lately there had been moments when she was working late, and she'd automatically feel that sense of fear, of panic, about what she'd face when she got home. Then a sensation of utter relief would wash over her, followed by agonising guilt for being so glad, in that moment, that he was gone.

Sue swung the car into Kingston police station and headed into the office where she took out the Medford file and began perusing it one more time. The multi-agency teams were working flat out on Onslow Avenue and had made several arrests, but so far there was no link to Eaves or any trace of communications with Medford. Perhaps there was something she had missed, some clue to where Medford might be.

She'd been over and over the main file, but this time she decided to wade through the enormous pile of brief sightings and 'tip-offs' Mike had boxed and labelled with a Post-it note as 'nutters'. Reports had come in from all over the world. Sue smiled to herself. Medford had even been glimpsed on a roller coaster in Florida.

That's when she saw it. An anonymous tip-off, phoned into Kingston Police.

Gave her name as 'Cleo'. Said she had sex in The Fairmont Hotel just outside Cobshott with Medford every Thursday, then hung up.

Cleo. Medford had mentioned a Cleo in the salon. She put the note on a separate pile. Might be worth checking out.

Two hours later, she came across a second note.

Caller gave her name as 'Cleo'. Said we should be looking for a man.

She checked the date. The call was made before the DNA results were released.

'Lauren,' she called, grabbing her jacket. 'We need to get to The Fairmont Hotel. *Now.*'

The campsite was at the top of a cliff, and after a one-pot dinner of corned beef and Smash, cooked over the campfire, washed down with a beer – Mike said he wouldn't tell if Tom didn't – the young lad crawled into his single-man tent and fell into an exhausted but relaxing sleep. He loved spending time with Mike. The dad he had never had. With Rob, he'd always been on edge. The awkward silences. The sulking. The temper. And, worst of all, the sense of utter helplessness when the violence came, pretending to his mum that he hadn't seen it or heard it, knowing that the truth would break her heart. Life without him was a relief.

The only reason he missed him was because he'd always been there.

It was late on their final night when Mike pulled on his thick skiing jacket and walking boots, and quietly unzipped his tent, heading into the blackness with a thin pocket torch. He climbed over the campsite's low stone wall into a field, where a flock of sheep froze as the torch panned around, its beam leaving them rooted to the spot. They'd walked this route earlier, so Mike knew roughly where he was going, up and over a stile, and through a second field to a rough stone path which led to the cliff. Below him, the Atlantic waves roared and crashed, biting through the soft sandstone cliffs. Scanning round with his torch, he chose a large rock and placed it at his feet. Mike reached in his pocket, took out Rob Fisher's burner phone and turned it on. The unsent message, *114b Onslow Avenue, Mayfair. 9pm. Tuesday* glowed on the screen.

Mike placed the phone on a rock, where he smashed it again and again into tiny pieces, and still he smashed it, his fist bloodied from the impact. Sue must never know, could never know. Mike had no idea how Rob was caught up in it. But any link between Rob and Onslow Avenue would devastate Sue and Tom. Their lives had been wrecked by the bastard quite enough.

Sweeping the pieces into his hand, he walked to the edge of the cliff and hurled them into the black, churning sea.

~

'The records show they always paid in cash,' The Fairmont Hotel manager told Sue, poring over his computer. 'Every Thursday. Regular as clockwork. Under the name Mary Jones. I've checked the address they gave. It doesn't exist.'

Sue looked around the foyer. It was a warm, welcoming hotel, attached to a pub, surrounded by fields and horses. 'What about the receptionists? Would they remember anything?'

'One's working in the bar. Let me get her.'

Moments later, a young, blonde girl appeared.

'I do remember the lady,' she said. 'Chloe, I think. Actually, maybe Cleo.'

'Can you describe the other person with her?'

'Quite run-of-the-mill, really. Guy in his late twenties with short brown hair. Skinny. Bit younger than her, I'd say.'

'Did they arrive together?'

'No. The lady, Cleo, would get here first. I served her in the bar once. Waited there with a drink. The man always went straight to the room.' She paused. 'But I do remember a woman with red hair turning up a couple of times after Cleo. In a Land Rover or Range Rover. Skyscraper heels. Very Cobshott.'

'That's also Medford. One of his aliases. Did you ever hear or see anything that could help us find them?'

She thought for a moment. 'There was one time, I'm sure, when Cleo asked me to order red roses. And she didn't have enough cash so she paid with a card.'

'When was this?'

'Near Valentine's Day. Whichever Thursday was the closest.'

'I need that card number,' Sue replied, her face determined. 'Urgently.'

As the train crawled to yet another halt outside London Waterloo, Sue checked her watch and looked across at the Shard, glinting in the autumn sunlight. Once she had the card number, tracing Cleo had been easy. Mr Charles Wright. She'd called Cleo at work, and said they needed to meet straightaway. Cleo asked if it could be on the Southbank. Somewhere anonymous. Sue didn't need to ask why. But she already had armed officers watching Cleo's office, in case she tried to run.

It was mid-afternoon, and The Southbank Centre was quiet. A vast, cavernous space with tables and chairs scattered around, it was yet to fill up with the evening's chattering classes, enjoying a glass of wine before a concert. Sue took a seat by the window and sent Cleo a text to say she'd arrived.

'DCI Fisher. I'm Cleo.' Dressed in a suit and tie, Cleo took a seat opposite her. 'Thanks for agreeing to meet me here, and not barging into the office. My wife, Helen… I have children… I'm not ready to have that conversation with them. Not yet.'

'I understand,' Sue replied. 'I'd like you to tell me everything you can about Medford. I know it will be difficult, but he's a killer, Cleo. I need to find him before someone else gets hurt.'

'He called me.' Cleo spoke urgently, and Sue saw a haunted, fearful look in her eyes. 'On the run. Just the once. A few weeks ago. He didn't say where he was. I-I asked him, but he wouldn't say. I did ring the hotline twice. Is that how you traced me? From the phone calls?'

'Yes. That led us to The Fairmont Hotel. You'd paid with a card once.'

'We used to meet there. Every Thursday. I'd been going to the salon for months when he asked me if I had time for a drink. And if I could keep a secret.'

'Which was?'

'That he was male. That his whole gossipy "Melinda Medford" act was just a persona he used in the nail bar, because it was good for business.' Cleo paused. 'Whenever we got to the hotel he'd strip off all his makeup, the blonde or red wig, every scrap of the disguise if he was wearing one, and just be himself. I enjoyed his company. And he was always so thoughtful, right from the first time I went to the salon. I felt understood. I thought we were two people who when we were together could finally be ourselves. Now I realise I didn't know him at all.'

'So he phoned on the run? What did he say to you?'

'He said it wasn't his fault. None of it. And he wanted me to wait for him because he'd find us somewhere to live and be together. He didn't trust anyone, really. Always said he liked having the disguises so he could keep his real self safe from the world. And disappear and reinvent himself if he needed to.' Cleo broke down, burying her face in her hands. 'I never dreamed his real self would be *this*. Murdering defenceless *children*. That he'd need to disappear because he was a serial killer. I just can't believe it. All the while he was torturing those poor girls.'

'Did he tell you his real name?' Sue asked gently, taking a tissue from her bag.

'No.' Cleo shook her head, blowing her nose loudly. 'I just called him "Mel". All I know is he grew up in Great Yarmouth, and his father abused him. For years. We only spoke about it once, briefly, because he wouldn't let me touch him when we slept together, and he wanted me to understand why. ' She shivered with disgust at the memories. 'I do know he moved to London when his mother died. Lived in Camden for a while, I think. I saw the reports about the flat there.' She let out a sob. 'That could have been *me*.'

'Did he give you any idea what his plans were when he called?'

'No. I tried to keep him talking but he hung up. I would have reported it straightaway if there was any clue at all. He hasn't been in touch since. I swear to you, DCI Fisher, I didn't know about any of it. He was always so kind to me, understood what I was going through. If only I'd seen a sign, those girls would still be alive. I thought he *loved* women. Why would he do that to them? Why?'

Cleo was clearly heartbroken, and Sue was certain she was telling the truth. She glanced at the undercover officers sitting at a table nearby, to indicate there was no immediate threat.

'Does he have any links apart from Yarmouth?'

'Mel never mentioned anywhere up North. His past was all in Norfolk as far as I know. He said he went back sometimes just to rub his father's nose in it.'

'Did he ever mention Riverdell?'

'No. Never. He told me he had a cheap flat in Surbiton, which was handy for the salon, but I never went there. He never invited me, and I didn't push it. Usually he drove a Mini, but more recently he'd turn up at the hotel in a Range Rover sometimes, in expensive designer clothes. I wondered if he'd come into some money, but he told me business was booming, and I didn't want to pry.'

Behind her, someone dropped a tray of drinks. Cleo jumped, and glanced fearfully over her shoulder. 'Sorry. I'm so nervous. Am I in danger? Will he come after me?'

'We don't think so, but we'll station officers very discreetly, to keep an eye on your workplace and home. Don't worry, no one will know.'

'Thank you. And I'm sorry I haven't been much help.'

'You'll need to make a full statement,' Sue added. 'We'll arrange that. Every single piece of information is useful, even the tiniest thing you can remember. Did he ever talk about any place he'd love to visit? Anywhere that was special to him?'

'We only ever met at the salon or the hotel. But he always said he wanted us to live by the sea. Ibiza, perhaps. Or Brighton. He said the seaside was somewhere you could disappear. Mel always said the past was dead to him.' She paused. 'He loved classical music, you know. Bach. Debussy. But I do remember one thing. He talked about a pub where he played the piano as a child. The Black Horse. His father knew the owner.'

Chapter Forty-One

I'm walking along Brighton seafront, and a chilly, early autumn wind is slicing right through my thin coat. Sleeping rough is starting to take its toll, especially now the weather is turning. All I have is the dirty clothes I'm wearing, my short blond wig, and the few notes that were stuffed into my pocket. Oh, and a sleeping bag which some kind soul placed over me one night.

I should never have left the hotel. But after almost a month there, the owner asked me cheerily one morning how long I'd be staying in Brighton. She was only making small talk. But I knew it was time to move on. Whitley Bay, perhaps. I hadn't made it there last time.

He was on a moped. Pulled up beside me on the street and punched me in the head. When I came round, a circle of worried bystanders around me, my case had gone. One of them tried to tend the wound on my head but I pushed her away and ran, disappearing into the crowds of shoppers on the Laines, and taking refuge in a shut up shop doorway, silently railing at the world.

Night-time is the worst. From time to time someone will bend down and talk to me, a kind face in a sea of disapproving ones, and invite me to a shelter, but I never go. I can't. What if they discover who I really am? I don't even have my music – my iPod is gone, so I can't disappear into a soundscape, escaping this world. I spend any coins I find on cans of Special Brew.

I look out across the grey-blue water, churned lightly by the wind, and the smell of chips from the takeaway near the pier makes me nauseous. I'm shivery, and the scissor wound on my leg is hurting again, oozing, so I go down the stairs into the stinking public toilets and shut myself in a cubicle, trying to clean it with paper. Livid red streaks are spreading on my leg now, and my pulse is racing. I vomit.

'You all right?'

It's the toilet attendant. He's seen me before.

'Yeah.' I flush the chain, wash my grimy hands and hurry back onto the streets. This is my home now, a lawless, desperate place, a parallel universe to the Brighton I knew before with its candy floss and deckchairs and sunsets. They're all still there, of course, but they're fuzzy, out of reach, part of a world I no longer inhabit, and a constant reminder of what I've lost. I miss all of it – my salon, my Riverdell, my Cleo, my nights with Shauna in Camden. Shauna was the only one who never left me. Not really.

I glimpse my face in a shop window. It's gaunt, dirty, stressed. The posters of me are long gone, faded and torn by the wind. If I see the news on TV in a shop window, I'm never on it.

My stained sleeping bag slung over my shoulder, I trudge towards the Hare Krishna van, not for food, but for silent company, where a queue of homeless people has formed. Anything to blot out the relentless loneliness, and the fear. Some I recognise from the streets. One of them probably stole my iPod, and gave it away for a crack pipe. The darkness doesn't come anymore, swallowed up by a terror that utterly engulfs me. I'm afraid of everything now, even too afraid to take my own life.

The Hare Krishnas wear orange robes, with shaved heads, and they are always smiling. Sometimes they chant. They give away free food every lunchtime – always vegetarian – and today it's curry. I join the queue, just for something to do, and one ladles a big dollop onto a paper plate while another spoons on some rice. 'Welcome,' says another, handing me a plastic fork. I'm not hungry at all, but perhaps eating will make me feel better. So I squat down on the kerb and shovel the food into my mouth, the first hot meal I've had for days. My belly groans unpleasantly, and stomach cramps almost make me double up. Sweat drips down my temple.

'You don't look too good,' says a gentle voice beside me.

It's one of the street pastors. I've seen her before, a middle-aged woman in a dog collar, long grey hair tumbling down. Kind face.

'Why don't we get you to the doctor's?' she adds. 'I can take you.'

I can't see a doctor. I can't see anyone. No one can know who I am. Panicking, I drop my plate and stagger off towards the back streets. There's an alleyway between houses I've used before. It's not safe at night, but maybe I can sit there for a while. I stumble down it, and curl up on a fetid piece of cardboard.

My vision is blurring now and my breath is coming in gasps. Something is wrong, very wrong. Spots are all over my arms, tiny red pinpricks. I'm terrified, more frightened than I've ever been. That's when I see her.

'Shauna?'

She's there, her grey hair blurred and fuzzy. I hear music, soft and soothing. Debussy's piano solo. And a voice.

'It's all right, love. We'll get you to hospital.'

Shauna's arms are around me and I nuzzle into her neck, safe and loved, swept away by the music's gentle, lilting rise and fall as the shadows begin to close in.

Chapter Forty-Two

The house in Great Yarmouth was a shabby Victorian terrace with a small crazy-paved front yard and tall weeds sprouting through the cracks. A uniformed officer opened the front door.

'DCI Fisher and DI Barley,' Sue said.

'Come in.' She opened the door fully and pointed to a back parlour. 'He's in there.'

The dingy hall was a grimy brown, stained with nicotine. Piles of old newspapers were stacked against one wall, making it even narrower. A single, shadeless bulb cast an eerie glow, and on the other wall a stuffed turtle was displayed, with its baby on its back.

Peter Baker was sitting in an armchair beside a flickering fire. He looked much older than his seventy-three years, with an almost completely bald head, a deeply lined face and steel-blue eyes, rheumy but just like his son's. The room had a distinct smell of urine, and on the dusty mantlepiece were several framed photos of Mark and his mother, beside a large blue bottle of Milk of Magnesia. In here, too, the light was weak, coming from two old-fashioned velvet wall lamps.

'Mr Baker,' Sue began. 'This must all be quite a shock.'

Fixing Sue with a watery gaze, he nodded, before picking up a poker and gently prodding the fire. 'Local police told me you were coming to talk about Mark. That he has something to do with them murders down South.'

'That's right.' Sue's voice was calm, controlled. 'Mr Baker, we believe that your son, Mark, is responsible for the deaths of three people, and the torture and imprisonment of a fourth.'

Sue wasn't sure how he'd react. Anger, perhaps. Disbelief. She'd even known relatives lash out, and Mike moved closer, ready to react. But Peter Baker stared straight ahead, with such a deep sadness in his eyes that Sue sensed he knew it was true.

'My wife wanted Mark to see a psychiatrist. I refused.'

'That's not in his medical records.'

'It was after the cat. Smokey. My wife was sure Mark killed it. He threw it out of the bedroom window.'

Sue listened, intently, as he described finding Smokey's broken body. Peter Baker was old, and frail. But he was also – if Mark had told Cleo the truth – a child abuser.

'My wife arranged a private visit. A psychiatrist in Norwich. But I cancelled it.' His face was burning red now. 'If I'd let Mark go to that psychiatrist, maybe those poor girls would be alive now. And that girl who survived wouldn't have been *tortured*. I read about it in the paper.'

Tears were welling up in Peter Baker's eyes, and Sue realised she had never seen anyone look quite so haunted.

'Mark didn't want to be himself. Do you want to know why? It wasn't his mother's death. It was … it was … because of *me*. What I did to him.'

'I'm listening,' Sue said gently.

In that moment, Sue realised the full horror of what this man was about to tell her. Sickened, she listened in silence as he confessed, and when he'd finally finished, he slumped back in the chair, mentally and physically exhausted.

Sue cleared her throat. 'We are also here to tell you that a young man was found collapsed in Brighton yesterday. He was taken to hospital and a doctor recognised him from the press coverage. Urgent DNA tests have confirmed his identity…'

'Can I see him? I just want to tell him I'm sorry.'

'Mark died of sepsis shortly after without regaining consciousness.'

The old man's rheumy eyes, full of tears, drifted to the mantlepiece, settling on a photo of Mark and his mother. His gnarled, brown hands gripped the side of his armchair and he pushed himself to his feet.

'Peter Baker. I am arresting you on suspicion of historic child abuse. You do not have to say anything, but it may harm your defence…'

'I don't need a defence.' He held out his hands meekly, his blue eyes unable to meet Sue's. 'I deserve this.'

Chapter Forty-Three

The sprawling cemetery in Brookwood, Surrey, lay alongside the main railway line, surrounded by trees, its neat, soft green lawns criss-crossed with paths and roads, and only the occasional rhythm of a train disturbed its tranquillity. All death was there, all faiths, from row upon row of war graves to mausoleums and monuments, from grand headstones to unmarked ones. On a chilly December morning, as a weak sun thawed the light frost and the headstones cast their long shadows, 'the girl in the bath', as she was known by the press, was laid to rest there.

No one knew her name. She'd made good headlines, and after her discovery the public had clamoured to know who she was. But the summer days turned to autumn, and they soon lost interest.

Unidentified, unknown, only Sue, Mike, Tom and a council officer stood by as the undertakers lowered her flimsy coffin into an unmarked pauper's grave, paying their respects as the remains of the young girl they'd worked so hard to identify were buried at last.

Sue bent down, took a handful of cold earth and threw it gently onto the coffin.

'Sleep well, sweet girl,' she whispered.

Mike took Sue's hand as they walked back to the car.

'I'm glad I came, Mum,' Tom whispered. 'I know how much this case meant to you. And she deserved some mourners. People to say goodbye.'

'I just wish we knew who she was,' Sue replied. 'Somewhere, her family are hoping she'll walk in the door. But she never will.'

'But it was you who realised Medford was the killer,' Mike added. 'Who knows how many more girls you saved. And there's his father, too. Ten years minimum and a lifetime as a registered sex offender. He'll die in prison.'

'You're right, Mike.' Sue sighed. 'We did everything we could. And at least Medford's gone. Cremated. No mourners, no trace. Not like this.'

Mike put his arm around her shoulder. 'Come on, let's all go for a drink. Raise a glass to all of them. Anna, Shauna, Sky, the poor girl we buried today. And to Cindy's recovery.' He paused. 'That pub you like, love. By the river.'

Sue nodded. She didn't say it, but she'd also silently raise a glass to Rob. And maybe even to Mark Baker. To the tiny part of their tortured, broken souls that was innocent. In so many ways, they were victims too.

As the car drove slowly away, Tom looked back out of the rear window, where two gravediggers were already shovelling the gritty earth, covering the cheap coffin like snow.

Tanya was finally at peace. Only her nan missed her.

Acknowledgments

First up has to be Charlotte 'Legend' Ledger, my publisher and editor at One More Chapter, who saw *something* in an early draft and transformed it into the thriller I hope you've just enjoyed, or are about to. Charlotte's vision and hard work made *The Nail Salon* happen and it simply wouldn't exist without her.

Lucy Bennett, for the stunning cover design which made me want to read my own book.

The entire One More Chapter team, especially Emma Petfield and Chloe Cummings, for getting *The Nail Salon* 'out there'.

Ed Wilson, the world's best literary agent, and his team at Johnson & Alcock, for *everything*. See you in the West Wing–mine's a gin and tonic.

Tarne Sinclair, for reading each chapter as I wrote it, and for those lovely long walks around Primrose Hill with Mary Comerford putting the world to rights.

Judith Cope, who first took me to a nail bar, for helping me to see the blue sky when the dark clouds came.

My boys Jasper and Justin (Jab and Lougle), my daughter-in-law Tiana (Princess T) and my husband Gino– who were all with me in Paros back in 2019 when I decided to write the book–for always believing, and for making the world shine.

Coco and Birrle-oove, my rescue cats, for not walking on the keyboard *too* often.

My parents, my nana, and the Mantripp family, for giving me the loving childhood that Melinda could only dream of.

And you, for reading.

Read on for an extract from *The Publicist*

PR guru Lola Lovett's client has gone missing, but that's not the problem. It's the fact that he's meant to be at home. Already dead.

Coming August 2023

Available to pre-order in eBook and paperback now

The Publicist: Chapter One

LOLA

It was dangling his balls in the prosecco that did it.

I've told him, a thousand times, that if you go to an awards ceremony, you're on show. It's all part of the job. You're there to be seen. Including the after-party. Did he listen? Did he fuck. Three bottles down and he'd whipped them out in front of the Head of Drama and shown her his party trick. It was even her prosecco.

This is going to take some smoothing over. Damage limitation. That's my job. And why my clients pay me so handsomely. Personal publicist to the stars. I've got plenty of A-lister actors and footballers, but I'm not that fussy. Soap stars, snooker players and those actors who pop up in serial dramas – the ones where you know the face but can never quite remember the name – are just as rewarding. It's not all about the money, either. I get a kick out of keeping their sordid lives out of the press. Reputation management. When a celeb is in trouble, they'd better call Lola.

If the *Daily News* gets hold of this, it'll be all over the front page. But that's not always a bad thing. I've built careers back up after a fall like the fucking bionic man, or woman. Depends if they've got that magical quality that means no matter what they do, the public is ultimately ready to forgive them. Because 'he's a nice boy really', or 'she didn't mean it'. For my clients, that magical quality is me.

It doesn't always work, of course. Like the prosecco. Some don't listen. Some – despite everything – are hell-bent on destroying the carefully manicured character you've created for them. Some just can't handle fame. And others are just shits.

Prosecco guy falls into the first category. It's not the first time he's done it and it won't be the last. But I like him. He's a jobbing B-list actor who – unlike many – has accepted Hollywood isn't interested and just wants to enjoy his fame while it lasts.

My phone lights up. It's a message from my assistant, Olivia. *Only one person got that on camera. Kym Sylvian.*

Ah, Kym. Also one of my clients. Word is bound to get out, but without video evidence, the papers won't run it. And even if they threaten to, I've got a few tricks up my sleeve. Offering them an exclusive on a footballer's wedding – I'm sure I can persuade one of them to tie the knot – in exchange for dropping it should work. I drain the rest of my sparkling water – I never drink on the job – and text Kym: *Meet me in the ladies by the entrance. Good news. URGENT!*

She'll be there, of course. Kym, like all my clients, is wedded to her phone. The London Sunset Plaza is a soulless place at the best of times, all glass, steel and fine dining dinners the size of a 10p, in a skyscraper with all the charm of a Travelodge. But I've done plenty of business here, especially in the entrance loos, which after the flurry of arrivals dashing in for their pre-party pick-me-up, is usually empty.

The attendant – whose main task this evening has been to clean the coke off the toilet seats – is quickly dispatched as usual with a twenty-pound note and a smile. 'Ten minutes, sweetie.' She nods. She knows me well at this point.

Kym sweeps in, her pale-blue Oscar de la Renta gown – loaned, of course, in exchange for a mention on the red carpet – showing unfortunate red wine drips. Inwardly, I wince. I can't bear red wine. Her eye make-up is smudged and she's slurring.

'Whassa news?'

'Kym, *darling*. I've been chatting to the Head of Drama. They think you're *wonderful*.'

'Really?' Underneath her up-do and borrowed jewels, she's a little girl from Liverpool, excited to be at the ball.

'Have a wee, now we're here, and I'll tell you all about it. Here, let me hold your stuff.'

Dutifully, she hands me her evening bag.

'Oh, darling, can I use your phone?' I add. 'I've left mine on the table. I know, I'm stupid. I'm always telling you never to do that. I need to call Olivia.'

'Sure,' she slurs. 'Passcode is… I can't 'member…' She puts her wobbly thumb on the phone and unlocks it before teetering into the cubicle.

The video is deleted in a flash. Gone, from her phone, the cloud, all her devices. Five minutes later, her ego pumped from top-secret tales of a non-existent drama series in the works, and which she'll have forgotten by morning, she's back on the cocktails. Job done.

It's four a.m. by the time my last client leaves, shoved into the back of a waiting taxi as the last few paparazzi by the exit grab a blurry shot. No one pays any attention to me as I leave ten minutes later, slipping out the front entrance and across Park Lane to the underground car park, where my black Tesla is fully charged, its blackout windows protecting anyone inside it. Three awards, two nominations, and apart from prosecco guy, no damage done. I'm tired but elated. The Head of Drama had taken some smoothing over, but with a client list like mine, keeping me onside outweighed the 'pathetic schoolboy prank', which I promised would never happen again. I blamed it on the stress of his wife's fictitious *affair*. I'd dispatched him in a cab straight after Bollockgate, but I'll keep Prosecco Guy on the books because I like him. Because it was funny. And because – despite my 'no touching the talent' rule, I slept with him once. Just once. He'd got all emotional and said he loved me. I'd laughed, but I was touched. We'd never mentioned it again.

I'm just about to drive off when my phone lights up. It's Tim Thacker, the editor of the *Daily News*.

'Lola? What's the deal with Sam Stevens? We're hearing he's gone missing. Wasn't he at the awards tonight?'

I freeze, but my voice stays completely calm. 'Missing? I haven't heard anything. He told me a few days ago that he couldn't make it tonight. Just finished a shoot. Who says he's missing?'

'Police sources. Seems his latest boyfriend has turned up at Kingston Police Station just now in a right state. Says he's not at either of their homes and his phone is off.'

'Probably just gone off on a retreat. He's into that. Likes meditating and finding himself. Had they had a row?'

'That's all I know. If this has legs, we're gonna need a statement from you.'

'Sure. But keep this low-key for now.'

'He's A-list, Lola. If he's missing it's huge.'

'I know. But I'm sure he isn't. Just the boyfriend going off on one. Keep me posted, Tim. And thanks for the heads-up.'

Missing. Now I really do have a problem.

Because Sam Stevens *is* supposed to be at home. Dead.

The Publicist: Chapter Two

Tuesday 6 September

Detective Chief Inspector Sue Fisher rolled over in bed and looked at the crumpled pile of bedcovers beside her. Mike, her former deputy and now her boyfriend, was in the seventies-style avocado bathroom, singing as he loudly brushed his teeth.

On the bedside table, her phone buzzed. Chief Constable Steve Biller. It was unusual for the boss to call.

'Sue? I need you in. Now. Missing person. Sam Stevens. The actor. This is obviously very high-profile, and we need to show we've got the best team on it.'

'Sam Stevens? Doesn't he live in Hollywood?'

'Cobshott. Somewhere you're very familiar with, Sue. So the press will expect us to assign you to it. And he has a flat in Hampstead. One in LA too, though he hasn't been there for months, according to the housekeeper. Get in and I'll brief you. We'll need you on camera.'

Sam Stevens. Sue wasn't one for fangirling, but he was up there with Tom Cruise in her book. Cobshott, though. Just a few miles away, but so many memories. Too many.

'That was the boss,' she told Mike as he emerged from the bathroom with a towel around his portly waist. 'Missing person. Sam Stevens. The actor.'

'God, even I've heard of him. Isn't he American?'

'No, just good with accents. British. Lives over here, apparently. Cobshott. Can you believe it? I thought I was done with that village and the super-rich. But they want me on it.'

Mike ruffled her hair. 'Only the best. The press will love you being on it. You did put Cobshott on the map solving the Medford case.'

Sue swung her legs out of bed and smiled. '*We* put it on the map,' she replied. Mike had never once appeared remotely jealous of the glory that had poured down on Sue after Medford, and she loved him for it. 'It'll feel weird going back there. I haven't set foot in Cobshott since.'

It had been four years since the Melinda Medford case had thrown both of them into the spotlight, and they'd started dating a year or so later. Sue shuddered as she recalled being left for dead in Cobshott, and what happened in the 'House of Horrors', as the papers had labelled the Medford crime scene.

'What happened to Medford's nail salon?' Sue called

thickly from the bathroom, as she brushed her teeth. 'Surely it's not still there?'

'Funnily enough, I drove up Cobshott high street the other day on that fraud job,' Mike replied. 'It's been turned into a Costa.'

Sue snorted. She loathed anywhere that sold overpriced coffee in toddler-like sippy cups.

'People still go there to take photos,' Mike went on. 'Even though that hideous house – Riverdell – was demolished, people still turn up in the village looking for it and wanting to see where it stood. Vultures.' He picked up his phone from the bedside table. 'That's history now, though. Do you want another cuppa, love?'

'Yeah. Strong one. Ta.'

She listened as Mike's slippered feet padded downstairs, followed by the predictable sound of the kettle. Cobshott might be history for Mike, but the scars still ran deep with Sue. She'd been lucky to survive the attack there.

Cobshott was bringing back too many memories, thoughts that she'd long driven deep inside, crunched so tightly that their darkness, their pain, rarely escaped. Memories of her late husband, Rob, exploded. How he secretly used to beat her, burn her with cigarettes. How he hated himself afterwards. And how, for years, she covered it up, pouring every scrap of energy into caring for their son, Tom, and catching men – and women – like Medford who inflicted such pain on others. Seven rapists and three killers were now off the streets thanks to her. Plus countless domestic abusers.

Sue turned the cold tap on full, splashing water on to her face. These days, her arms bore no bruises, and she no longer feared what might happen when she walked in the door at night. She was safe, free. But she still missed Rob. The part of him that, underneath the twisted, toxic mess he'd become, loved her.

Even though she cared for Mike dearly, and he'd been there for her and her son Tom during the most god-awful times, through the whole Medford case, she didn't love him like *that*.

Love, as she'd always known, was messy.

'Here you go,' Mike said cheerily, placing a steaming mug of builders' tea on the dressing table. He placed his arm gently round her shoulders. 'Don't worry, love. You've laid those Cobshott ghosts to rest.'

Sue wasn't so sure.

***

Dressed in a black suit, crisp white shirt and patent black shoes, with enough make-up to hopefully hide her late forty-something wrinkles on camera, Sue drove to the police station car park, wishing she had Mike by her side. He'd been the perfect deputy, but police rules meant that once they were dating, they couldn't work as a team, and pleas to Chief Constable Biller to make an exception in their case had fallen on unsurprisingly deaf ears.

She missed having Mike by her side at work. These days they were more friends than lovers. Sex with him had always been more cosy than passionate, but even that had dwindled. With Tom now eighteen and preparing to head off to university, they'd settled into a routine. Mike made the six a.m. cuppa. He always sang in the bathroom – Abba, usually. Today was 'Fernando'. They tried to organise their shifts to spend time together. A curry on a Thursday – veggie korma for her, chicken madras for him. Cinema on a Saturday if the job allowed. Occasional sex on a Sunday morning, always followed by Mike mowing the lawn. Sue hated him doing that, though she didn't really know why.

After the Medford case, she'd stayed in the same 1930s house in Surbiton, a commuter-belt town in Surrey. It was Tom's home, after all, and despite everything, it helped her feel close to Rob. His death was something that stayed with her every single day, something she felt responsible for. If only she'd got him the help he so clearly needed, to learn to cope with his anger rather than breaking her bones. If only she'd been *better*.

As the years had passed, she'd go for minutes and then hours without thinking of Rob, but then it would come back, all of it, enveloping her in a thick, ugly fog, blotting out all that was good in the world.

Now she had to go back to Cobshott, where she'd almost died, and where the truth about her life, and Medford's, had come out.

A small group of paparazzi were gathered by the car park entrance. Clearly the story had started to leak. Recognising Sue from the Medford case, they thrust their cameras at the car windows and photographed her as she waited for the barrier to rise. Her knuckles whitened as she gripped the steering wheel, a sense of panic rising in her belly. Thoughts of the Medford case, of Cobshott, flooded back. But Sue kept her face inscrutable, her eyes staring straight ahead as she drove inside and parked. Mike's insight – and emotional support – on the ground would have been invaluable. But Sue was too professional to let her thoughts linger. There was a missing man to be found.

Inside the station there was a real buzz, an unspoken sense of urgency that always happened when a major case was brewing.

'Morning, ma'am.'

Sue's new deputy, DI Dev Basu, handed her a coffee.

'What's the latest, Dev?'

'Biller wants us to go straight to his office. I've never seen him so worked up.'

'It's an A-list Hollywood celeb missing on his patch, Dev. He's only eight months off retirement. I reckon he was hoping to sail quietly into the sunset.'

Dev was right. Chief Constable Biller was pacing around his office like a man possessed.

'Ah, Sue, Dev, come in. Here's the file. It goes without saying that this is seriously high profile. We'll be under intense scrutiny. The whole world wants this man found.'

'Of course, sir,' Sue replied, calmly, fighting the urge to roll her eyes. The *whole world*. Biller had clearly got his knickers in a twist. 'What do we know?'

'His boyfriend, Tyler Tipping, called it in. Turned up,

actually, in the middle of the night. The duty sergeant did his best to cope as the man was *hysterical*. His statement's in there. The press office is setting up an on-camera appeal for later today. We'd like you to appear with Tyler. After the Medford case, it's good for the public to see we've got you on it.'

'Of course, sir.'

'We've got officers at his two homes now. No obvious signs of a break-in, or anything untoward at all, but Forensics are on their way. The paps have already got wind of it. Christ knows how. Bloody leak at the station if you ask me. More holes than a colander. Tyler's downstairs.'

'Any suggestion he's a suspect?'

'No. But we can't rule anything out. Including blackmail. There's been no ransom demand yet, but Stevens is *very* famous and super-rich, so it's a definite possibility.'

'What about activism?' Dev asked. 'Anyone or any groups he's annoyed lately?'

'Not that we know of,' Biller replied. 'His profile's been squeaky-clean up until now. No drugs, not even a driving offence. Doesn't even *drink* anymore.' Biller spat out the words as if being teetotal was utterly shameful.

'Almost too clean…' Sue pondered. 'Is Tyler up to being questioned?'

'He's pretty tearful but yes. Keen to do anything he can to help.'

'What about Stevens' parents? Still alive?'

'Yes. Dafydd and Gwen Morgan. Stevens changed his

name by deed poll. They live in the valleys in South Wales. Just outside a village called Tony-something. Tonyrefail, I think. Sounds like a dodgy cabaret singer. They've got a detached bungalow. Not at home, but neighbours say they're likely at their caravan, which is somewhere near Porthcawl, so local force are checking the sites. Seem to keep themselves to themselves. Neighbours also said, as far as they know, the parents haven't spoken to Sam for years. What was the quote?' Biller launched into a thick Welsh accent. '"They don't approve of his *ways*." I'd hoped to notify the parents before we went public but as it seems they haven't spoken in years I won't lose any sleep over it.'

Sue picked up the file and stood up. 'We'll get straight on it, sir.'

Biller nodded. 'We need to find him, Sue. I don't want it to drag on. His agent is Lola Lovett, so if we put a foot wrong, she'll be all over it. Bloody female Max Clifford. Without the paedophilia. I've asked Uniform to bring her in. She's bound to know more about Stevens' personal life than anyone.'

Back at her desk, Sue read through Tyler's statement. He claimed to have been with Sam for just under a year, ever since they met at an AA meeting. Tyler had addiction issues after growing up in care in Farnborough, Hampshire. Now clean, he worked for the Climate Crisis charity as a campaigner, which, Sue noted, might explain Sam's recent Instagram posts promoting veganism to save the rainforests. Tyler's own social media was full of pictures of him at work, glued to petrol pumps and setting fire to a bin in Trafalgar Square, but for the last year, it was *only* work. No pictures in restaurants, bars, of him socialising at all. That made sense, Sue thought. Stevens – no doubt with the help of Lola Lovett – had always kept his private life private. Tyler was thirty-one, Sam was forty-two. Bit of an age gap, but nothing that remarkable.

'So they didn't live together?' Dev asked.

'No,' Sue replied. 'Looks like Tyler often stayed over at Stevens' house in Cobshott and the one in Hampstead. But he has his own rented flat in Soho.'

'How does he afford that as a charity worker?'

'Dunno. Probably paid for by Stevens. Get on to the lettings agent and find out whose name it's in. Tyler last saw him in Cobshott on Saturday. They went out for dinner; he stayed the night and went home Sunday afternoon. Started to worry when he didn't get his usual "goodnight" video call – I'm thinking phone sex – that night. No replies to anything on Monday including phone calls and came in here panicking early hours of this morning.'

'What's your feeling, boss?'

'Multitude of options. A Grindr hook-up that went wrong. A crazed fan and he's tied to a bed like *Misery*. Stevens has fucked off somewhere for the hell of it. Gone all Stephen Fry on us and is driving to France or on a plane. Maybe the boyfriend did it. Get PC Evans to check all the passenger names on flights out of London to Los Angeles since Sunday afternoon, if he's got a home there. Like Biller said, we can't rule anything out. Let's go downstairs and talk to Tyler.'

~

Ready to find out what happens next…

***The Publicist* is available to pre-order in eBook and paperback now**

The author and One More Chapter would like to thank everyone who contributed to the publication of this story...

Analytics
Emma Harvey
Maria Osa

Audio
Fionnuala Barrett
Ciara Briggs

Contracts
Georgina Hoffman
Florence Shepherd

Design
Lucy Bennett
Fiona Greenway
Holly Macdonald
Liane Payne
Dean Russell

Digital Sales
Laura Daley
Michael Davies
Georgina Ugen

Editorial
Arsalan Isa
Charlotte Ledger
Nicky Lovick
Jennie Rothwell
Caroline Scott-Bowden
Kimberley Young

International Sales
Bethan Moore

Marketing & Publicity
Chloe Cummings
Emma Petfield

Operations
Melissa Okusanya
Hannah Stamp

Production
Emily Chan
Denis Manson
Francesca Tuzzeo

Rights
Lana Beckwith
Rachel McCarron
Agnes Rigou
Hany Sheikh
Mohamed
Zoe Shine
Aisling Smyth

The HarperCollins Distribution Team

The HarperCollins Finance & Royalties Team

The HarperCollins Legal Team

The HarperCollins Technology Team

Trade Marketing
Ben Hurd

UK Sales
Yazmeen Akhtar
Laura Carpenter
Isabel Coburn
Jay Cochrane
Alice Gomer
Gemma Rayner
Erin White
Harriet Williams
Leah Woods

And every other essential link in the chain from delivery drivers to booksellers to librarians and beyond!

One More Chapter is an award-winning global division of HarperCollins.

Sign up to our newsletter to get our latest eBook deals and stay up to date with our weekly Book Club!
Subscribe here.

Meet the team at
www.onemorechapter.com

Follow us!

 @OneMoreChapter_

 @OneMoreChapter

 @onemorechapterhc

Do you write unputdownable fiction?
We love to hear from new voices.
Find out how to submit your novel at
www.onemorechapter.com/submissions